PARADISE GIRL

PARADISE GIRL

Phill Featherstone

Matador
9 Priory Business Park,
Wistow Road, Kibworth Beauchamp,
Leicestershire. LE8 0RX
Tel: 0116 279 2299
Email: books@troubador.co.uk
Web: www.troubador.co.uk/matador
Twitter: @matadorbooks

ISBN 978 1785898 723

British Library Cataloguing in Publication Data.
A catalogue record for this book is available from the British Library.

Printed and bound in the UK by TJ International, Padstow, Cornwall
Typeset in 11pt Aldine401 BT by Troubador Publishing Ltd, Leicester, UK

Matador is an imprint of Troubador Publishing Ltd

MIX
Paper from
responsible sources
FSC
www.fsc.org   FSC® C013056

For Sally

I am free to walk on the moors, but when I go out there alone, everything reminds me of the times others were with me, and then the moors seem a wilderness, featureless, solitary, saddening.

Charlotte Brontë after the death
of her sisters and her brother

The mind is its own place, and in itself
Can make a heav'n of hell, a hell of heav'n

Milton, *Paradise Lost*

THE SHAPE OF THESE HILLS has barely changed in a thousand years. Until now. Now across the valley the margin of the land is no longer marked by the peaty moor. Instead wind turbines stalk the skyline. The planners ordered that they should be white, so as not to stand out. It doesn't work. They are too huge. The poles thrust sixty metres into the air and are topped by trios of blades, each the length of an articulated truck. Every day there is wind and every day they turn, like a row of spindly giants pirouetting in a ponderous ballet.

Granddad hated them. He lived here all his life and he saw these intruders as the work of some nameless, capitalist Satan bent on destroying our glorious heritage. His father had not fought Hitler to allow such vandalism in our green and pleasant land.

'It's them buggers in London,' he'd say. 'I bet they wouldn't put up with the bloody things in the south. They wouldn't stand for it.'

Of course he was wrong. Turbines were built everywhere, and everybody – well, almost everybody – did stand for it. Many welcomed them. So it would have pleased Granddad to know that the power the turbines are generating as I watch them today is of no use, no use at all. No one will turn on the TV or boil a kettle. No one will switch on a light. The factories will stay silent and the offices and schools dark. It was like that yesterday and it will be the same tomorrow, and for all the days to come.

These diaries tell you why.

The Purple Diary (before)

You should read this one first

INTRODUCTIONS ARE BORING, but unless I take time to explain things it will be confusing for you. Me first. Not very polite, I know, but it's probably the best place to start. My name is Kerryl – or that's what my family and friends call me. It's a funny name but there's an explanation for it. I'll go into that later. (There, that's a reason for you to keep on reading, isn't it?)

My proper name is Cheryl. Cheryl Alison Shaw. They call me the Paradise Girl. Don't get excited – it sounds sexy but it's not. I'm seventeen years old and still a virgin. I'm not a nun, I've been out with loads of boys – Tim, Mark (two of them), Nathan, Jake, Tristram, Steve – but I wasn't that keen on any of them and they didn't last. The exception was Mark II. He was older than me, fearsomely good looking and he had a nice car. I thought he was really hot. When I wasn't with him I was texting him or phoning him or on Face2Face, and when I wasn't doing that I was thinking about him. But it seems he wasn't as keen as me, and one day my best friend, Josie, told me that he was going out with Monica Woodbridge and saying I was a frigid cow. It seems everybody knew I'd been dumped and I was the last to find out. I felt as though I'd been kicked by Joey and I cried for a week, but I was angry too.

The worst thing was the shock. I thought Monica Woodbridge was my friend. As well as that, all the girls in our group had been going out with the same boys for a long time, but I seemed to keep a boyfriend for only a few weeks. Was there something wrong with me? To be honest, I'm not a great beauty. I don't mean I'm a train wreck or anything. I'm not bad looking, but I'm not like Charlene Brooker or Suzy Simmonds. They're electric, both of them. Charlene could be a model, and Suzy's always surrounded by a gang of drooling boys.

They're gone now: Charlene, Suzy, Josie, Monica, all of them.

★

Sorry for the break there. I had to stop to have a little weep. I'll try not to do too much of that. I suppose I can console myself with one thing: with everyone else dead, I must be the most beautiful girl in the world!

I'VE ALWAYS KEPT A DIARY. Not every day. Sometimes I'd go ages without writing anything; then I'd do five days on the trot. I was talking to Miss Dove, who used to teach us English at St Winifred's, and she said that was a good thing.

'Only write when you have something to say,' she said.

I didn't ask her whether I should apply that advice to the essays she sets us, because if I did there'd be times when I wouldn't write anything!

Lander, my brother, used to tease me about my diaries. He resented them because he didn't understand why I wrote them. One of the worst rows we ever had was when I caught him in my room reading one of them. I went berserk. I had a pair of scissors in my hand, and I swear I would have impaled him if he hadn't jumped over the bed and kept it between us. He couldn't understand why I was so mad.

'Why write it if you don't want anybody to read it?' he said.

He called me pathetic and I didn't speak to him for more than a week. Not till he realised how much he'd upset me and apologised. I think he was jealous. Not so much jealous of me writing my diary, but of the diary itself. He liked to think I told him everything, us being twins and all, and here was stuff the diary knew and he didn't.

Lander's not here any more and I don't know where he is, but I don't think he's dead. They say twins can sense these things. That may or may not be true, but I don't get any kind of death vibe, like I did after our Dad had gone. I have a feeling that Lander's alive. Somewhere.

The diaries I used to write didn't just record things that happened to me. I used them to help me work stuff out, and to say things I couldn't share with anybody, not even Josie, and certainly not with Lander. This diary is different though. It's different from anything I've written before.

Why?

Because I know I'm going to die.

Why?

Because the people I lived with – Gran, Granddad and our Mam – are already dead. So are all my friends and so is everybody else. And if Lander's not dead he might as well be.

Am I scared? The crazy (but true) answer is, 'I don't know'. Sometimes I wake up in the middle of the night feeling that something is eating me from the inside. I have to get up then, because going back to sleep is out of the question. But most of the time in the daylight, it doesn't seem real, even now, and I just get on with things. I can't believe that it won't all come right again, that life won't get back to normal. I mean, they'll sort it out. Won't they?

Anyway, I'm going to write about the things that happen to me now and I'm going to try not to be emotional. I'll tell you what I do, what I see and hear, what I think and what I feel. I'll keep writing as long as I can, until I'm too sick to do any more, and should there be anyone left, perhaps in another country, my diaries will tell them what happened here, in England, and particularly in this little corner of it, at this time in the twenty-first century.

I've got two notebooks, a purple one and a green one, and I'm going to use them for two different diaries. In the purple diary, the one that you're reading at this moment, I'm recording what's already happened. That's the part of the story I've called *Before*. My other diary, the green one, is my day-by-day account of what's gone on since then. I'm calling that one *Now*. I'm writing them both at the same time (well, not at *exactly* the same time, but you know what I mean), putting down each day's events in the green one and then catching up on the back story in the purple one. Purple past, green present, get it? Is that confusing? I hope not. Feel free to skip about from one to the other if at any stage you get bored. I'm not going to label the entries in either of them with dates. The passage of time is largely irrelevant now, and it doesn't matter whether something happened on a Monday in May or on a Tuesday in June. Actually, I'm not sure that I'd know to tell you, anyway. One day is very much like another.

DID YOU SEE WHAT happened back there? There was a question and I answered it. The question wasn't from me, it just popped into my head, as if there was a reader sitting beside me and whispering in my ear.

According to Miss Dove, a writer writes for herself; if she worries too much about the reader she ends up writing what she thinks they want to read instead of what she wants to say. It becomes false and she loses her voice. When she said 'loses her voice' I thought at first she meant like when you have a sore throat or a cold, but then she explained it and I understood. Rudy Fothergill, our other English teacher, didn't agree. He said that people like Dickens knew exactly who their readers were and what they wanted, and there was no question he wrote for them. I think Miss Dove would have known best because she'd been to conferences and met some actual writers. Besides, she'd done an Arvon course, and she'd had a short story published. By the way, I hope you noticed the smart use of the semi-colon at the beginning of the paragraph. Miss Dove would have given me an extra mark for that.

Mr Fothergill wasn't really called Rudy. That was just our name for him because he'd stroll round the tables looking over our shoulders. He was pretending to check our work but really he was trying to see down our tops (rude = Rudy, get it?).

Anyway, I'm going to imagine you, my dear reader, so I do know who I'm writing for. I'm going to think of you as tall, dark and mysterious, like Heathcliff. You have a firm but quiet voice and an infectious laugh. Oh, and you have an awesome six-pack! Of course, you might not be the way I'm imagining you at all. You might be an old man, or an old woman. You might be somebody ordinary, like me.

Should I give you a name? Maybe later.

Lander kept a diary too. Well, it wasn't really a diary because he never actually wrote anything in it (writing didn't interest Lander). As soon as it became obvious that the Infection was something to worry about, which I suppose to be honest was not until it reached northern Europe, he started to collect information about it. Some of it was things like leaflets from the Government, some was newspaper cuttings, but most of it was stuff he got off the internet. There were a whole bunch of them doing it, sharing information. They had their own website: www.thetruthwillsetyoufree.net. They'd post on it, and tweet, and they'd swap messages on iKnowU and QuickChat.

As the news of the Infection became more serious he got worse. He was always on his computer. Our Mam would go on and on at him about it. 'If only you'd put as much effort into helping around the farm we'd all be much better off,' she used to say. Then suddenly he stopped, around the time our Mam got ill. No more surfing, no more tweets; no more beckoning me over to his screen saying, 'Have you seen this?' or, 'Look at this, you wouldn't believe it!'. He'd spend as much time at his computer, but not doing anything, just staring at the screen. Sometimes it wouldn't even be turned on. I tried to talk to him about it, about how he was feeling, what we'd do if Gran and Granddad caught the Infection and we were left at the farm on our own, but he didn't want to discuss it. 'What's the point?' he'd say. 'If it happens it happens.'

I've kept some of the papers Lander collected. Here's a cutting he took from *The Times*.

African Ghost Town
by Andrea Ellis

I first visited the town of Konso, in Ethiopia, four years ago. Then it was a thriving, bustling place, an administrative and commercial centre and home to some 4,000 people. It had a petrol station, two hotels, a basic clinic, a bank and a twice-weekly market. It had electric power and a telephone system. I visited it again last week to find it had become a ghost town.

What has devastated Konso is not drought or famine, scourges we have seen many times before in this part of Africa, but something which is proving even more deadly. Virus I/452 is so new it doesn't yet have a proper name, although the people of Konso call it 'waga', a word they also use to mean a grave marking.

I/452 was first observed about a year ago in Senegal, although it may have been around longer, and in other areas. It is not only extremely infectious but also incurable. Moreover, it's unstoppable, there being so far no known way of protecting against it. It spreads most rapidly in hot climates and in areas with high population densities, poor sanitation and low standards of hygiene.

I interviewed Dr Genevieve Amblée, the regional officer for Médecins Sans Frontières, who is coordinating the local effort to combat I/452. 'One of the main problems with this infection,' she told me, 'is the period of incubation. The virus settles in a host and is with them for seven to ten days before there are any signs of illness. This means that there are a lot of secret carriers, people who are already infected but don't know it yet, and all the time they are passing on the virus to others. By the time the first symptoms show it's too late.

'The chief difficulty in trying to come up with a vaccine,' Dr Amblée explained, 'is that the virus mutates constantly, so that what may work against it one day is completely useless the next.' She warns that unless the scientific community can find tools to fight the disease she can see it spreading across the whole of the African continent, and even beyond.

The Disasters Emergency Committee has launched an appeal for funds to fight the infection, and the Department for Overseas Aid and the Commonwealth Office have together earmarked £5 million, which includes the costs of redeploying a mobile emergency treatment unit.

Scary, isn't it? That's not the half of it.

LANDER CAN'T HAVE BEEN interested in the pictures of what was happening, because with the article about Konso was a photo of what the place must have looked like, but he'd snipped most of it off. There are some more cuttings in his collection from around the same time, when the Infection was taking hold and becoming a serious problem in Africa but before it had spread anywhere else. There's one from the *Daily Mirror* headed 'Cursed Continent' and another from the *Daily Mail* called 'Africa's Lost Opportunity'. They both accuse African governments and unnamed individuals of pocketing billions of aid money instead of spending it on health, education and hygiene, and the authors imply that the countries have only themselves to blame for what they're going through. That seems to me terribly unfair, writing off the people because of what their leaders have done.

I can remember Granddad looking at one of the articles and going very quiet. Before, when he found anything that interested him in the news he would read it aloud to everybody as a preamble to one of his rants about 'them buggers in London', or taxes, or the way farmers were treated, or Leeds United, or the state of Yorkshire cricket. It used to drive Gran crazy. But now when he saw something in the paper that troubled him he'd say nothing. He'd just put it aside and go out to the barn, looking worried.

The Infection – and it was starting to be spelt with a capital 'I' – was closer now and getting more coverage on TV. Lander kept these two reports. The first is from *The Guardian*.

Africa's Scourge

Is Africa's scourge our nemesis? (*Insights* BBC Events Channel, 9pm) presented a grim picture of the latest in the catalogue of woes that have afflicted this great but sad continent. It also contained a stark warning of what might happen to the rest of us, although it was less clear about what we can do about it.

Michael Lockwood, who is rapidly making this Monday evening slot his own, provided a detailed account of the nature and spread of I/452, the World Health Organisation classification of the disease which is now rampant in several sub-Saharan countries. Not much is known about it, and even the singular might not be accurate. It could be that I/452 is actually several diseases spread by different viruses but sharing common characteristics.

It's likely that it started in Senegal, although some say that Mozambique has an equally strong claim to this dubious honour. It's spread by contact, and there is some evidence that it's also present in fauna and is carried by animals and birds, although they themselves are simply transporters and don't manifest any of the symptoms. One of the most dangerous aspects of this infection (or infections) is that a human host can harbour the virus for a week or more before starting to feel ill. In that time it's possible to infect scores, hundreds, of others.

Following the initial explanation were harrowing shots of the effects of the disease: suppurating sores, bleeding babies, heaving hospitals, desperate people.

So far, so good. What was lacking was any sort of suggested response. There were a number of questions. What will happen if the disease reaches Europe? How can we guard against it spreading through our own cities? How can we help those who are afflicted? All of these turned out to be rhetorical. All right, it's not the programme makers' job to come up with public health policy, , but they should at least have provided us with access to the people whose responsibility it is. There were spokespersons from the opposition parties, who had two messages: something must be done, and anyway it won't happen here. There was no one from the Government, but instead a bland and, in truth, insulting statement that implied the easy spread of the virus was Africa's own fault for squandering billions of aid money instead of using it to improve living conditions and build hospitals.

Despite this, the programme was a timely swake-up call. Let us hope that those who should hear it do.

The next clipping is printed from the online version of the *Daily Mail*, from the same date as the one above.

Look, a Wolf!

Whenever the BBC Events Channel has surplus airtime it sends somebody out to find something nasty to scare us. Last night it was Michael Lockwood, who was dispatched to report on yet another infection rampant in Africa. In *Is Africa's scourge our nemesis?* he told us what he knows about it (not much) and showed us footage of people suffering. His message was, 'Look, this could happen to you.' Well yes, it could. We might also get run over by a bus. Or win the Lottery. Then Lockwood wheeled out some politicians who were expected to have the answers to stopping it. Surprise surprise, they didn't. Wisely, the Government declined to take part in this pointless exercise.

More interesting, and definitely more entertaining, was *I married my dad (Real*

People, ITV5). This was about an adopted young woman who had an affair with, and eventually married, an older man, only to discover that he was her biological father. As luck would have it, what triggered this revelation was the man's insistence on a paternity test when his bride became pregnant, whereupon the doctors found out that the couple shared DNA. Naturally cats were among pigeons and the father…

And there the page ended. Lander hadn't bothered to print any more of the article. I was disappointed because I wanted to know what happened. Either Lander knew or he wasn't bothered. He never had much time for celeb stuff and gossip.

ME AND LANDER (Yes, I know, Miss Dove, it should be Lander and I, but this is my diary and I'll write it how I like) were born on the same day on this very farm where I am now. Lander was first and I came out an hour or so later. My, how he traded on that hour! 'I'm the oldest,' he'd say when I argued with him. 'Oldest first,' when we were in line for treats. He'd call me his 'little' sister, 'junior', 'kiddy', and when our Mam gave us jobs to do he'd leave the crappy ones for me. 'That's one for the youngest,' he'd say.

The farm belongs to Gran and Granddad. Our Mam wanted to be with her mam for the births, so she came to stay here to have us. She had a bad time and things weren't easy. The whole business did her some damage. She never went into the detail so I don't know exactly what went wrong, but it meant she couldn't have any more kids. I think our Dad always felt a bit resentful about that. He loved Lander and me, make no mistake, but I got the impression that he held us somehow responsible for what had happened to our Mam.

She stayed on with Gran and Granddad after we were born, and not much later our Dad moved in too. He'd had his own business making bespoke furniture but it hadn't been going well, and he packed it in and came up here. The farm's not big enough to support us all, so some of the time our Dad worked on the land with Granddad and for the rest he had a job as a driver for an agricultural supplier in the valley. Our Mam helped Gran around the house and with the hens. She shared some of the cooking (although to be honest wasn't much good at it) and she worked part-time in the newsagents in Walbrough, the town at the bottom of the hill.

We were happy. Me and Lander ran wild on the farm. We'd go down into the woods to make dens and up on the moors to look for remains. Lander said you could find dinosaur bones in the peat, but the closest we came were the skeletons of sheep. The moors scared me, particularly when it started to get dark or when heavy clouds came over and the light went. Lander said there were sucking bogs on the moors that you couldn't see till you were in them. You'd be walking along and the ground would look normal and then, whoosh, it would give way and you'd be in a sucking bog. They were called sucking bogs because the mud sucked at your feet and trapped you and pulled you under. 'Stick to the track,' Lander would say, 'and don't ever stray off it.' I did and I didn't.

On the edge of the moor, out of sight of the farm, there are some giant stones around a shallow pool, in the shape of a horseshoe. Lander said they were haunted, and we used to play around them, hiding and scaring each other and our friends. They're called the Bride Stones and there's lots of local folklore about them. One story is that they're people who were petrified (I mean turned to stone, not scared) for blaspheming. Another is that they're folk who pissed off a local witch. There's a legend that if a girl sits on the flat slab at the edge of the pool – the Bride Stone itself – on Midsummer's Day she'll see her true love. There's also a story about a bride who went there for her wedding and drowned herself in the pool when the groom jilted her. At one time people used to get wed up there, but I haven't heard of anybody doing that for ages. The stones are big and black and to me they look menacing. According to Betty Crowther, our neighbour who lives nearer to them than we do, the last people to get hitched at the Bride Stones were a couple of Goths from Rochdale. I bet a creepy place like that suited them perfectly.

Anyway, back to our childhood. As we grew older we began to help with things, particularly the hens and the sheep, and of course at haymaking everybody pitched in. We went to St John's Primary School in Walbrough. Then, when we were eleven, I moved up to St Winifred's Girls' School in Halifax and Lander to King's Heath Boys'. We hated being sent to separate schools – we'd never been apart for such long stretches at a time – but in the end it probably turned out for the best. It meant we became more independent of each other, yet at the same time it brought us closer together. And we were close, even though we used to fight sometimes.

Our Mam and Gran got on really well, and our Dad was all right, although looking back I think felt a bit left out and resented what he thought of as accepting charity from his wife's parents (that's how he saw it, I don't think they did). I was talking to Lander the other day about the time when we were kids and used to roam free.

'Bit different now,' he said.

I said, 'Not really, it's still the same place.'

That made him angry. 'Oh yes, of course it is,' he said, 'people dying all around us. It's fucking paradise.'

We were round the back of one of the sheds where, before the Infection, we used to pack the eggs. There was a blackboard that we'd put out at the end of the lane when Gran used to do B&B. It said, 'Welcome to North Hey Farm'. Lander snatched a piece of chalk, scribbled over North Hey and wrote Paradise over the top: 'Welcome to Paradise Farm'.

'There,' he said, and he threw down the board and walked off. He was doing that a lot then. Walking off, I mean.

I sat on the sun-warmed wall and looked out over the fields. The meadow was so full of buttercups it looked as though it had been dusted with yellow powder paint. A pale blue sky rimmed the hills across the valley. The trees at the end of the field were entering their first flush of green and masked the valley town. Beside me a drunken bumble bee made an uncertain landing on a dandelion. Yes, it was still paradise, but was Lander right? Were we losing it?

We'd been reading *Paradise Lost* at school. Not all of it, just some parts that Miss Dove picked out for us. We did the bit where Adam and Eve part for the first time and go in separate directions to work on the land, and Satan gives Eve the apple. Adam comes back and there's this really great scene where, although he's horrified at what she's done, he eats the fruit too because he'd rather share her fate, whatever that might be, than go on without her. It's awesome! I learnt some of what he says to her by heart:

... with thee have I fixed my lot,
If Death consort with thee, Death is to me as Life;
So forcible within my heart I feel
The bond of nature draw me to my own,
My own in thee, for what thou art is mine;
Our state cannot be severed, we are one,
One flesh; to lose thee were to lose my self.

Those lines really get to me. They make me well up every time. That's the sort of boyfriend I want.

I don't expect I'll find him now.

OUR DAD DIED when me and Lander were nine. It must have been gruesome, although to be honest I don't remember much about it. There was a lot of fuss and rushing about, and an ambulance, and the police, and my Auntie Madge coming. Everybody looked solemn and our Mam was crying. Nobody took much notice of us, and we sat in the corner trying to figure out what was going on.

I can remember Lander saying to me, 'Our Dad's dead.'

I'd already reached the same conclusion, although no one had told us. Hearing him say it out loud like that really hit me and I started to cry. Nobody took any notice; they were all too busy.

We didn't discover the details until later. Dad was killed in a farm accident, quite a common one it seems. A walker found his body and raised the alarm. Nobody knows for sure what happened, but our Mam told me and Lander what the police and the insurance investigator thought. Dad was down in the bottom field on the tractor. He parked it on the slope and got out. He can't have put the brake on properly and the tractor started to move. They think he tried to get into the cab to stop it, but he must have got caught on something. The tractor carried on down the hill and across the lane, dragging him with it. It ran into the clough and rolled over, squashing him underneath it.

'Would Dad have died straight away?' I asked our Mam.

She said, 'Yes, he would. He wouldn't have felt a thing.'

She was just trying to make me feel better, though. Much later I talked to Dr Carmichael and he said our Dad bled to death and it could have taken a couple of hours.

Me and Lander wanted to go and see where the accident had happened. It wasn't that we wanted to see the blood, our Dad's life splattered on rocks, staining the grass, soaking into the leaf mould, but we wanted evidence, proof that he was dead. It seemed so unreal. That morning when we'd gone to school he'd been splitting logs in the yard. He checked that we had all our stuff, gave us a pat and told us to have a good day. I didn't know I'd never see him again. I should have given him a kiss and a hug. I should have clung to him and refused to go to school. Then he wouldn't have gone out on the tractor. I didn't, and when we got home everything had changed.

We were sent away. Auntie Madge took me with her and Uncle Ernest to their house in Scarborough. Lander went with Auntie Jessie, our Mam's other sister, to Doncaster. I'd been to stay at Auntie Madge's before, with our Mam and Dad and Lander, and then it had been a big treat. This time, though, I didn't want to go. I wanted to be with my brother. So at the very time Lander and I needed each other most, they split us up.

'It won't be long,' Auntie Madge said. 'Just while your Mam gets things sorted out.'

The sorting out seemed to take Mam a long time and I was really homesick, desperate to go back to the farm. Soon, I was told, soon. It wasn't soon, though. We didn't go back home until after our Dad's funeral. That meant we never got to say goodbye to him.

AFTER THE ACCIDENT our Mam seemed constantly angry. She was mad all the time now, as if what had happened was somebody's fault – Gran's, Granddad's, even our Dad's, as if he'd chosen to get himself squashed and die. Incidentally, she never used the word 'die' in connection with what had happened. She'd never say, 'Jimmy died'. Instead it was always, 'Jimmy was killed'. As if it was something for which he was blameless, like being shot or blown up by an IED, like Monica Woodbridge's brother. Whereas the NFU man said our Dad had been careless and our Mam was lucky to get the insurance.

Once the insurance company had paid out, money wasn't a problem for our Mam any more, although she always behaved as if it was. I suppose she couldn't get used to having a bit to spare after all those years of struggling to make do. I was going through her papers the other day and I found she'd got £36,000 in her savings account at the bank, and a few hundred more in her current account. As well as this there were some Premium Bonds and a couple of ISAs, and £12,500 in the farm account. She was rolling in it, but that didn't stop her acting as if she was skint. I remember the parents' evening when Miss Dove suggested I apply to Cambridge.

Our Mam looked horrified. 'Cambridge?' she said. 'I can't afford to send her to a place like that. All those posh people, you need a fortune to go there.'

Miss Dove told her that it didn't have to cost more than any other university, but Mam didn't believe her.

The school took no notice and arranged some extra classes to get me ready for the entrance exam. All the other unis rely on your A levels to find out whether you're suitable, but Cambridge has its own exams. They were hard. There were two English papers, a general paper and French.

'French?' said Lander. 'Why French? I thought you were supposed to be doing English.'

I didn't know why they needed to test my French either but they did, so I mugged up what I'd done for GCSE. It was tough, though. Miss Dove talked to me a lot about what it would be like to be a student there: the lectures, the 'supervisions' (their name for tutorials), the libraries and museums, the social life. Our Mam never mentioned it. Even when I went for the exams and the interview she just behaved as if I was going for a sleep-over at my friend Josie's, and when I got back she didn't ask me a thing about it. Not how it had gone. Not what the place was like. Not anything. I was disappointed because I thought she might have been proud of me. Gran and Granddad were.

'What about Lander?' you say. 'Was he aiming for Cambridge too?' Well, the answer to that is, no chance. Oh, it's not that he wasn't clever. I think he was always brighter than me, and he was fantastic with computers. He just wasn't interested in school work. Apart from gadgets his other great passion was sport, especially cricket. He was a fearsome fast bowler, with a perfect line and length (whatever that means; it's what people said). He was in his school's first team when he was only fifteen, and even then hardly anyone could deal with him. He played an invitation game for Yorkshire Colts and took 5 for 16 against Derbyshire Youth XI. They offered him a place at the Yorkshire Cricket Academy and he was over the moon, but our Mam wouldn't let him go. She said he had to finish his schooling first, so he had something to fall back on if the cricket didn't work out. The Academy people said they'd take care of all that, he could finish his courses and take all his exams with them, but she wouldn't have it.

'It's madness,' she said to him. 'What happens if you get injured? Or if in the end it turns out that you're not good enough?'

I don't think Lander ever forgave her for that. Afterwards he seemed to lose all interest in cricket. The Walbrough Cricket Club offered him some games. They were a good side, high in the Lancashire Leagues, and they had a couple of professionals who'd played for Pakistan, but he wouldn't hear of it. It was Yorkshire or nothing.

As well as giving up the cricket he stopped trying at school. He took to hanging out with a bunch of wasters. Our Mam used to go on at him but it made no difference.

'No point,' he'd say when she asked him why he wasn't doing any work. 'There's no point doing anything, because I might not be good enough. Or I might get injured.'

I was on his side, he knew that, but I felt I had to say something because he was throwing away all his opportunities. 'You've got to try,' I said. 'There's more to life than cricket. And besides, you can always take it up again later.'

We had a terrible row and in the end he yelled at me. 'You sod off to your precious Cambridge if that's what you want,' he said, 'because I'm doing what I want.'

We didn't talk about it any more after that. Eventually the school threw him out. They didn't expel him exactly, they simply said that he should take a term off 'to reorientate himself'. He never went back. He helped a bit on the farm, though not nearly enough to satisfy our Mam. Most of the time he'd be in his bedroom, on his computer.

I SAID I'D TELL YOU about my name, why I'm called Kerryl. Well, as you know, my proper name is Cheryl. So why am I called Kerryl? Simple. When I was a kid I couldn't say Cheryl, and when I tried what came out was Kerryl. I couldn't manage Shaw either, and if anybody asked me my name I'd say 'Kerryl Kaw'. Everybody used to laugh at that. Our Mam thought Kerryl was a cute name and it stuck. People called me Kerryl right through primary school, until I got to secondary. There my friends would still call me Kerryl but to the teachers I was Miss Shaw, right from Year 7. Miss Dove used to call me Cheryl, but when I was a senior and went to see Dr Fawcett, the Head, she called me Alison. I expect she thought Cheryl was a bit common. I don't much care for it myself. I think there was a celeb called Cheryl on the TV around the time I was born and our Mam liked her so she chose that name for me. Some people at school called me Rick. Rick-shaw, get it?

And Lander? A bit the same. His proper name is Alexander James Shaw (our Dad's name was James). The closest either of us could get to Alexander was Lander, so that's what he was. My school nickname was all right but his was 'Shit-face' (Shaw (sure) as shit, all right? Oh they were so clever, the King's Heath lads!). I'd have hated it but he didn't seem to mind. When I asked him about it he just shrugged and said it was no big deal, I should hear what he called them.

Kerryl and Lander. That's the story of our names. It was worth waiting for, wasn't it?

I'M SITTING WITH A FOLDER of Lander's cuttings beside me. He must have started collecting them quite early on, before the Infection became really big news. Did he know what was going to happen? He couldn't have, but he must have had some inkling, otherwise why save all this stuff?

There are half a dozen clips that date from right back at the beginning, before the Infection got a capital 'I', but they're only short and they don't say much. You've seen the first few that went into any sort of detail. The next interesting one is a long report from *The Sunday Times Magazine*. It has maps and diagrams which show how the virus radiated from what was thought to be its starting point, and spread through South and North Sudan to Egypt, and thence to the Middle East and Europe. It's a long report and if I paste all of it in my diary it will fill it up. This extract is what turned out to be probably the most important part.

An emergency session of the United Nations General Assembly was preceded by a meeting of the Security Council. Unusually the latter was held behind closed doors, but it is understood that a number of radical emergency measures were discussed to prevent the further spread of the Infection, particularly to the Far East, Europe and the USA. Among the topics on the table were restrictions on international travel.

Sources refused to confirm that Saudi Arabia is under pressure to abandon the Hajj, the annual pilgrimage to Mecca due to take place later this month at the end of the Islamic year. The Hajj is the largest annual gathering of people in the world, and the World Health Organisation has suggested that it might be deferred, along with other major events across the globe. However, the Saudi Ambassador declared that 'the Hajj is a demonstration of the solidarity of the Muslim people and their submission to God' and that postponement was inconceivable.

Alongside the UN activity the President of France, M. Huilac, is convening an urgent meeting of the leaders of Portugal, Spain, Italy, Greece and Turkey (known along with France as the 'Midi Six') to agree plans for dealing with the possibility of the I/452 virus being carried into Europe by fugitives, migrants and other illegal traffic across the Mediterranean.

A spokesperson for M. Huilac refused to confirm or deny reports that a suspected case of the I/452 infection had turned up in Marseilles.

Lander has highlighted the last sentence. I can remember there being a lot on the TV about the possible Marseilles case, and others in Malta. The authorities denied them all at first, but eventually a relative of one of the Maltese cases let the cat out by publicly attacking European governments for not doing enough to help the families. By then the Infection had taken hold in a number of other places in Europe. People were saying it was only a matter of time before it was everywhere, although I don't think anybody realised exactly what that meant: that all of us, everybody, would one day catch it.

THERE'S QUITE A LOT of this stuff of Lander's and I can't fill my diary with every single bit of it. I mean, we know that the Infection eventually did spread everywhere, don't we? Otherwise why would I be here on my own writing this diary? And why, my imaginary reader, would you be reading it? If you are. There's one thing that needs to go in, though, because it's really important. It shows the stupidity of the politicians whose job should have been to protect us against what was happening, but who turned out to be incapable of doing anything useful. It's a print-out from Lander's computer. I don't know where it came from or how he got it, but I guess he hacked into some site somewhere (he was always doing stuff like that). Or maybe it was circulated by his mates in thetruthwillsetyoufree.net. It seems to be some sort of official memo.

From: Controller, BBC News
To: Director, Media Monitoring Unit, 10 Downing Street
Subject: Interview – Elizabeth Harley (Minister for Health)/Gavin Martin (Anchor, BBC News Review), BBC1, May 29th, 21.30.

Malcolm

As required by your masters, I send you herewith a transcript of the interview with Bessie Harley that we broadcast last night. I hope you will agree with me that Gavin was very gentle with her and extremely fair, and that the session was free from the anti-government bias of which the BBC is often accused, and the policing of which is your raison d'être.

By the way, this would be an appropriate time to remind you that the BBC offers consultancy to public figures on techniques for handling interviews. You might want to suggest to Ms Harley that she sign up for a session!

Regards to Margot, and to your lovely daughter.

Quentin

Attachment:

Gavin Martin	Good evening. Those of you who watched the *Insights* programme on the BBC Events Channel two weeks ago will have seen our report on the mysterious virus which has ravaged the African continent. You may also have heard over the weekend of the alarming speed at which it seems to be spreading. There was news on Sunday of cases being found as far apart as Sardinia, Istanbul and Marseilles, and this morning there were further reports of possible cases in Lille and Antwerp.
	The Government has been accused of not doing enough quickly enough to prevent the virus reaching the United Kingdom. Tonight we have with us the Right Honourable Elizabeth Harley MP, Minister for Health, to answer those criticisms.

Elizabeth Harley	Good evening.
Gavin Martin	Minister, you'll be as aware as I am of what is being said. Is the Government doing enough?
Elizabeth Harley	Well yes, of course. We are taking all necessary action to protect the people of these islands.
Gavin Martin	Can you tell us what that action is? Because from where I sit it's hard to see what, if anything, is being done. In fact a headline in this morning's *Guardian* asks, 'Is the Government asleep at the wheel?'
Elizabeth Harley	Well you would expect that from *The Guardian*, wouldn't you? And you would expect the BBC to pick up on it. We have certainly not been asleep at the wheel. The Government has been monitoring the situation very closely from the very beginning, and some time ago we issued guidance to travellers to avoid a number of areas. The Royal Navy has played a major part in the Mediterranean blockade which was put in place, largely on the initiative of the United Kingdom, to seal off southern Europe and prevent the virus being brought to Europe by migrants and others running away from infected areas in Africa.

Gavin Martin	The blockade hasn't worked, though, has it? As I said in my introduction, we have cases of the infection recently reported as close as Belgium and northern France. What do you plan to do now?
Elizabeth Harley	I agree with you that the situation is serious. This very morning I chaired a meeting of COBRA to discuss our response to these reports.
Gavin Martin	And that is?
Elizabeth Harley	Well, I think we have to retain a sense of proportion. As I understand it the diagnoses from Antwerp and Lille have yet to be confirmed, and we're only talking about one case in each city. If they are confirmed, then we need to establish whether this strain of the virus is the same as the African one.
Gavin Martin	And in the meantime, what steps are being taken to stop it coming here?
Elizabeth Harley	Well, Gavin, as you know, the Government has been running a series of pubic information announcements on radio, television and in cinemas. These give valuable guidance on hygiene and on keeping homes and workplaces germ free. We're supplementing these with information leaflets which will go to every home in the country. They tell people what to do if they...

Gavin Martin	But all this seems to be based on the assumption that the virus *will* get here. What are you doing to ensure that it doesn't?
Elizabeth Harley	Well, if you'll let me finish, Gavin, it's the Government's duty to see that people are as well informed as possible about the virus and what to do if they encounter it. It's part of a two-pronged strategy, the other aspect of which is to make sure that the health services, and in particular our major hospitals, are prepared to deal with a widespread outbreak of the infection.
Gavin Martin	So you do think it's unstoppable, that the disease will spread to these shores.
Elizabeth Harley	I didn't say that, I didn't say that at all. We're working very closely with our European partners to contain matters. The European Health Executive has set up an early warning system to notify members immediately of any new outbreaks.
Gavin Martin	But what about travel restrictions? The opposition is calling for prohibitions on all but essential travel from and to mainland Europe, and for the establishment of screening units at ports and airports.

Elizabeth Harley	Yes, well, I notice the opposition is very good at making calls without spelling out the consequences. What's 'essential travel'? Travel that's essential to you might not seem so to me. And if we were to screen everyone coming into the country, think what chaos that would cause. People would be waiting for clearance for days. The whole system would seize up.
Gavin Martin	Better to be held in a queue than to die in agony, surely.
Elizabeth Harley	Now let's not be dramatic. These blanket controls are not as simple as people make them sound. We would need approval from our European partners to impose the sorts of restrictions that are being suggested. And would you really want us to shut the door on those British citizens living abroad who may want to seek refuge here? Or on European friends who want to come here to escape infection in their own countries? Pulling up the drawbridge isn't the answer. We live on a group of islands, and that has stood us in good stead in the past. I'm sure it will again.
Gavin Martin	I think people would be happier if they thought the Government was relying on more than the Channel to protect them. Is it true that the Americans are set to extend to the UK their ban on flights from the European mainland unless we impose our own restrictions on people coming here from the rest of Europe?

Elizabeth Harley	I think you've been listening to gossip, Gavin. I haven't heard that.
Gavin Martin	So you don't think it's inevitable that the infection will come here, and you're confident that everything that can be done to prevent such a thing is being done.
Elizabeth Harley	Yes, I am.
Gavin Martin	Minister, thank you very much.

The next one is the last of the clippings in Lander's collection. It may be the shortest but it conveys the bleakness and desperation of what happened better than any of the others. It's simply the whole front page of the *Daily Express*. There's the masthead, the date, and then just two words, in a black-edged box filling the whole of the rest of the space:

It's Here!

That's it. No photos, no text, just the headline. After all, what more was there to say?

THE NEXT DAY – or was it the day after? – I arrived at school as usual with my friend Josie to find Mrs Pritchard ('Pritt Stick'), the Head of Upper School, at the door of the sixth form block. She told us to go to the hall for a full assembly. Full assemblies were rare. The school hall was small, and getting 1,200 girls and the staff into it was a bit of a squeeze. For that reason they were saved for the beginnings and ends of terms, and there were still a few weeks left before the summer holiday. We were to go straight to the hall, Pritt Stick said. She wouldn't even let us drop off our bags in our form room first.

Me and Josie sat with Mandy Ross and some other Year 13 girls, hoping they knew what it was all about, but they were just as much in the dark as we were. Most of the staff were already in their seats on the stage, all in their gowns. They looked very solemn. Was there some trouble? Were we going to be told off? Was somebody going to be expelled? Miss Dove was on the front row. She was wearing a short summer dress and looked fabulous. Josie whispered that she probably wouldn't have worn that dress if she'd known she was going to be on the stage because it gave everybody a grandstand view of her legs. I said I couldn't see why not, because her legs were terrific. She was sitting next to Rudy. He was leaning towards her to say something in her ear, much too close, I thought. She smiled at him and shook her head.

Everybody stood when Dr Fawcett ('Forceps'), the Head, came in, and there was a hush as she swept down the hall to the stage. She was a very tall woman with a pointed nose and grey, almost white, hair tied back. She got to the lectern and made a downward gesture with her hand, and we all sat. She waited a long time before she started to speak, as if she hadn't quite worked out what she was going to say, or at least how to start.

'Girls,' she said at last, 'you will all be aware of the serious and highly contagious infection that has devastated Africa.' We were. Only a couple of weeks before, Year 11 had organised a collection for African children orphaned by the outbreak. 'You will also have heard,' she said, 'how the disease has spread beyond that continent and is now rampant in Asia and mainland Europe.

'A few days ago,' she went on, 'it was reported that a case has been diagnosed in Kent, and yesterday there was further evidence, this time from Birmingham and Norwich, that the Infection has arrived on these shores. The Government has therefore decided that immediate action is necessary to prevent it spreading further. As part of this, all places of education have been ordered to close immediately, until further notice.'

There was a stifled cheer from a group of Year 9 half way down the hall. They got Forceps's most regal glare. When she continued she said that the closure was a measured and sensible precaution. She apologised that there had not been time to inform parents, but it had been necessary to act quickly.

'At the end of this assembly,' she said, 'the house captains will be at the doors of the hall, and you should each collect from them a letter to take home. You are to go straight home and not spend time saying goodbye to friends or teachers. It is not the end of term, merely a temporary closure, a precaution. There is nothing to worry about, and I am sure that this situation will last for only a short time.

'Twenty minutes from the end of the assembly the school warden and her staff will check the building and close it,' she said, 'and shortly after that the main gates will be locked. All school premises will remain in that state until the all-clear is given.'

There was total silence for what seemed an age. Forceps stood erect at the lectern and surveyed her school, her eyes fixed and her mouth grim. Behind her some of the staff were looking flabbergasted, others were staring at the floor, and an old girl at the back whose name I didn't know appeared to be crying into her handkerchief.

Forceps spoke again. We were not to linger on the way home, she said, but to go straight there. Once home we were to avoid unnecessary contacts, follow the instructions given by the authorities and our parents and guardians, and stay safe.

'Your subject teachers will be putting homework for you on the school's website. You are expected to complete it conscientiously. Those of you in Years 11 and 13 will be wondering about examinations. The examination boards have announced that they are suspending all examinations, and new arrangements will be made when schools resume. I have been assured that candidates' performances in the papers they have already taken this summer will stand.'

She wished us well and looked forward to seeing us all together again, happy and well, in the near future. Then we all stood while Millicent Wainwright, the Head Girl, read a prayer.

O Almighty God, who in thy wrath didst send a plague upon thine own people; and also, in the time of King David, didst slay with the plague of pestilence threescore and ten thousand, and yet remembering thy mercy didst save the rest: Have pity upon us miserable sinners, who now are visited with great sickness and mortality; that like as thou didst then accept of an atonement, and didst command the destroying Angel to cease from punishing, so it may now please thee to withdraw from us this plague and grievous sickness.

Don't think I knew this prayer by heart. When I got home I looked it up because it sounded so powerful and so musical in that room full of silent girls.

I collected my letter at the door and shuffled along the corridor towards the main entrance with Josie, Monica, Charlene and a few others. Just before the door I felt a hand on my arm. It was Miss Dove.

'I thought you might like these,' she said.

She held out two books. One was *The Turn of the Screw* by Henry James. We'd read *Washington Square* and she'd been talking to us about James's other work and encouraging us to read some.

'It's a ghost story, of a sort,' she said. 'You said you were thinking of writing one. I think this might interest you.'

'By telling me not to bother?' I said.

'By helping you to write a better one,' she said.

The other book was a fat paperback. It was called *Mimesis: The Representation of Reality in Western Literature* by Eric Auerbach. I opened the front cover. On the flyleaf was her name, Angela Dove, and 'Girton College, Cambridge'.

'Read it,' she said. 'You're the only one of my students who I think would get anything from it.'

I thanked her. I felt really moved. She wasn't waiting for any of the other girls to lend them her books, and I was welling up. 'Where are you going?' I said, thinking that maybe I could cheat the rule and look in on her.

As if she was reading my thoughts she shook her head. 'I'm going to Chepstow,' she said, 'back home to my parents.'

'Can I email you?' I said. She nodded and said she'd text me her email address. She smiled at me and her eyes looked moist.

I never saw Miss Dove again. She never did send me her email address.

I WALKED WITH JOSIE to the bus stop. None of the other girls in our crowd seemed to be around. I think a lot of them had gone to say goodbye to their teachers, despite what old Forceps had said.

'Are you scared?' I asked Josie.

'Course I'm scared, you silly moo,' she said. 'Aren't you?'

'I suppose so. I don't know,' I said. 'It doesn't seem real. All those people dying so far away and you and me walking along the road here in the sunshine to catch a bus. It doesn't seem like it's actually happening.'

'It'll seem real enough when somebody round here catches it,' she said.

I laughed at her. 'You sound just like my gran,' I said.

She gave me a playful nudge. 'It just shows how wise your gran is then, doesn't it?' she said.

A car pulled in beside us. It was a dark grey Skoda Scabbard. I knew whose it was. I had been on its back seat. Monica Woodbridge leaned out of the passenger window. Mark II, behind the wheel, ignored us.

'Hello, you two. Do you want a lift?' said Monica, flashing her dazzling teeth.

I looked at Josie. I think she probably did but I didn't want anything to do with Mark II.

'No thanks,' I said. 'We'd rather walk. Plenty to think and talk about.'

'You can say that,' said Monica.

'I just did,' I muttered under my breath.

Monica didn't hear me. 'Okay,' she said, 'suit yourselves. See you around.'

She gave us another opportunity to admire her dental work and the car blazed off with a screech of tyres and a noise like an elephant farting.

'Show off!' I shouted after it.

'She's only trying to make it up to you,' said Josie, 'because she's sorry about taking Mark off you.'

'I don't care,' I said. 'She can have him. He's a prick.'

Neither of us said anything at first on the bus. Then Josie said, 'It's all right for you. You're lucky, living where you do. You'll be safe. There's no way the bugs will make it up the hill to you.'

I hadn't really thought about that. Josie's dad was a baker. They had a little shop on a street of terraces in the middle of the town, and Josie, her mam, dad and kid brother all lived above it.

'You've got loads of room,' she said. 'We're packed in like sardines. If anybody in our street gets it all the rest of us will. That's for sure.'

I gave her arm a squeeze. 'Come up with us,' I said. 'Please. We've got plenty of space We can make some for you, I know we can.'

Josie pulled out a tissue and shook her head. I could see she was crying. We didn't say any more until we got off the bus in the middle of Walbrough.

'I suppose this is it, then,' Josie said. 'You to your place, me to mine, to wait for what fate has in store for us.'

'It'll be all right,' I said, 'I'm sure of it.'

Josie forced a smile. Her eyes were red. 'You always look on the bright side,' she said. 'That's one of the things I love about you.' She leant forward and kissed me on the cheek. I hugged her. 'We shouldn't meet till it's over,' she said, 'but let's keep in touch.'

'I will,' I said.

BACK AT HOME LANDER was in his bedroom. I tapped on the door and without waiting went in. It looked like somebody had ransacked a jumble sale. Clothes, magazines, a guitar, books, crisp packets, chocolate wrappers, cans and all sorts of unmentionable stuff on every surface. Lander was at his desk, on his computer. He looked annoyed at being disturbed. I sat down on the edge of his bed.

'Make yourself at home,' he said. He didn't mean it.

'I will,' I said. I did.

'Lander,' I said, 'what are they doing about the kids?'

'How do you mean?' he said.

'The Government,' I said. 'What are they doing about the kids? Josie's brother, Simon, is only four. The Government must be doing something to protect the children. Aren't they?'

Lander turned back to his screen. 'Look at this,' he said.

He clicked a few keys and a video appeared. It was of some people demonstrating. They had placards with slogans. Some of them said 'GIVE US BACK OUR KIDS', 'GOVERNMENT CHILD SNATCHERS' and 'OUR NARK IS THE ARK'.

'What's going on?' I said.

'It's a demonstration,' he said. 'The Government started to set up what they called Children's Arks. They were supposed to be places insulated against the Infection, staffed by teachers and nurses, where kids would be safe. This was the first one, in Croydon, for kids under five.

Except instead of inviting parents to take their children along, they sent the police round their houses to collect them up. They said there wasn't time for consultation and that was the only way to get the arks set up in time. The parents protested. It got nasty after that,' he said, nodding towards the screen. 'They stormed the doors, got the kids out and set fire to the building.'

I watched over his shoulder images of people running, mothers and fathers carrying small children, a blazing building, fire engines, police in riot gear.

'What happened?' I said.

'The programme's been scrapped,' he said. 'Had to. There were only a couple of arks anyway, both in the south, and they've shut them down.'

'Where did you find that clip?' I said. 'I didn't see it on the news.'

'You wouldn't,' he said. 'The news is censored.' He moved his mouse and clicked through to a home screen. There was a circular portal blazing with light, set in darkness and in the centre the words 'The Truth Will Set You Free'.

'What's that?' I said.

'It's a group that shares information,' he said. 'The Government's only telling us what it wants us to know. The papers lie and the TV news is all over the place. This is an open access site where people can post what they see and hear and say what's actually happening to them. It's free, uncontrolled. It tells you what's really going on.'

'The truth will make you free,' I said. 'Sounds like something Hitler would have come up with.'

'No,' said Lander, 'it's just the opposite.'

I got up to go, but I wanted to be reassured so I stopped at the door. 'Josie says we're going to be all right up here,' I said. 'She says that even if the Infection takes hold in the valley it won't get up the hill to us. She's right, isn't she? We will be okay, won't we?'

Lander took a long time to answer. 'It depends,' he said. 'We'll have to be careful. Disinfect everything, avoid contact, keep everywhere clean.'

'Starting here?' I said, pointing to the mess that surrounded us.

'No,' he said, 'I don't mean this. But you can take down those bird feeders of yours for a start.'

'Why?' I said, surprised.

'Because they say that the Infection can be spread by birds,' he said.

'Oh.' I was disappointed because I like birds.

He turned back to his computer and I left him clicking away.

I COULD SEE THAT it was a sensible precaution to close the school until the threat of the Infection was over, but I was disappointed. We all grumbled about St Winifred's but I liked the rhythms and routines of the place. I liked the lessons and I liked my teachers. Well, most of them. I was especially gutted because I wouldn't be able to finish my exams. I'd got four more papers to go, and I thought I'd done well in the ones I'd already taken. Actually, because of Cambridge's entrance exams my results didn't matter, but I wanted to get A★ in everything. It was a challenge. I'd got eight A★s in my GCSEs. Maths and French let me down – I only got Bs in those – and I was annoyed that I hadn't managed a full house. This time I was determined it would be different. I'd been revising hard, doing two or three practice questions every night when I'd finished my jobs around the house or the farm. I have a tendency to write too much (you'd never guess, would you?!), so I was working to get my ideas down in the time allowed.

Lander thought I was mad. 'School shut, exams scrapped, that's paradise,' he said.

I explained that I really wanted to take my exams and he rolled his eyes.

'Smart-arse,' he said, and threw a cushion at me.

'Thick twonk,' I said, and threw it back.

'Twonk?' he said. 'Twonk? What sort of posh twatspeak is that? What's a twonk?'

I didn't tell him that twonk was Elizabethan slang for a dildo, at least that's what Rudy told us, although he might not have been right because I tried to look it up but I couldn't find it anywhere. Instead I returned the cushion, which had come my way again, and was pleased to catch him on the side of the head with it.

Me and Lander often bickered. Most of the time it was good humoured, like just now, but other times we had full-blown rows, like when I caught him looking at my diary. I wonder if he'll ever read this one. Don't get jealous, imaginary reader, you know it's for you, but he might one day find it and read it, if he stays alive. And if I do, I might even give it to him.

Even though the schools closed I didn't expect that everything else would too, but it did. New instructions from the Government came out every day, and we got used to turning on breakfast TV to see what was the latest thing to be shut down or axed. At the same time as the schools, churches and other places of worship were instructed to stay locked and suspend their services.

'They'll never do it,' Granddad said. 'There'll be a bloody revolution.'

There wasn't, although there might have been. An imam in Bedford flatly refused to close his mosque. He was on TV saying that life and death were in the hands of Allah and the faithful had an obligation to attend Friday prayers. The army threw a cordon round the mosque and there were some nasty scenes. Religious groups in other places joined in. It went on for a few days, and who knows what would have happened if the Infection had not eaten into the protesters and the crowds melted away.

Cinemas, theatres and clubs were ordered to close too. There was a club owner in Shoreditch who tried to start a 'Right to Rave' movement. He set up a website and defied the ban, saying it was his duty to offer music to the people ('And to collect twenty quid off each of them at the door,' said Lander). Police in biohazard outfits raided his place, he was dragged away and everybody in the club arrested. A band calling themselves The Virals set up a free gig in Roundhay Park. There were about 3,000 fans there when the police arrived in riot gear, and that was the end of that. It was widely reported, the same footage playing again and again. Some people posted messages calling the police pigs and fascists but I think they did a good job. The band was crap!

Very soon after that, sports grounds were closed and sporting events cancelled, so I was surprised when Lander asked me if I wanted to watch Arsenal v. Leicester City on TV.

'I thought football had been stopped,' I said.

'It has,' he said, 'except for the Premier League. Those matches can go ahead but in empty stadiums, with no crowd.'

We turned on the TV and watched the game, the players doing their thing in front of tier above tier of empty seats.

'This is weird,' I said.

'Duh,' said Lander. 'But why particularly?'

'Where is everybody? You can hear a crowd but there's no one there.'

'That's the director,' Lander said. 'He's dubbed in crowd noise to give it some atmosphere. But look.'

An Arsenal winger had the ball and one of the Leicester players robbed him from behind, then lost his footing and the ball rolled into touch. There was a huge roar from the 'crowd' and shouts of 'goal'.

Lander let out a yell. 'What a plonker that director is,' he said. 'You'd think he'd at least make the sound fit the game.'

Just then the invisible crowd started up with *You'll Never Walk Alone*. 'Isn't that a Liverpool anthem?' I said.

Lander started to laugh and so did I. It became more and more bizarre, the players doing one thing and the 'supporters' cheering another. We couldn't stop. We hooted until our cheeks and our sides were aching and we couldn't take any more. It was the last time we laughed together like that.

ALL THE TIME THE ROLL of victims of the Infection silently grew. Within three weeks there were cases in every major town and city. Hospitals were full and A&E departments struggling. There were constant instructions not to go out, to stay at home. As well as the football, the TV offered an endless stream of old comedy shows and blockbusters, just like at Christmas. Off-air or subscription, the channels were all the same. I suppose this was intended to reassure people and keep them in, but it seemed to me more likely to drive them out. I'd seen all the shows and movies before, so mostly I stayed in my room watching moviesticks on my iPad and reading.

I revised *Washington Square*. I felt really sorry for Catherine Sloper and murderous towards her father. He was so bossy. Why couldn't he just leave her alone and let her live her life? I wasn't sure about Morris Townsend. I don't think he was a bad man. Even if her father was right and Morris really was after Catherine's money, that doesn't mean that he couldn't have loved her and made her happy, if they'd been left alone. I think that despite her controlling dad Catherine was a girl to be reckoned with, and I think she could have sorted out our Morris.

I read *The Turn of the Screw* as well. It's a strange story. Are the ghosts real? No, I don't mean that, I know ghosts aren't 'real', what I mean is, who sees them? Of course the governess does, but does Mrs Grose, the housekeeper? Do Miles and Flora, the children? Can ghosts exist for one person and not another? Is it all happening inside the governess's head?

I started thinking about Miss Dove. I wonder why she hasn't married. She's great looking, funny, clever – and, if old Rudy's anything to go by, blokes like her. So why no boyfriend? Perhaps she's got a girlfriend instead, but she's never mentioned anyone.

I put *Washington Square* aside and started on *Mimesis*, but it was hard going. I've read only a few of the works Auerbach talks about. Some of the early quotes are in Latin, and although there's a translation it puts you off. I've never done Latin and it makes no sense to me! I made a list of the books I need to read to help me understand it. Where would I get them? The libraries are closed. I decided it would be better to wait till the libraries open again, and I put it aside and went back to the moviesticks.

I wish that I'd not already seen them all. It would be good now to have some fresh ones. Also I should have been choosier when I recorded them. I can watch *The Hunger Games*, *Jane Eyre*, *Titanic*, even *Diary of a Teenage Girl* again and again, but *Celebs in the Jungle* or *Essex Hen Nights* pall after a mere dozen plays!

I settled into our new routine far better than Lander, although he should have been used to having time on his hands. I helped with the animals and did odd jobs around the farm. I've always done the milking during the school holidays and now I took it over completely. It meant getting up early, but even on a chilly morning sitting in the semi-dark in the sweet-smelling barn, my head against Bonnie's or Dolly's ample flank, music on my iPod (I was developing a taste for classical music. Who'd have thought it?) was very soothing. The world of the Infection seemed another planet. I felt safe. Like most farms we had no near neighbours, there were no callers and we saw nobody. There was plenty of food so we had no need to go down to Walbrough. How could the Infection get to us up here? All we had to do was carry on as normal, sit tight and hope that the people in the valley would be all right too.

Our Mam had laid in a stock of antiseptic wipes, and she made Lander and me go round twice a day wiping everything: doors, furniture, drawer handles, surfaces, anything that anybody touched. I volunteered for the mornings and left the evenings for Lander, because he's hopeless in the morning. I didn't think all the wiping was necessary but I did my stint thoroughly to please our Mam. Lander skived off and did his badly.

'What's the point?' he said when I grumbled at him. 'Either we're safe up here or we're not, and a bit of wiping isn't going to make any difference.'

'How do you know that?' I said. I was angry with him and I told him he was a selfish, lazy slob.

'Great,' he said, 'you want to do it, knock yourself out!' and he flung down the packet of wipes and stamped out. I finished off for our Mam.

Lander had a problem: he didn't seem able to settle down. Although the news reports were upsetting and I felt very sorry for the poor people who were suffering, I was content with our lives at the farm. I didn't want it to go on like that for always, but I had no doubt that things would soon get back to normal, and while it lasted it was quite cosy. Lander, on the other hand, fretted. He missed his friends and whatever it was they did when they were all together. He didn't want to be here, but there was nowhere else he could be.

WE HAD PLENTY of warning that the Infection was coming closer. It got to Birmingham, then Derby, Nottingham, Sheffield, Wakefield, Leeds, Bradford, Stafford, Manchester, Oldham. It was like an advancing army, throwing a ring round us. Even though it seemed clear now that it would reach our valley we thought we'd have more time to prepare. We didn't. It was as swift and unexpected as a knife from a stranger in the dark. In the cities it spread amazingly quickly because people lived and worked close together. One infected person on a tram in Manchester could give it to all the other passengers, and they would take it home and pass it on to their families and friends. The people on the tram wouldn't know they were carrying it and those they met wouldn't know they were being infected. They would all consider themselves fine. Then a week to ten days later the passengers would start to feel ill, and soon after that all their contacts would too.

We all knew the Infection could take hold easily and quickly, but nobody had realised what that actually meant. So it was all a scramble, and it seemed that everything the authorities did could be described in the same way: a good idea that might have been useful if it had been done sooner, but was now far too late.

Take, for example, the biohazard suits. Apparently there were loads of these, and masks, which had been put into store a few years ago when MI5 uncovered a germ warfare plot by AWA terrorists and there was a big scare. The problem was that at first no one knew where they were all kept. It took days to locate them, and then even longer to transport them and give them out. And they weren't much use anyway. Because they were old and hadn't been stored properly the plastic of some of them had deteriorated so that they split easily. Also there weren't enough of them, and a rule was made that only essential workers, people under thirty-five and pregnant and nursing mothers could have them. That meant that me and Lander got one each, but our Mam, Gran and Granddad didn't. I wanted our Mam to have mine but there was no way she would. 'We're expendable,' said Granddad. I don't think he was being bitter. He was just stating what seemed to him to be an obvious fact.

The Government set up Infection Control Centres (ICCs) in every town. These were supposed to take some of the pressure off the hospitals, as well as assuming a civil defence role. The ICCs offered first-line care and were meant to give out the bio suits and the literature. However, they were badly organised and the staff poorly trained. The ICC for Walbrough took over the Health Centre. It commandeered the premises and seized the ambulances and emergency vehicles. However, it was all done in a rush, communications went adrift and orders were misunderstood. The existing Health Centre staff, including the doctors, nurses and ambulance drivers, suddenly found themselves with no premises, no equipment and no jobs to do. They were skilled people but there was no one organising them and they drifted away.

Later, after the Infection had taken hold, the job of the ICC changed to collecting and cremating the corpses.

It couldn't do it. There were so many bodies and some were being left to rot. I know this because I saw them. Of course, once people working in the ICC themselves got ill the whole operation fell apart.

As well as this, a lot of time and effort were wasted. Take the last leaflet. It was delivered to every home in the country. Think of the resources it took to do that. Think of what else, more useful, those people could have been doing. I remember when Billy, our postman, delivered ours. 'Here,' he said, adjusting his face mask and extending a blue-gloved hand. 'A bit of bedtime reading for you.' That was the last time I saw him.

I'm going to paste the leaflet in my diary here. (Why am I telling you this? You'll know that's what I did because you can see it!)

Beating the Infection

Say goodbye to 452-I!

The Infection known as I/452 is on the move. It's reached mainland Europe and could come here. The way to beat it is to be prepared. Here's what to do.

1. Try to avoid busy places, and don't spend long in them. Do your shopping online and get your orders delivered.

2. Cancel travel, and plans for special events such as concert, cinema or theatre trips. Postpone holidays.

3. We suggest you also postpone parties, weddings, birthday celebrations and other gatherings, even if you know all the people who'll be attending.

4. Food is safe but wash everything before eating it. Wash your hands before and after eating.

5. You may hear people say that pets can carry the infection. This is unlikely, but we recommend that you keep cats and other small animals indoors. Keep dogs on a lead when walking them and don't allow them to approach strangers.

6. The virus spreads easily but it is also easy to kill. Wash your hands frequently using antiseptic soap. Wipe door and drawer handles and surfaces in your home with antiseptic wipes at least once a day. Do the same with your car, wiping the steering wheel, all controls and the door handles. Wash your

clothes using antiseptic detergent. There is a list of recommended brands on the website.

7. The law requires your employer to take these precautions too. Make sure he does, and report him to the nearest Infection Control Centre if he doesn't.

8. If you feel at all unwell, particularly if you have a headache, joint pains or a fever *don't go to your family doctor.* Instead go straight to an Infection Control Centre. There is one in every town. The address of your nearest is on the leaflet that has been delivered to your house (or soon will be). You can also find it online at www.doh.gov.uk/fighttheinfection. Just enter a postcode. Write down the address and phone number and put it somewhere prominent so that everyone in your household is aware of it.

9. If a person you have been in contact with develops symptoms of the Infection ten days or less after you have been with them, go straight to the nearest Infection Control Centre to get yourself checked out. *You can attend any Infection Control Centre and you don't need an appointment – just go!*

Stay informed. Watch the news and check out www.doh.gov.uk/fighttheinfection and Twitter @fighttheinfection for the latest updates and information.

Together we can beat this!

It's all good advice, and you can see that it might have been useful when it was written, but by the time it got to us it was out of date. On the day I took the leaflet from Billy all the offices and factories had been closed for several days. So had many of the shops. People in the valley were ill and some were already dead.

Every night on TV there were news updates. They were trying to say that the situation was under control and everything would soon be back to normal but we knew that wasn't true. As well as thetruthwillsetyoufree.net, people called each other and QuickChatted and posted online, so it was easy to find out what the real situation was.

The TV reports kept telling people to keep calm and do what they would normally do, except for going out. By now, though, the internet sites were buzzing with gossip about shortages and it was impossible to get online grocery deliveries. Some sites started offering basic things – eggs, milk, bread, cereal, jam, soap – for silly money. Others offered to do your shopping for you, sterilise the packaging and bring it to your door. There were rumours of people panic buying and there was looting. The police were attacked in Bradford when they were trying to stop a crowd breaking into a supermarket.

A couple of days after the mad football game I heard our Mam bang on Lander's door. 'Come on,' she said, 'stir your stumps. I'm going into Walbrough to get supplies and I need some help.'

There was the usual grumpy Neanderthal grunting from my brother, but he did get up.

'Suits on,' said our Mam, when Lander eventually appeared downstairs. Me and Lander put on our bio suits. I certainly felt foolish and I'm sure he did too, and I felt embarrassed that we had suits and our Mam didn't.

'Ooh, you do look a picture,' said our Mam, reaching to chuck Lander's cheek. He pushed her hand away. We climbed into the Land Rover and Mam drove us down the hill.

'Well, will you look at that?' she said as we approached the town.

There were police and army everywhere, all dressed in orange biohazard suits. Some of them had guns. A lot of the shops had been boarded up and only ones selling essentials were open.

'There's nothing much about, so at least parking won't be a problem,' our Mam said as she swung into the supermarket car park. 'Looks like we'll have to queue, though.'

We joined the straggling line of would-be shoppers waiting patiently outside the store. Some of them were wearing biohazard suits, but a lot weren't.

'Keep apart,' a soldier barked. 'Stay at arm's length from everyone else. Don't close up.'

There were two suited people at the door. One of them gave us hand wipes and told us to cover our eyes and mouth and step one at a time into a sort of plastic tent. 'Stay inside until you hear the buzzer,' she said. As soon as we were inside the tent a flap closed behind us. Me and Lander pulled on our masks, Mam held a cloth to her face and the space filled with a very fine mist. Then the buzzer went off and we walked out the other side of the tent into the shop.

What we found was not a supermarket any more. There was just a long counter across the tills, with some of the shop people behind it, all in bio suits. We weren't allowed to go to the shelves. Mam had to show them her ID and they looked on their computer to check our household entitlement. Then we had to tell them what we wanted, up to the number of points we were allowed, and they fetched it. When we'd finished, our Mam paid and we went out by a different door.

'I paid for all that,' said our Mam, 'but I wonder if money's going to be any good for much longer.' I expect she was thinking about her £36,000.

When our Mam told Granddad about our trip he decided to take the tractor and trailer into the town to see what he could find.

'We've got to get what we can while we can,' he said to Gran. 'There'll be no end of useful stuff lying around down there and soon it'll all be gone.'

He took Lander and was away for hours. I don't know what we expected, Gran, Mam and me, but we didn't think he'd come back with the trailer piled high with wooden pallets. He looked pleased with himself.

'Is that it?' said Gran. 'Is that all you could get? What on earth have you brought those for?'

'We found them at the back of Lamb's Sweets,' said Granddad. 'There must be another hundred there. I'll go down again tomorrow for some more.'

Gran thought he was mad and told him so.

'You never know what will come in handy if things go on like this,' said Granddad. 'Pallets are very useful. I can make things out of them. We can use the wood for repairs. We can burn them. You'll be glad of these, mark my words.'

He took the trailer round the back of the barn and I helped him and Lander stack the pallets against the wall. I didn't know then what I would eventually be using them for.

I WAS MISSING my friends, especially Josie. I'd known her forever. We'd been in the same class at primary school. We took the entrance exam for St Winifred's together and we both got in. There was only us and Minal Akram from our primary who did. Me and Josie were put in the same tutor group.

I went to school with Josie every day. I'd meet her at the bottom of the hill and we'd catch the bus together. I'd go round her place some evenings and at weekends, or she would come up the hill to ours. Sometimes we'd have sleep-overs. We'd spend hours in her room or mine. We might be doing our homework, but more likely we'd be dancing to tracks, practising make-up, trying on clothes. Or we'd lie on her bed, talking about boys we fancied and bitching about other girls. We started our periods within two months of each other, even though Josie's nine months older than me. We went into the sixth form together. Josie almost didn't make it. You needed mostly A or B grades in your GCSEs to go on to higher level studies at St Winny's. Josie got a lot of Cs.

'If they don't let you into the sixth form I'm not going either,' I told her, and I think I meant it. Anyway, it didn't have to be tested because they gave her a place on an advanced practical course. I was really pleased. I may be cleverer than Josie but boys think she's really hot. I've never had a steady boyfriend but Josie's been going out with Bobby Ainsworth for a year now. She sees him a lot but she still has time for me.

After the school closed I talked to Josie every day on my mobile. I texted her and sent her messages and pictures on QuickChat and iKnowU and we'd spend hours on Face2Face. This was okay, but I missed her.

Two days went by and I didn't hear from her and she didn't answer my calls. I texted her and said I didn't care about the Infection, I wanted to come and see her and I'd walk down the hill and we could meet at the park. Within a few minutes my phone rang and I saw it was her.

'Josie?' I said. There was no answer. I thought maybe she didn't want to see me. Then I realised she was crying.

'Don't come,' she said. 'Don't come anywhere near me.'

'Why ever not?' I said. 'What's the matter?'

'My mam's got it,' she said. 'She went down with it yesterday and George (her brother) has got it too and I expect I'll be next.'

I cried too then. It was the worst phone call, neither of us saying anything, neither wanting to drop the call and both of us crying.

I messaged Josie that evening and she replied. She said that I was the best friend she could have and she loved me. I messaged her again in the morning. She didn't respond. I called her number and there was no answer. I tried the landline but got a number suspended tone. I wanted to go to her house to find out what had happened but Lander talked me out of it. He said I was being selfish.

'What happens if you catch it and bring it back here?' he said. 'Do you want to infect all of us?'

Of course I didn't, but I was really cut up about Josie. I called some of my other friends. Penny Cross lives in the same street as Josie. She said she didn't know about Josie herself but she'd seen an ambulance outside her house. I said that might mean they were taking somebody to hospital.

'No,' she said, 'nobody goes to hospital any more. They're using ambulances for hearses now.'

I asked her what things were like down the hill. She didn't want to talk about it. I called Suzy Simmonds but it went through to voicemail. I went on iKnowU but nobody in my pod had posted for two days. I put out a *Holler*. There was one reply and that took an hour. It was from Steve, the last boy I'd gone out with. We hadn't really broken up but he'd moved to Ayrebridge along the valley and we'd just not connected since. We did a Face2Face. The picture kept jumping, but I could see he was wearing a black anarchist T-shirt and his hair was a mess. He looked awful. He said everybody there was dying and all the young people were having a 'Death's Doorway' party and they were all going to dance and drink and shag and get high until one by one they dropped. He said that people were breaking into the stores and taking what they wanted and there was no one there to stop them, no police or army or anything. He said I should join him, because if you've got to go that's the way to do it.

He held out his phone and swung it in an arc so I could see what he meant. There were a lot of people in the streets, mostly young but a few adults too. Some of them were half naked, some had bottles, some were dancing. Several were lying on the floor, either drunk or apparently dead. He lingered on a couple making out. In the background another girl was puking up. It made me feel sick.

I told Lander about the pictures. 'Good for them,' he said.

I got angry then. How could he not see how awful it was? 'Why don't you go and join them if you think it's so fucking fantastic?' I yelled at him.

'I think I will,' he shouted back, and he walked out.

He didn't go, though, because later I heard him in the field with his .22. I think he was trying to shoot rabbits. Lander and I seemed to be quarrelling a lot now. We didn't used to, well, not as much. We might have gone on as we were for who knows how long. We might all have survived, because as long as we kept to ourselves up here how could the Infection get to us?

Bryst put an end to that. I don't blame him. He didn't set out with the intention to kill us. He was just looking for some way to help his boy.

I'M GOING TO PUT this down in detail, even though it means a lot of writing. 'So what?' you say. 'What else have you got to do?' Even if I was busy from morning to night this story would need to be told. It's how the Infection broke into our haven on the hill, how it tipped out our lives and used them up, and you need to know.

I was in bed. It was time to get up but I was putting it off. I'm usually pretty good in the mornings but that day was unseasonably cold. Granddad wouldn't run the heating in the summer, and the house was chilly. Our Mam used to go on at him about it. 'We've got free electricity from the solar panels and the wind turbine,' she'd tell him, 'so why on earth do we have to be cold?' He'd just ignore her. Anyway, I digress (again). That morning was cold, and I made a cocoon with the duvet and hung on until I could stay there no longer.

I passed Lander's bedroom. The door was open and he was on his back with his mouth open, snoring. Buster sleeps with me now but then he used to sleep on the landing, and as I passed he looked up and his tail thumped the floor. He didn't get up, though. He was Lander's dog and he wouldn't stir till his boss did. I stamped down the stairs but I knew Lander wouldn't hear me. A bomb wouldn't wake him before nine o'clock. Then he'd arrive in the kitchen, rubbing his eyes and expecting breakfast.

I took my parka from its peg and opened the door. Rain slapped my face and I shut it again while I pushed my arms into the sleeves and pulled up the hood. Then I went across the yard to the barn. I remember hearing the wind slam the kitchen door behind me and thinking, 'Good, that'll stir you up.'

Once inside the barn I felt better. I always did when I smelt the sweet hay and the animals. Our three cows were waiting patiently. Their muzzles were glossy and their breath steamed. I gathered the bucket and the stool. Only two of them, Bonnie and Dolly, were giving milk. Molly was in calf but still a few weeks away yet.

I remember exactly what happened. I've rerun it time and time again in my head, wondering if I could have done anything differently. The problem is, I didn't see the danger until it was too late. It just never occurred to me. Does that mean I was to blame for what happened? Lander thought so.

Anyway, the story. Bonnie and Dolly are placid animals and don't need to be tied for milking, so I set the stool beside Bonnie, took a cloth, dipped it in a bowl of disinfectant and wiped her udders. Then I began to knead her teats, squirting the milk into the bucket in warm, frothy spurts. I felt guilty that I'd made such a racket leaving the house. I'd just been in a mardy mood. The milking wasn't bad once you got used to the early start, in fact I quite enjoyed it. Anyway, I told myself, I'd rather get up every morning for the milking than have to do the slaughtering. We needed Bonnie's milk but we hadn't needed her calf. At the best of times we wouldn't have got much for a male calf, but now with the markets closed it would have been impossible to sell. So Granddad had taken it behind the barn and shot it. Bonnie had wailed dismally for three days. I wanted to know why he'd killed it, why not just let it loose. He said that it wouldn't have gone away, and that Bonnie would have tried to go after it. It would have died anyway, so better to do it quickly. I can remember watching while he gutted and skinned it and cut it up for the freezer, and wondering why I wasn't a vegetarian!

I loosened Bonnie and she ambled away. I switched on the cooler and poured in the milk. The barn door was open and Bonnie was free to leave now but she wouldn't. I always milked her first and when I'd done she'd wait until Dolly was finished too. Then they'd both go out together.

After I'd done Dolly I drained off the cooler and filled a minichurn to take to the kitchen. Molly didn't want to go out – cows don't like rain – but I shooed her off after the others and stepped out to close the barn door, and that's when I saw him. He was about twenty metres away and standing perfectly still. I thought he was cradling a bundle of rags, but then I saw it was a child wrapped in a dirty blanket. I thought it must be dead because its limbs were hanging loose and its head lolled back. The man took two paces towards me and I retreated into the doorway.

'Stay there, don't come near me,' I shouted.

'Please, please,' he said, 'please don't go. I need help. Please.'

He had a slight accent, middle European, I thought. He took another step towards me and I backed away. *DO NOT ASSOCIATE WITH STRANGERS. DO NOT LET STRANGERS INTO YOUR HOME.*

Afterwards I tried to recall what he looked like. I remember that his black hair was plastered over his forehead by the rain, his jacket was old and sopping wet, and his jeans were muddy and torn. But I wasn't really concentrating on him. I was looking at the dead child he was holding and listening to the warning beating in my head. *DO NOT ASSOCIATE WITH STRANGERS. DO NOT LET STRANGERS INTO YOUR HOME.* That's what the *How to keep safe* leaflet said. Strangers were a threat, a new sort of stranger danger. I should have slammed the barn door there and then, but I didn't.

'What do you want?' I said. 'You can't come in.' My voice was hard and he seemed to flinch.

'My boy,' he said, 'he is ill. Please help me. Please.'

The child moaned and rolled its head towards me. The face was pale, the eyes bloodshot, and now he was closer I could see he was shivering.

'I mean you no harm,' the man said. 'We need help, somewhere to rest for a short time. That's all I ask, and some water, that's all. My name is Bryst. I'm a musician. I was on my way to my brother in Manchester when my boy got sick. It's only a cold, it's not the Infection. Please trust me.'

I didn't believe him. I could see the boy was infected, I had no doubt about it. I shouldn't have listened to him. I should have run back to the house and shouted for Granddad or Lander to go with a shotgun and drive him away. Then we should have reported it to the ICC. That's what Lander thought, and he was right, but I couldn't. The boy looked to be in pain, and the man who said his name was Bryst seemed so sad. He was desperate, but he wasn't threatening or grovelling, he was dignified. I felt sorry for them. I couldn't not help.

'Follow me,' I said. 'And stay back. Don't come any nearer.'

I led the way towards the house and pointed to a spot in the yard about three metres away from the kitchen door. 'Stay there,' I said.

I went inside and shut the door firmly behind me. Granddad was at the table with a mug of tea, watching the morning news. Gran was frying bacon. I wondered if Bryst was hungry. He must be, he looked starving. His face was so thin and the hands holding his son were long-fingered and boney.

'There's somebody outside. He's got a little lad with him,' I said.

Gran dropped the skillet and our Mam looked horrified. Granddad went to the door and looked out. He didn't say anything to Bryst but he shut the door again.

'The boy's ill,' I said. 'The chap says he's got a cold.'

Granddad went into the hall and came back with one of his shotguns.

'Where are you going with that?' said Gran.

'I'm going to see him off before they infect us all, that's where I'm going.'

'You're going to see off a sick child? With a shotgun?' Gran blocked the door to the yard and folded her arms.

For a couple of seconds they faced each other, but Gran held her ground and Granddad looked down. 'Anyway, it's not loaded,' he mumbled. He broke the gun and laid it on the table. He looked up at Gran and nodded. She'd won.

'Right,' said Granddad. 'This is what we'll do. Kerryl, you put on your bio suit. I'll borrow Lander's. You and

71

me'll go out and examine the boy to see if it really is just a cold he's got, or if it seems more serious.'

'Give you three guesses,' said Lander who'd come into the kitchen to see what all the fuss was. He was happy to get up now the milking was done.

'Well, we'll see,' said Granddad. He gave Gran a long look. 'There've been reports of gangs stealing from isolated homes, so Lander, take the .22 up to the back bedroom and watch the yard in case it's some trick to cover an attack on us.' He told our Mam to stand by with the first aid kit and Gran to lock the door and stay inside, ready to phone the authorities if anything went wrong.

When we were suited up and everyone was ready, Granddad eased the door open and led the way out. The man, Bryst, had disappeared. All that was left was the child, lying on the ground in a wet bundle.

I searched around to see if I could find Bryst but he'd gone. Meanwhile Granddad spread out some hay in a corner of the barn. Our Mam found some old blankets and we made up a sort of bed. Then Granddad lifted the boy and carried him into the barn. I think that's when he put the split in Lander's suit, because it was so tight on him. We dried the boy and wrapped him up. He had a high fever and the next day the diarrhoea started. Then the cramps came. We tried to help him, easing his limbs to sooth the pain. We tried to get him to eat something but everything we gave him came right back up again. There was nothing we could do. The next day the bleeding began, and then it was all over. It was awful when he died but it was a relief too. His cries had been pitiful.

The boy never spoke to us and we never knew his name. We guessed he was about seven. I thought that maybe Bryst had gone to get more help, but he never came back.

Granddad phoned the ICC and they sent an ambulance. Lander and I watched one of the suited men load the boy into the vehicle while the other went through the forms with Granddad. Bryst had left no clue about either of them, and all I could do was tell the man what had happened. He said he'd have to put it down as death of a male child, identity unknown, and if we discovered any more we were to report it. He said we shouldn't have taken him in and we should expect to hear more about it. He left a card.

After the ambulance had gone Lander turned on me. He'd hardly spoken during the time we'd been nursing the boy but now he was furious.

'What were you thinking of?' he said. 'You must be out of your fucking mind.'

I was angry with him for being angry with me. 'What could I do?' I said. 'Send a sick child away? Is that what you would have done?'

'Too fucking right it is,' he said. 'You've probably infected us all.'

'The boy didn't come into the house,' I said, 'and we had the suits.'

'The suits are useless, everybody knows that,' he said. 'We'll all get it now. Thank you very fucking much, sister.'

Our Mam told him to stop swearing and threw him some wipes. 'If you're so worried, wipe everything,' she said.

Lander was right, though. Or nearly.

ONE OF THE WORST THINGS about the Infection was that it made you scared of everybody. Our Mam had brought Lander and me up to be polite and friendly towards people. She said that most people were decent, and if you were nice to them they'd be nice to you. I think she was right, but the Infection turned every single person, even your closest friends and family, into someone who might kill you. Can you imagine what that was like? To look at every other human being as a threat, and therefore as an enemy? Well, if you're reading this of course you can, because you will have been through it.

I was the only one with an undamaged bio suit, so I raked up the hay in the stall where the boy had been and carried that and the blanket he'd used out to the old slurry pit behind the barn. Lander threw a pallet on top and set the whole lot on fire.

Granddad said we should tell our neighbours, in case Bryst had been on their land.

'We ought to warn them,' he said. 'The man might have been in their outbuildings and they'll need to wipe things down, just in case. Besides,' he said, 'they will have seen the ambulance and they might be thinking it was for one of us.'

'I'll go,' I said. 'I'll wear my suit.' That was as much to reassure them as to protect me.

The neighbours were not close, either physically or socially. The nearest, Highgate Farm, is further up the hill, about 500 metres away. The other two, West Lee and Broadstones, are about the same distance on each

74

side. We could go weeks without talking to any of them, just giving the occasional wave if we saw someone in their fields.

I knew the Crowthers at Highgate best so I decided to start with them. I got hot walking up the hill in my suit and I was soon sweating. When I reached their gate I stopped to get my breath. 'This will teach you to be so lardy,' I told myself. 'Time you went on a diet, girl!'

I turned into their yard and found they'd put a hurdle across the entrance and hung up a big iron plate and a mallet. There was a sign saying to stop there and bang the plate to get attention. I thought that was a really good idea. They could come out to talk to visitors without having them come right up to their door. I gave the plate a clout with the mallet and it rang like a bell. I waited. There was no response so I struck it again. Still nothing. Then I noticed – and I don't know why I hadn't seen it before – that there was no life in the fields or the outbuildings. There were no hens pecking about in the yard, no cows grazing, nothing. The Crowthers had two donkeys that were the children's pets, but their stable was shut up.

I ducked under the hurdles and went to the front of the house. There was a red and yellow biohazard sticker on the door and an official notice: DANGER. INFECTED AREA. KEEP OUT! The door and the downstairs windows were taped up. I couldn't take it in at first, but it could mean only one thing. The family was gone.

I felt really bad. The Crowthers had been nice. Ben and Sarah, the children, were my age. They had gone to the primary school over the hill in the next valley, not the same one as Lander and me, but I'd known them and we'd played together. They seemed to get on really well together and didn't bitch at each other the way Lander and I did. More recently, Ben had gone to agricultural college and was away, but I'd sometimes run into Sarah when she was out and about with her friends, and we'd chat. Mr Crowther and our Dad would borrow tools and other stuff from each other. When I was a kid Mr Crowther would sometimes bring one of the donkeys down and let me ride it, and when I went up to theirs Mrs Crowther would give me cake. Now it seemed they were all dead. They'd got infected, become sick, suffered and died and I hadn't known anything about it. We hadn't seen an ambulance. They hadn't called us and we had been unaware of the drama playing out so near. Had it happened to them all at once? Or one after the other? Had one of them been left till last? Who? I imagined Sarah, alone and afraid, patiently waiting for her own end after seeing the rest of her family die. I started to cry. For Sarah, not because I had any idea that I would soon be experiencing that very same thing myself.

Still sobbing, I walked across the fields to Mr and Mrs Baxter's place at West Lee. They were both elderly and didn't farm, they just had a couple of acres with half a dozen sheep and some hens. I was dreading finding the same red and yellow tape and the official notices sealing off their house too. It wasn't as bad as that, but it was not good. Nobody was around and that was unusual. Mr Baxter was always pottering in one of his sheds, making or mending something, but everything was shut up. I stopped a few metres from the back door and called. Mrs Baxter opened it a little, just enough for their dog, Maxwell, to run out to me.

'I won't come any nearer,' I said, rubbing Maxwell's ears. 'I just came to see that you're all right.' I made to move nearer but she held up her hand to stop me anyway.

She told me that she felt fine but she was worried about Mr Baxter. He'd been down to Walbrough a week ago to get some things he said they needed.

'I told him not to bother, that we could manage,' she said, 'but he'd insisted.' He'd found the town more or less deserted. 'There were no police or army around and everything was closed,' she said. 'The supermarket was locked up but somebody'd broken all the windows so you could just walk in.'

She'd been worried about him because they were both too old to qualify for protective suits. 'I made him cover his mouth and nose with a scarf soaked in disinfectant,' she said, 'and as soon as he got back we wiped everything and he showered. It wasn't enough, though.' He'd been all right for a few days, but that morning he had started to feel ill. She described his symptoms: shivering, fever, headache, aching joints. It was obvious what it was. I think she knew too, although she had to hang on to the hope that it might not be. I told her about Bryst and his little boy but she hadn't seen them. Neither of them had come across anyone else up here: no boy, no thin, dark-haired man. I told her about the Crowthers and she said she knew and wasn't it dreadful?

'We saw the ambulance at your place,' she said, 'and we thought it must be for one of you. I was going to call, but I didn't like to. He was thinking about coming over to see what was up, but then he started to feel a bit groggy himself.' She began to cry. 'Where will it all end?'

I took the news back home. Granddad was upset about the Crowthers; he'd known the family for a long time.

'Well,' said our Mam, 'it doesn't get us any nearer to knowing where this lad came from, does it?'

'Or how he got here,' said Lander.

I don't think Lander believed me that Bryst existed. 'You're the only one who thinks she saw him,' he'd said to me the night we found the boy, 'none of the rest of us did. When I looked there was no sign of him. Do you really think he'd just dump his sick kid and go off like that? Are you sure you didn't imagine him?'

It riled me. 'Don't be stupid,' I said. 'How do you think a sick boy got up here on his own? Or perhaps you think I went down into Wally to fetch him.'

He shrugged. 'Wouldn't be surprised,' he said. 'You're daft enough.'

I knew he didn't mean it. It was just Lander being Lander.

I ONCE READ A MAGAZINE article about how to cope with the impact of the death of a parent. I'd felt terrible when our Dad died, but I'd never really considered our Mam going. She'd had the odd cold now and then, but I'd never known her to be really ill. She had always been there and she always would be. So it was a shock when the next day I came down to do the milking and found Mam and Gran already up. Mam was in an armchair, a blanket round her and her head lolling back on the cushions. Gran was on the other side of the kitchen. Mam's hair was dank and stringy, and when she looked up at me I could see she was sweating and her face was flushed.

'What is it?' I said.

'What do you think?' said our Mam, and she smiled at me weakly. Her voice was feeble and she looked frightened. I moved towards her but she held up her hand. 'No, love, don't come any closer,' she said.

I stood away from her, awkwardly, like being told off at school. She told me how she'd been up most of the night. How she'd had a headache when she went to bed and she'd taken a couple of Paracetamol. She woke up after sleeping for an hour or so sweating, her head feeling worse and her joints aching. She shuddered. Gran wanted her to go to bed but she wouldn't.

'I'm all right here in the chair,' she said. 'If I lie down I won't ever get up again. I know that and so do you.'

Just then Granddad came in from the yard. 'It's all done,' he said.

He'd been getting a space ready for Mam in the barn, where Bryst's boy had been. 'A sort of isolation ward,' he said. He'd moved an easy chair across from the house, and a little table for her to put her things on, and he'd rigged up a light. He'd hung a curtain across the end of the stall to give her a bit of privacy, and brought a few of her personal things over from her bedroom. There was a jug of drinking water, and a bowl and toiletries for washing, and a little jar of flowers. It must have taken him a long time to get it all organised like that. He shook his head when I asked if there was anything I could do to help.

'Don't come and see me,' said Mam, getting up. She moved like an old woman, as if it hurt her. 'Nor Lander neither,' she said. 'Don't come near me, either of you.' She blew me a kiss. 'It's nothing,' she said. 'I expect it's just a bit of 'flu, that's all. I love you,' she said.

I stood in the kitchen and watched her hobble across the yard, feeling tears prickle my eyes. I'd heard so much about the Infection and seen its effects in countless news reports, but it had seemed a long way off. I hated to admit it even to myself, but people dying in Africa hadn't been as important to me as the other things going on in my life. But now here it was, the Infection, embedded in our family and attacking someone I loved. I felt completely useless. I wanted to get on the phone for help, or take her down the hill in the Land Rover. But there was no point trying to get treatment. Where would we go? The ICC would just send us away and tell her to go to bed. Anyway, we couldn't take her away from here. It was a criminal offence for someone experiencing the symptoms of the Infection to deliberately go out in public. If we were caught we would be locked up and forgotten. There were even reports of infected people seen out of their homes being shot, along with their carers.

Once our Mam was settled Granddad sent me to get Lander, and the four of us sat in the front room. Granddad told us that he had no doubt that our Mam had the Infection and it was inevitable she would die.

'No point beating about the bush,' he said. 'We've got to face the facts.'

Lander and me were the two with biohazard suits. Granddad had taped up the tear he'd made in Lander's suit but he didn't want to risk it splitting again, so it was agreed that Gran and me would put on the suits and take it in turns to nurse our Mam. That way someone would always be with her. Lander and Granddad would have to talk to her from the door.

She was too weak to say much, but she tried her best to smile at Gran and me whenever we came in to be with her. I sat on the milking stool at her side and watched her, lifting the water that she couldn't get enough of to her lips and wiping her brow with a hanky splashed with rose water, her favourite. I remembered when she'd done the same for me when I'd had scarlet fever. Her hair was plastered to her forehead with sweat. I moved it aside, and thought about how, when I was younger, she used to brush and plait mine before I went to school. I've got a lot of hair, thick and long. She doesn't plait it any more but on a Saturday night if I was not going out I'd wash it and she would brush it for me while we watched the TV together.

After the fever came the vomiting and the diarrhoea. Me and Gran had a real struggle to keep Mam clean. Everything we took off her we put into bags, took round the back of the barn and burnt. Next were the cramps. They were awful. All her muscles knotted. She couldn't breath, her body arched, her jaw locked and her sinews stood out like cords. She gripped my hand and squeezed it so tight I thought she would break my fingers. It hurt enough to bring tears, but I didn't mind. I thought that if I shared in her pain it might make it easier for her. Crazy, I know. When the spasm passed she'd lie panting, too weak to do anything except wait for the next one.

Towards the end of the third day she entered what I knew from the descriptions would be the final phase. The cramps eased but she had no strength. She coughed blood. She couldn't swallow so was unable to eat or drink. She could hardly speak. A lot of the time she slept, and when she wasn't sleeping she seemed disconnected, far away.

It was hard. The hoods and masks and gloves took away any possibility of intimacy. It seemed that the last contacts our Mam would have with us would be through layers of latex and plastic. It wasn't enough that the Infection racked the body, it punished a sufferer with isolation too. Loneliness can be a terrible affliction. I didn't fully understand then how terrible but I do now. I also know now that although extreme loneliness is a partner of death, it isn't reserved only for those who are dying. You'll see that when you get to the green diary.

It was because I didn't want our Mam to feel she was alone that I took a decision, and that was when Lander and me had the last of our big rows.

It was clear that our Mam was getting close to death. She'd gone through the vomiting and the diarrhoea and the cramps. It was awful and she was so brave, hardly making a sound even though she must have been in agony. Then a strange calm came over her. She was very weak and barely conscious. It was my turn to be with her. Lander came into the barn and stopped in the doorway, like he often did. He used to look in on her like this two or three times a day. He wouldn't go close but would stand well away at the end of the barn. I was holding her hand and dabbing her mouth with a tissue, wiping away the blood-tinged saliva. I'd taken off my bio hood, my mask and my gloves, and they were on the floor beside me.

'Jesus Christ, Kerryl, what are you doing?' Lander shouted at me. 'Your mask! Your hood! For fuck's sake put them on, now, before it's too late.'

'I expect it's too late already,' I said. The shouting had roused our Mam but she didn't look to be with us. I got up from the bed and went out into the yard. Lander followed me, keeping a distance between us.

'I don't want to live like this,' I said, 'afraid of people, avoiding them, not able to touch anybody without being wrapped in plastic. If this is all that's left for us, I don't want it.'

'So you decide to kill yourself? To commit suicide?' Lander said. 'And on the way infect the rest of us too. Wouldn't it have been an idea to talk to us about this first? To talk to me, your twin? Who gave you the right to decide something like that?' He was quivering with rage, as angry as I'd ever seen him.

'I'm sorry,' I said, 'I can't help it. I don't want to say goodbye to her trussed up like a mummy. I don't want that stupid mask to be the last she sees of me. Isn't dying bad enough without having to do it on your own?'

'Everybody has to do it on their own,' he said. 'You're a mad, selfish bitch.' And he walked off.

DO YOU THINK I'm a mad, selfish bitch? Do you think I'm cold, the way I'm writing all this down? Perhaps you do, but you have to understand how it was for me, for us all then. It isn't that I didn't feel things, but the sharpness of the pain that comes with the ending of a life lessens the more times you see it. When death is rare it affects you more deeply than when a lot of people are dying. I've read that this can happen in wartime. People get so used to the killing and the dying that a kind of numbness sets in and they begin to take the violence and the deaths for granted. It isn't that they don't hurt any more, it's just that you become desensitised, immune to the pain.

That's what happened with the Infection. The reports of the first deaths in Birmingham and Norwich were long and detailed. There was video of the funerals and there was footage of grieving families and friends, mounds of flowers, interviews. The TV, QuickChat, iKnowU and YouTube were full of it. For the second wave of deaths, in Colchester, Tamworth, Lichfield, Dover, there was less coverage. As the volume of cases grew the focus shifted away from individuals and their grief to numbers. There was just too much for anybody to take in, and the dead became simply arithmetic, tables of statistics.

I think that's what happened to me. The more people died the less it hit me. I cried for days when our Dad had his accident, and I cried when Bryst's boy died, even though I didn't know him. I cried when I found the Crowthers' place deserted and the notice on their door. But when our Mam got the Infection I didn't cry as much, even though I loved her to bits, far more than any of the others. I was becoming used to it happening. In truth, after the episode with Bryst's boy I was expecting one of us to get it, and it was almost a relief when it happened because the waiting and the dread were over. I wished it could have been me, but it wasn't, it was our Mam, and once it started in her I wanted her to die because I wanted it to be over for her. In the later stages, when there was nothing of our Mam left and only pain and vomit and fluids, the end couldn't come soon enough. I knew then that one by one the rest of us would follow.

Granddad rang the ICC and told them about our Mam, and the ambulance collected her. The next day Lander went down to Walbrough in the Land Rover to collect her ashes. I would have gone with him but he was still angry with me, so he went on his own. He brought Mam's ashes back in a little urn made of shiny black plastic. It looked and felt cheap, the sort of thing you might see in a pound shop or on a stall at the seaside. This was our Mam? This was what she'd come to? It was so grotesque that I laughed. It was a nervous laugh, not a full belly laugh, but it annoyed Lander and we had another row. He said I was a heartless cow. He told me it was no wonder I couldn't get a proper boyfriend because I'd got no feelings. I called him… well, never mind what I called him, let's just leave it that we had a row and it ended the way all our rows ended, with him walking away.

It was soon after this that Lander went. By 'went' I don't mean he died, I mean he went away. Just like that.

He'd carried on at me about not talking to him about taking off my suit when I was with our Mam, but did he discuss with me whether he should leave? It's Lander we're talking about here, so there are no prizes for guessing the answer.

THE FIRST INDICATION THAT LANDER was going to do something dramatic came that evening. I went into the front room to have a minute or two alone with the ashes. Granddad had put the urn on the mantelpiece, with the printed condolence card from the Government that everybody got. I think we all thought that there wasn't much point doing anything special with the urn because the rest of us would soon be gone too. I didn't turn on the light but stood before the urn in the gloom, thinking about our Mam. I was about to leave when I heard a noise behind me. It was Lander, sitting in a corner alone. There was a long silence while each of us waited for the other to apologise. I gave in first.

'What are you doing here in the dark?' I said.

'What does it look like?' he said. 'I'm just sitting here. I don't need a permit, do I?'

I didn't want another quarrel so I didn't answer.

After a minute he said, 'I'm just thinking how totally bloody pointless all this is.'

'What is?' I said.

'All this,' he said. 'Us, the farm, trying to go on like normal, like nothing was happening.'

I didn't know how to answer. I mean, it wasn't pointless, was it? He'd been angry with me when he'd accused me of trying to commit suicide, so how could he say that trying to stay alive and carry on was pointless? I sat down too. The grandfather clock ticked heavily. Neither of us spoke.

Then Lander said, 'I can't do this. I don't like dealing with sick people.'

'Nobody does,' I said, 'but it's not their fault, they don't choose to be sick.'

'What happens when you get sick yourself?' he said, 'and Gran, and Granddad, and me? Who'll look after us then? Who'll look after the last one left? Who'll turn off the lights?'

'I don't know,' I said.

I sat with him for a bit longer in the dark. I could see from his face that he was in a state – his jaw was working and his brow twitching – but I didn't know what to say to help him. I couldn't say never mind, it will all be better soon, like I used to when I comforted him when we were small. It wouldn't be, and none of the usual forms of words would fit.

He blew his nose loudly, and that made me think that before I'd come in he'd been crying. Then he stood up. 'I love you,' he said, and before I could say anything back he left.

I was thunderstruck. I should have been touched but instead I felt a prickle of unease, a premonition that something was wrong with him. We're twins, and we're close like twins are, despite all our rows. Each of us was always conscious of what the other was feeling almost before they knew it themselves, but we never said how we felt about each other. It wasn't our style, and it was completely out of character for Lander to come out with something like that. And he'd seemed upset, too. What was bothering him? What was going on? Was he feeling the first symptoms? Oh please, no, don't let it be that.

The next morning I came back from the barn expecting to see Lander at the kitchen table like usual, bleary eyed and waiting for Gran to give him his breakfast. Instead Gran asked me where he was.

'I don't know. Should I?'

'I thought he was with you,' she said.

'Why?' I said.

'Well, he's not in his room,' she said. 'I thought he must have gone with you to help with the milking.'

'Help with the milking? Fat chance!' I said.

I ran up the stairs and looked in his bedroom. The bedclothes were in their usual tangle but the bed was empty. I checked the bathroom, and our Mam's room, but he wasn't there either. There was no sign of him. I went back to his bedroom. His backpack was gone, and so were his biker's jacket and his trainers. I came downstairs and went out to the shed. His motorbike and helmet were missing.

'Where do you think he's gone?' said Gran.

'Oh, he's probably just gone for a ride around,' I said.

'I don't think so,' said Granddad, who had just come in. 'I didn't hear him leave, and that means he rode down the hill without starting his engine. He didn't want us to know he was off. I think he'll be away for a bit.'

I was suddenly angry. 'Well, at least it's one less mouth to feed,' I said, 'and it's not as if we'll miss his work because he does bugger all.' Gran frowned. She doesn't like me swearing.

After breakfast, while Gran cleared up and Granddad left to look out for the sheep, I went up to Lander's room.

I was feeling softer towards him now and I wondered whether to change his bed for when he came back. I flicked back the screwed up sheets, and there was a note. Lander had beautiful handwriting, better than many girls. He'd written, 'Sorry. I think I've got it. This is for the best. Take care, good luck. L.' And two kisses.

I was numb. I couldn't understand it, that he should leave just like that. If he was ill, where would he go? Why not stay here, where he could be looked after? I had a picture of him holed up in some old shed somewhere, on his own, waiting for the Infection to carry him off. Lander hated illness, he took it as a sign of weakness. If he really had the Infection he wouldn't want anybody to see him. Two kisses. Not even one each. I started to cry.

I cried again all through the afternoon milking, tears running down my face and dripping off my chin as I rested my head on Bonnie's warm flank. She looked round at me and gave a cud-laced sigh, as if she knew.

We talked about Lander again that evening. 'Where do you think he's gone?' I said.

Granddad didn't answer, but Gran said, 'Don't worry, I'm sure he'll come back.'

But he didn't. And even though later I found out the real reason why he left and learnt that it wasn't just selfishness, I haven't forgiven him for it.

THERE'S ONE LAST THING to write about in this purple diary, and it's very hard. It's hard because it's how I came to be finally alone. In a funny way it feels worse remembering it now than it did going through it at the time. At the time there was such a lot to do and no opportunity to think, and it was just a matter of coping.

Gran and Granddad were really upset about Lander taking off. He'd said goodbye to me, sort of, but he'd said nothing at all to them and it was a real shock when they found him gone. It wasn't that he was needed on the farm. I used to needle him for not helping enough, but there was actually very little to do. We could easily cope without him. What hurt Gran and Granddad was that they felt he'd blown them off, given them two fingers. I didn't tell them about his note because I didn't want them to know he was infected and had gone away to die somewhere. The thought of him suffering in a strange place with nobody to care for him was awful. It would have been more than Gran could bear. She would have scoured the area looking for him. It was better for them both to think he was well, and that for reasons of his own he had chosen to go somewhere else.

They talked endlessly about where that might be, and why, and Gran blamed herself for driving him away by nagging at him too much. It shows how little she knew him! Nagging never made any impression on Lander. He was able to blank it out so well that I don't think he even heard it. In the end Granddad said he thought he must have decided to go because he couldn't stand to be here after our Mam had died. That idea seemed to help them both.

They might have carried on and on talking about Lander if they hadn't got ill themselves. It was about a week after he'd disappeared and I came in from the morning milking to find the kitchen empty. Gran was queen of the kitchen and every single morning of my life she had been there and in charge, at the table, at the sink, at the stove. Today she wasn't. I called upstairs. I'd never known Gran or Granddad oversleep, but they might. It was then I heard a sound from the front room. I tried the door but it wouldn't open.

'Don't come in, love. Stay back,' I heard Gran's voice say.

I knew straight away what was wrong and my insides turned to lead. Ever since our Mam died I'd been waiting for the rest of us to start the symptoms. But a day went by, and then another, and another, and a week and we were all still healthy. A week to ten days for incubation, they'd said. A few more days and we'd have passed that. We'd be all right, we'd have dodged it.

'Gran,' I called, 'let me in.'

There was silence. Then I heard Granddad say, 'We don't want you to come in here, love. Your Gran and me, we're not well.'

Whenever anybody said that there was always the silly, irrational hope that it wasn't the Infection they'd got, it was something less serious. It never was, but I still said, 'Let me get you some Paracetamol. It might be just a touch of the 'flu.'

There was no answer.

'Look,' I said, 'let me in. I want to help you. I feel fine, I can look after you.'

'You mustn't come near. We don't want you to get it too,' said Gran.

'I'll wear my suit,' I said.

I took it out from its sterilising wrap and put it on, although it seemed pointless. If they really had got it they'd have been infectious for days and there wasn't the slightest chance that I'd escape.

'There, I've got my suit on,' I called. 'Let me in, please.'

There was a click, the door opened a crack and I squinted through the gap. Granddad was in a chair by the fireplace. He looked awful. He was covered in blankets and he was shivering. His face was flushed and shiny with sweat. His eyes were closed.

'When did it start?' I said to Gran. She was standing by the door. She looked better than he did, but not much.

'Middle of the night,' she said. 'He got the shakes and he said his knees and hips hurt. Then he got coughing and I saw there was blood on his pillow. Not a lot, just a few little specks,' she said, as if that made it less worrying. She gestured towards Granddad in his chair. 'He's been like this ever since,' she said.

They must have been here, in the front room, when I went out to do the milking. I hadn't noticed, although I remembered that Buster had been whining softly at the door. I'd just thought he wanted to go in and sleep on the couch, one of his favourite spots, so I'd ignored him. I helped Gran to a chair near Granddad and made her sit down. 'What about you?' I said.

'Oh, I'm all right,' she said, but I could see that she wasn't.

I took off my mask and slipped out of my suit. Gran started to protest but I said, 'Look, we've been sharing a house. If I'm going to get it, I'll get it. A poxy bit of plastic won't stop it.' I screwed up the suit and put it in the rubbish basket. Then I gave Gran a hug. She held back at first, as though still worried about contaminating me, but then she relaxed and kissed me on the cheek.

'You're a good girl,' she said. 'I expect you're right. Oh, Kerryl, what a business. That we should all end up like this.' She shook her head and let out a long sigh. 'It's God's punishment for all our wickedness, that's what it is.'

I couldn't believe that. What had Bryst's boy done that was so wicked? And Gran, well, there was no one less wicked than her. She was kindness itself. Everybody said so.

'Then let's make the most of it,' I said. I took the bottle of sherry that they kept in the sideboard and some glasses and poured a tumbler full. I looked at Granddad but he'd fallen asleep, so I gave it to Gran and poured another one for me. I don't really like sherry, I'm more a vodka kind of gal when I do go for it, which isn't often, but I knocked that sherry back fast enough.

I helped them upstairs and made them as comfortable as I could in their bed. They lay with the curtains closed, their arms around each other. They didn't want anything apart from water, which they drank and drank because of the fever. I dragged a rocking chair from our Mam's room and sat with them. I held Gran's hand for a long time, but I kept dozing off and nearly fell out of the chair. They both seemed asleep, so I kissed them and went to my own room. I was thankful they didn't seem to be in pain, suffering like our Mam had. I lay on my back in the dark and tears ran over my cheeks. Gran and Granddad were gone, there was nothing I could do to save them. I wondered when the symptoms would start with me and which I would feel first. The headache? The aching joints? The cramps? I moved my knees and hips and shoulders and elbows. Did I feel a twinge? I wasn't sure. Did my head hurt? It might have been the sherry. I fell asleep.

I woke in a sweat with my bed covers in a tangle. The horrible certainty struck me that it must be the fever, but I sat up and was surprised to find that I felt all right: no aches, no pains, and the headache had gone. The only symptom was that my mouth felt as though it had been stuffed with polystyrene granules, so I drank some water and felt better.

I got out of bed and went to Gran's and Granddad's room. They both looked to be asleep. I tip-toed away, splashed my face, and went down to do the afternoon milking. Actually they must have been dead already, because when I went back upstairs an hour later I reached for Gran's hand and it was stone cold. Granddad was the same.

For about an hour I didn't do anything. I was tearful and I cried a bit, but it wasn't as if their deaths were a shock, and mostly I was grateful that they'd not suffered as much as some people had. It's embarrassing to admit it, but I also felt sorry for myself. What would happen to me now? There was no one left. Everybody had gone. I was on my own. Who would put out the lights for me?

I went downstairs and made myself a coffee. I sat at the table, cursing Lander for being away and wishing that he would come back. I needed him. Buster padded across to me and nuzzled my hand. At least I had him. And Joey, my poor neglected horse that I only briefly saw now and hadn't ridden for weeks. And the cows, although conversation with all of them was limited.

There were two dead people in the house and I didn't know what to do. They'd died so quickly, not over days like our Mam had but in hours, and there'd been no time to prepare. I went upstairs. Of course I hadn't expected Gran and Granddad to move, but for a second I was surprised they were both exactly as before. When I'd found them their eyes had been shut as if they were sleeping, so I was spared having to close them. It looks so easy when you see people do it in the movies but I don't think it would have been. Their faces looked purplish in the dim light. Was I sure they were dead? The line between living and dying is such a fine one, perhaps they were still this side of it. There was a loose feather from a pillow on the floor and I held it at Gran's mouth and nose. It was absolutely still. I heard a cock crow from outside and remembered the hens. They were Gran's. I expect she hadn't seen to them since yesterday. I would need to sort out the nesting boxes and find the eggs.

I returned to the kitchen and took down the *What to do when someone dies* leaflet from the pin board. I got my mobile and started to tap in the number for the ICC. Suddenly I began to tremble, so much that I nearly dropped it and could hardly hit the right spots on the screen. I remembered that Lander had put the number in the memory of the landline phone so we could speed dial it. I'd told him he was being macabre and he'd thrown a cushion at me and told me not to use posh words just because I was going to Cambridge. My eyes started to water.

The number rang for a long time before an automated voice asked me for 'the full names and the National Insurance number of the person whom you wish to report deceased', and for the address and postcode of the location of the body. The zombie voice told me that the information had been recorded and a collection would be made as soon as possible, but that given the unprecedented demand there was likely to be a delay. It sympathised with my loss.

The system could only cope with one name at a time, so I did Gran first and then had to dial again and queue again and repeat the whole process for Granddad.

I put the phone down and wondered what to do while I waited. I would have liked to have gone for a ride on Joey, miles over the moors. I don't know why I should suddenly want that now. I hadn't thought of going for a ride in ages.

I cleaned the kitchen and the bathroom and tidied the front room. Then I started to sort out the papers on Granddad's desk, until it occurred to me that when they came from the ICC they might think I was searching for Granddad's will and that would look dreadful. Then it dawned on me how useless all that was because pretty soon I would be dead, too, and property and money and wills were meaningless now.

The ICC men came mid-evening, two of them, one short and one tall. They looked absolutely spent. It wasn't their faces, which I couldn't see well through their masks, but the way they stood and moved that made them seem worn out, used up. The tall one carried a folding stretcher and the other a large plastic equipment case.

'Where's your suit and mask?' said the short one as I met them at the door. 'Do you want to kill yourself?' He didn't wait for an answer but pushed past me.

'We'll be back for you next,' said the other one. 'Upstairs?'

I took them up to Gran's and Granddad's room. I don't know why I'd shut the door; somehow it had seemed respectful. When I opened it there was a smell that knocked me back. The taller of the men noticed my reaction and put his hand on my shoulder.

'Best if you stay out here, love,' he said.

I remembered reading in one of my endless internet sessions that when someone dies their bladder and bowels empty. I felt sorry for Gran and Granddad that I'd forgotten this and not thought to clean them up. It was undignified letting them be taken away in this state. Not that the ICC crew seemed to mind or even notice. They were brisk and businesslike. They covered Gran in a plastic sheet and rolled her over so the sheet wrapped round her. They sprayed something with a strong antiseptic smell into the bag they'd made and sealed it. Then they did the same to Granddad. They lifted both bodies on to the floor, bundled up the bedding and sealed that too in a plastic bag. Then they carried the parcels that were my Gran and Granddad downstairs, one at a time, to the ambulance. When they opened its doors I saw that it was fitted with racks for stretchers, five on each side. They were all full, so they had to put Gran and Granddad on the ambulance floor. They hooked a webbing strap round them so they wouldn't slide about.

Although they were tired and busy, the men were sensitive and gentle.

'I'm sorry for your loss, love,' said the tall one. 'Who were they? Family?'

'My Gran and Granddad,' I said.

He gave a sympathetic tut. 'They'll be cremated tonight,' he said. 'I have to tell you that while the emergency regulations are in force families can't attend the cremations. Nobody can, they're done behind closed doors.'

I gulped and nodded. I knew it from what had happened with our Mam.

The short one was filling in something on a tablet. 'It's a rotten business, this,' he said. 'Fingerprint here,' he said, and handed me the tablet. I hesitated, trying to understand what it was. 'It's just your agreement to release the departed to us,' he said.

The departed? It was such a quaint term. Then I understood he was being thoughtful. He could hardly call them 'the stiffs' or 'the corpses', could he? I put my finger on the tablet.

'They'll be ready tomorrow,' he said. 'They'll text you when you can collect them.' He meant the ashes.

'Are you going to be all right?' said the tall one. 'Is there somebody up here with you?'

'Yes, my brother,' I lied.

They climbed into the ambulance. I watched it as far as West Lee, where it stopped.

Somehow the night passed, although I can't remember how I got through it. I felt an awful emptiness. The house was so quiet. Before, even when we were in different rooms and no one was making any noise, I could feel that other people were there. Now there was nobody, just stillness and silence. I heard a scratching and went to the door. It was Buster. I knelt down and hugged him. He put up with it, a puzzled frown on his face. 'I'm going to need you, my old friend,' I said. He tried to lick my face.

I started to pass the time with games on my tablet, but that seemed somehow disrespectful so I put it aside. I found a classical music station on the radio, but they were playing something really gloomy and it made me feel worse. I found an old recording of a chat show online but that didn't work either. It had been made before the Infection and it seemed so trivial, the things people were talking about insignificant compared with what was happening now. I stood on the landing for a long time, watching the full moon. At one stage I got an antiseptic spray and drenched Gran's and Granddad's mattress. Then I thought, *Why? Nobody else is ever going to sleep on it.* I thought I might burn it, if I could get it downstairs. I wished Lander was with me. Buster rubbed his wet nose on my hand and I stroked his ears.

I went to my own room and took from a drawer the two notebooks: the purple one and the green one. I opened the purple one and wrote the title 'Before'.

Then I started on an account of what had happened, right from the beginning. I thought it was important to leave a record of my story. I didn't know how important writing the diary was going to become for me.

I GOT THE MESSAGE that the ashes were ready for collection at about three o'clock the next day. I got into the Land Rover, Buster settled beside me and we started out of the yard. Then I remembered my suit. If you were in one of the categories that had been provided with suits it was an offence to go out without one. The last thing I wanted was to be arrested for something so petty. Imagine being locked up and getting the Infection and dying in jail. So even though I knew that wearing my suit was pointless, I returned to the house, retrieved it from the rubbish basket in the front room, and put it on. Then I went down to Walbrough. I don't have a driving licence, but I reckoned people had more to bother about than that. Anyway, I'd been driving on our own land for years and I was good, better than a lot of the people on the roads.

I hadn't gone with Lander when he'd collected our Mam's ashes and I didn't know what to expect. The ICC had run out of space at the Health Centre and I was directed to some empty offices that they'd taken over. The building was a disgrace. It had been vacant for years and was covered with graffiti. Windows were smashed where local youths had broken in to do drugs or have sex.

The ICC people had taken down the boards that had covered the windows and cleaned the place up a bit, but it still stank. It was laughable that after sitting on a lemon for so long the owners were at last going to get some rent for it, when they probably weren't going to be around to spend the money anyway. You could say it was ironic. Just before our school closed we'd been working with Miss Dove on irony. Rudy Fothergill said it was just another form of sarcasm – and he should know because he was the most sarcastic teacher there. I wondered if they'd been infected, either of them, or were they all right. How could I find out? Miss Dove said she'd text me her email address but she hadn't. Come to think of it, I hadn't been on the school's website to download the homework Forceps said would be there for us. Should I do that? Was there any point? It might take my mind off things, although I was starting to realise that I would not be going back to school again. Nobody would.

There was a short line of people waiting in the reception area. I stood at the end, taking care to keep the regulation arm's length away from everyone else. People were touchy about that and there'd been on the news a report of a man in Sunderland who'd been stabbed because he stood in a queue too near to somebody else.

To collect the ashes you had to go up to a counter and show your ID. Someone would check on the computer and then go through the door to the back to get them. Every time the door opened I saw loads of cardboard cartons lined up on shelves. These were the ashes. Rows and rows of people, each one in a shiny little white box, in alphabetical order.

They gave me the cartons of Gran's and Granddad's ashes in a black plastic carrier bag. They made me take them out and confirm that the boxes had the right names, and to sign that I'd received them. The names were in copperplate on black-edged labels: Gilbert Michael

Stanley on one and Elizabeth Mary Stanley on the other, with the dates of their births and yesterday's date, the date of their deaths.

There was a man behind another counter which was stacked with black plastic urns and he asked me if I wanted to buy any. I hadn't thought to bring money with me and only had what was in the pocket of my jeans. I could just about scrape up enough for one. Would one urn do? Gran and Granddad had been married for over forty years and did everything together. It seemed wrong that they were now in separate boxes. Would it be disrespectful to put them all in one and mix them up? I thought they'd like that. Then it seemed mean to get just one urn, so I told the man I'd come back later.

I sat in the Land Rover with the ashes on my knee. This was my family, in cardboard cartons in a plastic bag, like a takeaway meal. The boxes were so small. Gran had been sixty-eight and Granddad seventy-one. Was that all that remained of all those years? I had to take off my biohazard mask because I was crying, my nose was running and the visor steaming up. Buster looked up at me with big brown eyes and licked me. He sensed something was wrong and I think in his doggy way he wanted to comfort me.

I drove back up the hill to the farm with the cartons on the seat beside me. I wasn't concentrating and part way up the track I hit a bump and Gran's box fell onto the floor. I stopped to retrieve it and saw that it had split and some of the ashes spilt out. It was less than a teaspoonful but it upset me. I got out of the Land Rover and stood in the middle of the track, howling with shame and frustration that at their end I couldn't give my grandparents a funeral or even look after their remains properly, and with rage at the fucking stupid, feeble ICC for putting something so precious in such a fucking stupid, feeble container. Then my anger subsided and an awful feeling of emptiness smothered me. I couldn't think, couldn't imagine what I was going to do now. How would I manage? There had been five of us, now there was just me.

I was still snivelling when I got home. I didn't know what to do with the ashes so I put them on the mantelpiece in the front room next to our Mam's. I drew up a chair and sat in the silent house looking at the pair of boxes. I wished I'd been able to buy some of the plastic urns.

SO THAT'S IT. That's how things got to be the way they are now, and it's the end of my purple diary. If, my dear, patient, imaginary friend, you've stuck with me this far and you want to find out what happened next, move on to the green one. If you've had enough, go and do something more interesting. But before you do either I need to flesh you out a bit. That includes giving you a name. I can't keep on calling you 'my imaginary reader' for the rest of my diary, however long or short that turns out to be.

Actually I've thought about you a lot, and since early on I've had a clear picture of you. If you've cheated and looked at the green diary, you'll already know what I decided. If not, this is how I got to settling who you are.

The first thing was to establish your gender. You had to have one. You could have been gay or bisexual or trans, but that might have made you more interesting than me and I couldn't risk that! So the question was, whether to make you a straight male or a straight female. If you were female you'd be a friend to chat to about girly things and exchange gossip with. Except there wouldn't be any exchange, it would just be me telling you, and I don't know any girl who could stand being constantly quiet while I did all the talking! Of course, having you as a girl would mean that I could say things to you that I couldn't or wouldn't to a boy, but in the end the idea of you being male is more exciting. You'll have to turn your back when I undress and stay outside when I go to the bathroom, but apart from that you can be with me all the time. And there's always the chance we might develop a romance!

I knew from the start what you look like: fair haired and hunky. You're broad, but not too much – I don't want to be seen out with a barn door. You're muscular, though, and strong. You've got powerful shoulders and great pecs. You can pick me up and carry me – and I promise to lose some of my lard to make that easier for you. You're clean shaven and have hardly any body hair, I don't like bears. You're tall but not too tall. I'm five foot eight and I can't have you shorter than me. At the same time I don't want you to be towering over me. Six foot seems right, a four-inch difference between us. We'll look good together, and if there is a romance it's a handy height for snogging! You're white but tanned, you have a strong chin, high cheek bones and twinkly blue eyes. Your hair is quite long and has a bit of a curl to it. Your voice is deep enough to sound manly, but not ridiculous, like a voice in a TV ad. Most of the time you wear jeans and T-shirts (plain, no logos or messages). You look good in shorts because of your muscular legs.

That's the physical bit done. Now what about your personality? Well, I've got to know you a bit now and I think you are kind and generous. You've got a great sense of humour and a happy-sounding laugh, the sort that makes me want to laugh too. You're intelligent, but not as smart as me. In fact, you're a bit in awe of how bright I am. You play the guitar. You're interested in animals, reading, clothes, the same bands that I like, cooking. I'll let you have some lads' stuff too: cars, motorbikes, football. Not computers though. I got enough of that with Lander.

The last job is to give you a name, and that's hard. It has to be timeless without being old fashioned. I thought about Mick, but that sounds Irish. Not that I've got anything against the Irish, I just don't see you as being Irish. I quite like the name Mark, but I've been out with two Marks: one was a dork and the other an arsehole. I flicked through a few of the romances Gran had got from the library. The love bunny in the first one is called Jake. I quite like the sound of that, except when Lander was little and wanted a pee he used to tell our Mam he wanted a jake, so it can't be that; I'd just be laughing at you all the time! Another from the romances is Brad. That has kind of an Australian twang but it doesn't seem classy enough. Sam might be a possibility, except there was a girl called Sam in our form at school and she was a bit weird (well, she was a lot weird actually!). Tod, Simon, Martin, Matt – maybe, but none of them seems quite right.

Then it comes to me: Adam. You're called Adam. It's short, virile, strong, and it fits you perfectly. So, Adam, meet your Eve.

The Green Diary (now)

TUESDAY

My new diary starts today. That's because it's different now. Up till two days ago there was always somebody else here asking, giving, ordering, wanting, or just being there. Now there's no one. I'm on my own. I don't like that. Once I thought that not having anybody making demands on me would be wonderful. Already I know it's not.

I stare for a long time at the little white boxes that contain my grandparents' ashes. Then I take them off the mantelpiece and put them on the table. I open them and look at the grey powder. There's about the same amount in each, but there's so little of it. The urn that holds our Mam's ashes has a screw top. I've never looked inside and it feels so light that for a wild moment I think it might be empty. I undo the lid. What's inside looks just the same as what's in the boxes. I know that the human body is more than half water, but surely there's not as much in here as there should be. Is this really all a person is? Have they given me all of them? Or just a bit, a sort of token? Is the dust I'm looking at really my Gran, my Granddad, our Mam at all? The ICC must be dealing with so many bodies, hundreds and hundreds of them. How do they know which is which? How do they keep them separate? These could be the ashes of complete strangers and I'd never know. And would it matter if they were? The Prime Minister said when he made a broadcast just before everything collapsed, 'We're all in this together.' He was right, but I don't think he meant all in the same ash can too.

I've stopped crying now but I'm still upset that Gran and Granddad are not getting their due. I'll go down the hill tomorrow with some money and buy a couple of urns for them. It seems only right. I don't know what I'll do with them then. Bury them? People talk about scattering ashes, but where would I scatter these? Wouldn't scattering them be like just throwing them away? And if that's what I'm going to do, why bother buying poxy plastic urns?

I feel as though I'm being crushed by a colossal weight. I must do something to cheer myself up. I switch on the kitchen TV and scan the channels. There's news (depressing), movies (old), soaps (also old), reality shows (older still), panel games (even older than those), sitcoms and chat shows (dull and out of date). I switch to the ads channel. The blend of seductive voices, bland slogans and chirpy tunes is soothing. I suppose that's why a channel that shows nothing but ads, old and new, is popular.

I must face up to the question that's been with me all the time since our Mam got ill. When will it be my turn? I switch on my tablet and go to www.doh.gov.uk/fighttheinfection. I click on the page headed 'Symptoms' and read the stark menu of what lies ahead for me. It's not new. I've read it a hundred times before, but I go back in case it's changed and I've been given some sort of reprieve, or in case they've suddenly come up with a miracle cure, even though I know that both those thoughts are rubbish.

The best I can hope for is that it will be over quickly. Gran and Granddad were soon gone. Although I could tell it was excruciating for them, they didn't suffer as badly as our Mam. I'm filled with dread, and I pray that I get through it without having to endure the Infection at its worst. Is that why Lander went? Because he couldn't bear to have anybody see him ill and in pain? If so, he should have told me. I'm his twin, for fuck's sake. I can't cure him but I could look after him. I could go through it with him. We could approach the end together and die caring for each other. I deserve better than just being left here on my own.

I stare at the screen. One thing the cold catalogue of symptoms doesn't mention is the fear. The prospect of the Infection is terrifying. It's like facing a death sentence. There is no appeal, no possibility of mercy. So why not save all the pain and finish it now? I'm not short of means. There are two shotguns in the cupboard in the hall. They're good ones: Purdeys, Granddad's pride and joy. There's a .22 rifle as well, that Lander used. It can't be that difficult to shoot yourself, look at some of the dickheads who manage it. And it would be quicker than the Infection.

I sit stone still while I consider this. Load, click, bang, gone. Easy. But is that what I want? Am I so desperate that I want to give up the little bit of life I have left? And suppose I botch it and die slowly and in agony over days? That's no improvement on the Infection.

Everything feels more intense. The breeze from the open window on my face is sharper, the air is clearer, the scent of the fields sweeter, the light brighter. Buster is at my feet, his head leaning against my ankle, and I can feel every single hair of his muzzle where it touches my skin. A bird sings at a thousand decibels. The sun shines. I can't kill myself. It's not that I don't have the guts. It's that I don't want to. Despite everything that has happened and despite what's in store for me, life, the world, is still precious.

WEDNESDAY

I open my eyes to the sun blazing through my bedroom window. The dark thoughts of last night have gone. I slept really well, and I get up with energy and a sense of purpose. I'm glad I didn't yield to the brief temptation to top myself.

How long have I got? A day? More? Incubation is seven to ten days. I check the calendar. It's been hard to keep track of everything that's been going on. It's almost three weeks since Bryst's boy died, so while I think our Mam must have caught it from him, and maybe Gran and Granddad did too, somehow I escaped. It's more than ten days since our Mam got ill, so if I'd caught it from her I'd probably be showing the signs by now. It's amazing that her bugs missed me when you think about how close to her I was, tending her without my bio mask and gloves. Gran and Granddad must already have been infected by the time our Mam died, because they went very soon after. I suppose Granddad might even have got it from Bryst's boy when the bio suit he borrowed from Lander split.

By the way, where is Lander's suit? I haven't seen it anywhere. Perhaps he took it with him. If so he can't have been infected when he went away, despite what his note said. Otherwise, what would be the point of taking the suit? The thought that Lander might be safe warms me. Perhaps he'll come back.

Today is Wednesday. I reckon I've probably got till Sunday, so I'm going to make the most of it. I need a plan. Buster nuzzles my hand, as if he knows what I'm thinking and agrees.

There's a roll of kitchen paper in the drawer. I tear some off, spread it out on the table and take a felt tip pen from the jar by the phone. I draw a circle in the middle of the paper and at the top write DAILY JOBS. Then I fill it with a list of the things that are most important.

Morning milking (must do that)

Afternoon milking (that too)

Hens – check their run's secure (essential, there are a lot of foxes around)

Hens – check nest boxes for eggs (nice, I like eggs, but not essential)

Joey – feed; groom; ride (poor old Joey, he deserves some attention and I'd like to spend some time with him)

Buster – feed; walk; feed some more (he wags his tail to show he supports that)

Go running on the moor (okay, maybe; I used to enjoy that, it was part of my 'fight the flab' routine, but I haven't done it for ages)

Cats – feed (where are the bloody cats? not seen them)

I draw another circle for each of the days I have left and write in it the other things I have in mind to do.

Wednesday

Get urns. Dispose of ashes – Mam, Gran and Granddad (some sort of ceremony?)

Thursday

Move my stuff downstairs. Bring down my bed and mattress & set up in the front room. (Easier for me to get to the rest of the house when I'm ill; also easier for the ICC people to deal with what's left of me.) *Clean the house.* (Okay, no one will see it, but I owe it to Mam, who seemed to spend all her life tidying up.)

Friday

Prepare kit for when I'm ill – plenty of water, Paracetamol, spare PJs, washing stuff & towels, bowl (to catch vomit), *phone, torch, notebook* (for important last thoughts).

Saturday

Text goodbye to all my friends.
Do a farewell message for my iKnowU wall.
Free Joey & the cows & the hens.
Turn sheep loose.
Buster?

Sunday

Yes, Sunday. Crunch day. If the Infection's not got me before, it surely will have by then.

I stand back and look at what I've done. I'm sure there's a lot more that should go down but I can't think of anything else. All of it assumes a sedate passage towards the weekend. Suppose it doesn't work out like that. Suppose I'm suddenly struck down tomorrow. I'll have to abandon this list and do the best I can. I highlight moving my stuff downstairs. I'm going to do that today, this afternoon, as soon as I'm back from fetching the urns. As well as it being easier in the front room, I don't want to be upstairs on my own, next door to the bedroom where my grandparents died. I won't bother trying to shift my bed and mattress. I'll doss down on one of the sofas.

The animals will have to take their chance. I think Joey will be all right. I'll open his stable, smack him on the rump and he'll be off. He's a big, strong horse and I'm sure he'll be able to live wild here. He'll find shelter and enough to eat. I'm not so sure about the cows. Bonnie and Dolly are still giving milk. They make a huge fuss when they're ready for milking so I expect they'll be uncomfortable if no one relieves them, but they should be all right too, so long as they don't get mastitis. Molly is more of a problem because she's close to calving. She'll have to cope on her own. So will the sheep and the hens. Buster's a different matter. There are a lot of stray dogs around in the town. They look half starved, and some of them are aggressive. All of them have scars and wounds. Buster is such a big, soft thing. How will he manage in an environment like that, where he has to compete for his food instead of just ambling to his bowl to find it? Would the kindest thing be to shoot him? Even if it were, the thought sickens me. I couldn't do it.

Food. I know I have enough for the next five months, let alone five days. Granddad always used to say that Gran kept enough in the house to withstand a siege. Well, now there is one, although not the sort he meant. I go to the pantry and look at the shelves. There's cereal.

There are jars and tins of all sorts: savoury and dessert. There's flour and bread-making kits, pasta, sauces, jams and pickles (home made and bought). I open the fridge: butter, milk, bacon, eggs, packets of meats, cheese. The freezer, too, is rammed.

I take a packet of chocolate biscuits (Lander's favourite) from the shelves and open it. I'm about to take a bite out of the biscuit but I stop myself. How am I going to manage this? How do I want my exit from the world to be? I have a choice. I can go the way Stuart and his lot decided: eat and drink myself into a stupor, drug myself up (I don't think I'd have much trouble finding some stuff in Walbrough). Or I could spend my last few days clear headed and knowing what was happening to me. I can't stop what the Infection will do to my body. It will break me physically, but I can fight it mentally. If I'm disciplined I can govern what it does to me emotionally. I put the biscuits back. Buster looks disappointed, although he's not allowed chocolate anyway.

THURSDAY

The revision to my plans meant that I didn't go for the urns yesterday. I'm getting them today. This morning I took some cash from our Mam's wardrobe. I've always known where she keeps – kept – it and it was not unknown for me (and Lander) to help ourselves from time to time. Not lots, just the occasional fiver to see us through. We thought she didn't know, but I think now she probably did, and didn't care.

I took £40. Twenty per urn seems a lot to me for a bit of plastic, but that's what they're charging. Why not give them away? I mean, what are they going to do with the money? I could have taken more cash because there's plenty: some fives and tens and some loose change, and £500 in twenties, tied with a rubber band. It's somehow reassuring to know it's there, even though it's obvious it's not going to be of much use to me.

I put on my bio suit and drove down to the ICC, expecting that I'd pick up the urns and go straight back home. I realised something was wrong as soon as I swung off the road and into the car park. The ICC was closed, doors shut fast and boards back on the windows. There were a few people hanging about on the steps, angry and confused. None of them was wearing a protective suit. A woman was crying.

'It's fucking shut,' a man said. I asked him why and he said how the fuck did I expect him to know? Clearly a man of few words. Well, one, really.

'It was open Tuesday,' I said, as if that was any help. 'Is it shut for good?'

'I don't fucking know,' he said. 'Who do you think I am, the fucking prime minister?'

'No, I don't think you're that,' I said. He glared at me.

'They've got my Derek in there,' the woman whimpered. 'They can't keep him like that. I want him, he's mine.' She began keening, a drawn-out, desolate wail growing in volume and intensity. The man stared angrily at her.

There was no point staying and I turned away.

It was a shock and a disappointment. I'd set my heart on getting the urns today, and I felt guilty I hadn't done so before. Still, I'm not as badly off as the others who'd turned up at the ICC today. At least I have the remains of my family. I climbed into the Land Rover and came home.

So, no urns. I think I'll just scatter Gran's and Granddad's ashes. Mam's too. It seems a better idea than trying to do anything fancy. There's a corner of the back field where cowslips grow. Our Mam always liked them so I'll scatter her there. Granddad told me that he planted the ash tree at the end of the lane the year he and Gran were married, so I'll put him there. Where shall I leave Gran? She loved sitting on a summer evening on the little wooden bench at the edge of the yard, where you can watch the sunset and see the lights coming on in the valley. That seems a good place for her. Then I change my mind. Gran and Granddad were together for a long time, much longer than they were apart. Shouldn't they be in the same place? I could mix the ashes together and divide them, and put half by the tree and the rest by the seat. But that can't be right. It must be bad karma, surely, splitting up a person's remains, like carving up their soul. I'll keep the ashes separate and have a ceremony for each.

I wish I was religious; I'd have a much better idea of how to do this properly. I've only been to one funeral. Lander and I were told to sit at the end of the pew, close by the wall. I was mesmerised by a spider's web, stretched across the corner of the window and sprinkled with a few dry flies. I could see the spider lurking. It was huge, and I spent the entire service praying that it wouldn't come out. It stayed put, which was enough to convince me at the time of the power of prayer.

Seeing the ICC shut like that was a real setback. It had seemed a place of order, a symbol of stability in the middle of the chaos that the Infection was creating. Its job was gruesome and dismal, but it was doing it. Even though they were exhausted, the men who'd collected Gran and Granddad had been friendly, thoughtful. They were doing things that had to be done and treating people, alive and dead, as if they were still important. The closure of the ICC is a message that no one is important any more. I'm near the end and there's no one to help me. The Infection has taken hold and there's no way it's going to let go.

How do you die? I don't mean the process of your soul parting from your body, if that's what happens. I mean how do you manage it? You can't just let go of your life, put it down like a bag of shopping that's got too heavy, can you? There ought to be more to dying than that. You should do something special to mark the second most significant thing that ever happens to you. I suppose that's why the deaths of kings, queens, emperors and so on were like shows, with people clustered round their deathbeds straining for their last words. There'll be no one to cluster round mine, but even so I want to make some preparations.

I'd put in my plan that I would text goodbye to all my friends. I've scarcely thought about them in the last few days, but suddenly contacting them becomes the number one priority. Except I don't want just to message them, I want something closer than that.

Of course, actually seeing my friends to say goodbye isn't possible. They wouldn't welcome me turning up on their doorsteps, having come from a house where three people have just died. I'll phone.

I tried Josie before and got no reply. I'll have another go. I remember what Penny Cross said about seeing an ambulance outside her house, and I wait in an agony of suspense, willing her to answer. This time it does ring but that's all, it doesn't go through to voicemail. I wait a long time and reluctantly I disconnect.

My insides feel hollowed out. I so desperately want to talk to my best friend. To anyone. I call Natasha, and Charlotte, and Suzy and Penny Cross. I even try Monica Woodbridge. Nobody answers. For Monica I get a number-out-of-service notification. Charlotte's asks me to leave a message (I don't). The others are like Josie's, no response of any sort. I call Steve. His phone, too, goes to voicemail. This time I do say something.

'Hi Steve, it's Kerryl. I just wondered how you're doing. Still partying? I'd really like to talk to you. Call me.'

I don't know why I say that last bit. I've never been that keen on Steve, and if you'd asked me before, 'Do you really want Steve to be the last person you speak to?' I'd have said no. Now it's different. Loneliness kicking in, I suppose.

I'm feeling desperate for human contact, and I do something I told myself I never would. Weeks, months ago I was having a tutorial with Miss Dove. She left her phone on the table while she slipped out. I hesitated for so long I thought she'd be back and I'd miss my chance, then I picked it up. I wasn't snooping, I didn't want to read her messages or anything, I just wanted her number. The school didn't allow pupils to have the private numbers of staff, and Miss Dove had never offered me hers, not even when I went for the Cambridge exam. But I could get it now. There was no password, and her phone woke up as soon as I grabbed it. I clicked on 'my phone' and jotted down the number that came up on the screen. I told myself that I'd never use it. Simply having it in my contacts was enough.

Now I choose it and press 'call'. It rings for a long time, then a man answers. 'Yes?' he says.

I'm surprised at the male voice and I don't know what to say. 'I'm sorry,' I mumble, 'I must have the wrong number.'

'Who do you want?' says the man.

I'm tempted just to cut off but I say, 'I was trying to get hold of Miss Dove.'

There's a pause. 'You have the right number,' says the man. 'Who are you?'

'My name's Cheryl Shaw,' I say. 'I'm one of her students at St Winifred's.'

'Oh,' says the man. There's another pause, so long that I think he might have put the phone down and gone to get her. Then he comes back on. 'I'm Miss Dove's father,' he says. 'I'm afraid you can't speak to her. She passed away yesterday.' There's a catch in his voice.

I can't answer him. I can't even say that I'm sorry. I disconnect.

I sit still, the phone in my lap, while the light fades. The banal sounds of the ads channel come from the kitchen next door.

I go upstairs and I lie face down on my bed and I cry racking, choking, inconsolable sobs. So much for getting used to people who are close to you dying. I cry till my pillow's soaked. Then I sit up, wipe my eyes and blow my nose. I open *Mimesis* and run my finger over her signature on the flyleaf: Angela Dove, Girton College, Cambridge. When she wrote that she was alive. She was bright, enthusiastic, everything before her. She saw and heard and tasted and touched. Her flesh was warm, her brain fired, her lungs sucked air and her heart pumped. She had no idea what was going to happen to her, to all of us. I close my eyes and try to see her face, but the image won't come. That makes me cry again.

LATER

I run my fingers along the books on the shelf beside my bed. Most of them are set books for our English course. Miss Dove had chosen the Women in World Literature module, so among the titles were *Anna Karenina*, *Madame Bovary* and *The*

Portrait of a Lady, all featuring women who were dominated and controlled by men who didn't understand them. At her suggestion I'd read *Middlemarch* before the Cambridge exam because she said that had the same theme.

I pull out my letter from its place between two books. I've read it so often – at least once a day to begin with – that I know it by heart.

Dear Ms Shaw

I write in connection with your application to this college to read English, and your attendance last week to take part in the selection process.

My colleagues and I thought you presented well. Your answers to the questions we put to you at interview were relevant and direct, and showed you to be intelligent and thoughtful. This impression was confirmed by your performance in the entrance examinations. Your papers were of a high standard. All your essays were well expressed and indicated insight and imagination. However, you have a tendency to over-write and should work to cultivate conciseness. Your General Paper showed sound general knowledge and a good understanding of a broad range of social, moral and political issues. Your English paper demonstrated your ability to analyse your A level set texts and interpret them sensitively, and provided strong evidence of reading around. Only your unseen French paper left something to be desired.

I can now tell you that as a result of our assessment of your application it has been determined not to offer you a place at this college for the next academic year. However, we would be pleased to admit you for the year following. Part of the reason for this is that, having been born in August, you are among the youngest in your year group. We feel you should take advantage of this by using a year after you leave school to broaden your experience and widen your reading. I am sure your teachers will be able to suggest how you might employ this time. I would urge you to travel, perhaps combining this with voluntary work of some kind.

I hope you will accept this offer and that we will welcome you to Cambridge in due course. I would appreciate notice of your decision at your earliest convenience.

With kind regards
Dr Hilary Smith

Tutor for Admissions, English

Cambridge! Me! The same college Miss Dove had gone to! Although our Mam had ignored the whole business before I got my offer, once the letter came she was made up, so proud. Gran and Granddad too. Even Lander had been pleased, although he pretended not to be. I look at the letter again, for a long time. Then I tear it into pieces. There's no point keeping it. Whatever happens about the Infection I know I won't be going to Cambridge now.

FRIDAY

I still haven't moved my things downstairs, but last night I slept on the sofa anyway. When I woke up I had back ache and a headache and I thought, *All right, this is it.* I hadn't made all the preparations I'd planned but there was no time for that now. The ashes would stay where they were and the animals would have to fend for themselves. I lay on the sofa, staring at the ceiling and waiting for things to get worse. Buster sat on the floor beside me and licked my hand. I fell asleep.

When I woke up I looked at the clock on the mantelpiece and couldn't believe it: three o'clock, the middle of the afternoon! The other amazing thing was I felt better. My headache had gone. I stretched cautiously, feeling for the tell-tale stiffness, but my joints were fine. I got up, and decided I was more than all right; I was good. I dressed and went over to the barn to milk Bonnie and Dolly. They were very reproachful at being missed earlier. I threw some food into the hen run, had a few words with Joey and gave him some carrots. It was so wonderful to see them all again, after thinking only that morning that by now if I was not actually through death's door I'd be standing on the welcome mat.

I spent the evening watching old movies on the TV. I couldn't understand why I was so tired after sleeping most of the day. It was only then that I realised I couldn't remember when I'd last eaten. I thought about it. I didn't feel hungry. If I wasn't hungry I didn't need to eat. That would be a good thing because I could do with losing some weight.

I dropped off, but this time I didn't sleep as well. I dreamt about Miss Dove. She is in Cambridge, riding a bike along Huntingdon Road towards Girton, like I'd seen students doing when I went for my interview. She offers me a lift on her crossbar.

'I can't,' I say, 'it's against school rules.'

'It's all right,' she says. 'No one will mind.'

I try to get on the bike but she doesn't slow down, she says she can't. I scramble to try to get on but I slip and fall in the road. Then I see that she's riding towards a river. I shout to her to stop, and she turns round to look at me and as she does that her bike goes over the edge of the bank, which has suddenly become steeper. She races towards the water and disappears.

SATURDAY

I got up this morning feeling stiff and cramped. It's strange, but I don't feel scared any more. I almost wish the Infection would come and get me, and it would be over.

I make myself some coffee, proper coffee using Granddad's grinder and percolator, not the instant that Gran would make. 'If I'm heading for the end of the world I might as well have a decent cup of coffee on the way,' I say to Buster. I'm talking a lot to him now. He leans against my legs and licks me. I give him a biscuit (not chocolate).

I go over to the barn for the milking and after that I visit the hens. There are nine eggs today, which must include yesterday's too. I've already got more than a dozen and they're laying them faster than I can eat them. I break one for Buster. It disappears in one extended slurp. He loves eggs, but Gran said it's not good for him to have too many.

I go upstairs to get the rest of my things to bring down. Before I start I open the door to Lander's room. I missed it out from my cleaning and I've not been in there since he left. The place is a tip. Every surface is covered with mess. There are clothes dumped on the bed and on chairs. There are magazines, books, tissues. Some of the magazines are about computing and some are lads' stuff, with huge-breasted girls in tiny bikinis on the covers.

I don't throw anything away. I put the magazines in piles. I go through the heaps of clothes on his chair and his bed, and the ones thrown in the bottom of his cupboard. Those that smell bad I put to wash, the others I hang up, or fold and put away in his drawers. I straighten the sheets and make up his bed. I don't like things not to be tidy, and I want his stuff to be ready for him when he comes back.

I pick up some T-shirts and open a drawer to put them away, and there's his computer. I'm surprised. Separating Lander from his computer usually required a surgical operation. I assumed he'd taken it with him, and wonder what the fact that he didn't means. I take it out and turn it on. I might be able to tweet or message some of the people he'd been exchanging with and find out if anyone knows where he is. Besides, it would be interesting to look through the rest of the material he's collected about the Infection.

The computer seems to take forever to boot up, then the home screen appears. There's nothing. There are no folders or files, no diary or address book. His mailboxes are empty and there are only the basic apps. There's not even a personalised desktop. He's wiped the lot. I'm puzzled. Why has he cleared everything out? Whatever the reason, it's obvious that he didn't want anybody to read any more from his archive. It's all gone, and the only things left are the documents he'd given me copies of, the ones I've pasted in my purple diary. I go through the other drawers looking for his iPad. I don't find it, and that comforts me. He must have thought he was going to need it, and that means he wasn't expecting to die. At least, not yet.

I go downstairs. The ads channel is still on in the kitchen. I find it comforting. It's like having people around me but it makes no demands. It's all I want. I don't want news bulletins, or useless statements from the Government about how to manage something that everybody knows is already way beyond control.

I fill the kettle. In a minute I'll have a shower, but first I'll make a cup of tea. The ad for Guys' fragrance comes on the TV, the one with Jason Ford with his shirt off. I put the kettle down to watch.

There's a small click and the picture and sound vanish. 'Fuck,' I say out loud. I try the switch, turning it off and on again, but although the green light comes on the screen stays blank. I fiddle about with the wires at the back but they all seem properly connected. I try the TV in the front room because that gets its signal from a satellite and not over broadband. That doesn't work either. I flick through a dozen channels and they're all the same: snowy screen, hissy sound.

I have a think. I wonder if there's a power cut. We have solar panels and a wind turbine, and they make most of the electricity we need during a normal day, so provided they were producing enough to power the TV and boil the kettle I wouldn't notice if the public supply went down.

I go across the yard to the barn where all the power stuff is: the inverter, controller and the meters. Granddad dealt with all that after Dad had gone. I frown at the dials. I wish I paid more attention to how it all works.

As far as I can see, everything is all right. There's energy coming from the solar panels and from the turbine. Some of that is being fed into the mains, which must mean it's working. The problem, therefore, is that there's something wrong with the TV. Not our TV sets, but the TV broadcasting system. All of it.

I go to my bedroom to get my radio. At least I can listen to that. Except I can't. I turn it on and scan through the stations, but on all of them there's only hissing. I switch from FM to DAB. Nothing there either. What's happened?

An emptiness sits in my stomach. It's as if I've been cast adrift and the rest of the world has disappeared.

SUNDAY

The TV and radio going off means that something is very, very seriously wrong. I mean, at a time like this wouldn't the Government do everything it could to keep the broadcast networks going? If it can't do that it can't communicate, it's lost control. I didn't expect my iPad to connect to the internet but I tried it anyway. I couldn't connect to anything with my phone either. It seems that our broadband is screwed; that, or the whole of the world wide web has gone.

It sounds stupid, but I can't do anything except try to be normal. I mean, if I don't do the normal things, what do I do? So I do the milking and the feeding. When I get back in the house I hook my phone to my Bluetooth speakers and put on Far Sighted, my current fave band, very very loud. Buster reclines in a corner. I don't think he really has his paws over his ears, I think it's just the way his head's lying.

According to my plan, yesterday I should have turned Joey and the other animals loose and got things together for my sick bed, but I don't feel at all ill. I feel very well. Doing things to close everything down when I feel so good is crazy.

I decide to go for a ride. Joey needs the exercise and Jesus, so do I, and it could be my last chance. I saddle him up and take him for a canter around the bottom fields. We both enjoy it, but we don't see a soul. On a normal Sunday there'd be plenty of people on the path that winds up the hill beside the farm – walkers, mountain bikers, people taking their dogs and children out – but there's nobody.

I get back, unsaddle Joey, rub him down and go back to the house. I am not sick. I am not sick! I haven't been near enough to anyone else to be infected since our Mam went, and the time is almost up. If I get through tomorrow without any symptoms it proves I'm safe. I will have survived. I WILL HAVE SURVIVED. I wonder who else has. Where is Lander?

It's a lovely day and I don't feel ready to go in yet. I put on some boots and take off up the hill behind our house. When people first come to our farm they think it's the top of the world, but it's not. There's still plenty above us. Buster's up for a walk and he trots along beside me.

For no particular reason I decide to make for the Bride Stones. It's only about half a mile to the stones but it's a toughish climb. Buster races ahead of me and rushes back so many times that he covers the distance at least twice.

The semicircle of monoliths is on one side of a shallow, peaty pool. On the other is a horseshoe of rock, about ten metres high. At some time in the past the face has been quarried, and there are rejected stones around its base, some of them the size of a horse. How did they move such enormous objects back in the days when this quarry was used, when there were no motors, and pack horses tracked the hills?

The Bride Stones themselves are seven huge pillars. They look like a prehistoric monument, dolmen driven into the earth, but they're not. They're natural, some geological freak created when the glacier that once filled the valley retreated at the end of the Ice Age. Lander used to say they look like seven stone pricks, and I think he has a point. One of them even looks to have a fold of foreskin. Local lads scale the stones, treating them as a challenge. Lander once told me that he could climb all seven but I never saw him do it.

The place has the reputation of being creepy, and when me and Lander were kids we'd come up here at twilight to play dare and scare. It doesn't seem in the least threatening under today's blue sky. Despite that, I experience a sudden, short shiver, a lurch, like falling. It's a feeling Gran used to get and she ascribed it to 'somebody walking on me grave'. It only lasts a second but it disturbs me for a moment or two. Is there really something other worldly about the stones? Are there supernatural forces at work here? I take a deep breath. Get a grip, Kerryl Shaw. You don't believe in that sort of stuff.

I clamber up the easiest of the sun-warmed stones and sit on its top. It's too high for Buster to jump and I'm not going to lift him, so he whines at the bottom. I look out at the spread of moorland on the hills across the dale, and Walbrough laid out like a toy town below. In the far distance is more high ground, the faint edge of the Derbyshire peaks. Normally from here you can pick out the landing lights of the planes coming in and out of Manchester airport, tiny pinpoints of light like fireflies, but today there are none. Normally the sky would be laced with vapour trails; there are none of those either. A road, a railway, a river and the canal jostle for space through the narrow valley. All are idle, all still.

It's only when I'm actually up here that I know why I had to come. It was to prove that I am still able to manage the climb up the hill, and because if I do succumb tomorrow to this sodding, evil plague, this is the last time I'll see the glorious landscape that has been the backdrop to my life.

I look down at the pool, dark and still, with a few reeds at its edge. In the library at St Winny's there was a copy of a picture. It was of a girl in a long dress lying on her back in water. She was holding flowers at her chest and she was dead. I'd seen the original on a school trip to a pre-Raphaelite exhibition in Leeds. It was supposed to be Ophelia, who had drowned herself because Hamlet had dumped her. *If you wanted a pool to drown yourself in,* I thought, *this one here would be a good choice. A bit shallow, perhaps, but water's water, and that's all you need.*

I remember the legend that from this rock you could see your true love on Midsummer's Day. Is it Midsummer's Day today? No idea. I've lost track of the days. I scan the moor around the rocks. No one. I sit on the stone until the sun lowers and I feel chilly. Then I go back to the house.

The TV and radio are still useless, and when I look out there are no lights on anywhere. There is nothing moving in the town, except in one place where I can see a thick column of black smoke, like burning tyres. Should I go tomorrow to see what's happening down there? I'm not sure. Truth be told, I'm nervous about venturing into Walbrough. When I went down to try to buy the urns the atmosphere was decidedly unfriendly.

MONDAY

A bad night. Despite my euphoria yesterday, I'm still scared of the Infection. I woke up what felt like every five minutes expecting to be sweating and for my limbs to be aching. I got a savage cramp in my leg. It was probably only the result of scrambling up to the Bride Stones yesterday, but in the silent darkness it felt fatal.

The verdict this morning is that I'm okay but I'm knackered. I look in the cupboard for breakfast. There's plenty there but I don't fancy any of it. I'd love to get some fresh bread, like Josie's dad used to make. I wonder if there's any in the town. It's a lovely sunny morning and the valley doesn't look threatening the way it did last night. I'm all right. I could go and look for some.

The trouble is, I don't feel like doing anything, not even reading. I always have a book on the go, but not at the moment. That's crazy. I have a lot of books, and there are books I should be reading for Cambridge. No, correction: there is no Cambridge. There is no exam or syllabus to read for now. Maybe there's no reason to read at all, and never will be again. Has the line of fiction, the chain of creative narrative that is unpicked in *Mimesis*, ended? Will nobody ever write a story again? And if they do write, who's to read it? They don't all have you, Adam.

I learnt to read early, much sooner than Lander. It seemed easy to me. The meaning of the marks on the page was so clear that I couldn't understand how it was that he didn't get it. At primary school I used to bring books home from the class library. We were allowed one a week, and I'd always finish mine in the first day and then I'd have to spend the rest of the week reading it again or making do with something I could scrounge from somebody else. I had an arrangement with Lucy Kershaw. She hated reading and wasn't very good at it, so she'd pass her library book to me and I'd read it and tell her the story so she could write it up in her reading record. It never occurred to me to ask the teacher if I could have another book. I expect I could.

I pick up one of Mam's old magazines but I don't fancy it. Our Mam only read gossip and celeb stuff. Granddad read *Farmers' Guardian* and books about the wars. And sometimes he'd read a paper when our Mam brought one back from her shift. Gran was a bit of a dark horse and she'd get bodice rippers from the public library, but it would take her ages to read one, weeks and weeks. Nobody minded me spending so much time with my head buried in a book, but nobody encouraged me either. It was something I did for myself, and because of that it became extra special.

Whenever anybody asked me what I wanted for a birthday or Christmas I'd say a book. Sometimes they'd buy me one, sometimes they didn't, and sometimes they bought me a book that maybe they'd liked when they were kids but was now ancient. They'd ask me about it and I'd have to be enthusiastic, even if I hated it. Sometimes elderly, well-meaning relatives would give me something they thought a girl of my age ought to want: crap like *Rainy Day Puzzles*, or *50 Exciting Activities for Girls*, or *Sarah* bloody *Sunshine*. In the end I'd just ask for money, which I'd spend at the second-hand bookshop in Walbrough.

One of the things I liked most about moving up to St Winifred's was the school library. It was open at lunchtimes, and I'd go there every day to read. I'd even sneak in my packed lunch, although it was against the rules. Girls who'd been excused PE and games spent those lessons in the library, so I used to con, persuade and nag our Mam into writing me sick notes. She usually did because she knew I hated games, and on the rare occasions when she was in a bad mood and wouldn't provide me with a note I'd forge one.

'You're the only girl I know who has her period every fortnight,' said our games teacher, 'and it's always at its worst on games days.' I don't think she minded really. Unlike Lander, I was crap at games and she was probably glad to be rid of me.

I used the library as a refuge, and the characters that peopled the books were a diversion from the things that troubled me during the rest of the day. I became the girls I read about: Anne of Green Gables, Rebecca, Jane Eyre, Scout Finch, Hermione Granger, Katniss Everdeen. I took books home, too. When you were in Year 7 you could have two at a time, Year 8 three, Year 9 four, and so on up to Year 11, when you could have half a dozen at once. And you could change them whenever you wanted, every day if you felt like it. I didn't read on the bus because Josie liked to talk, but as soon as I got home and had finished my evening jobs I'd start. Sometimes I read at the expense of doing my homework, and often I'd put the light on again after I was in bed and our Mam had been in to say goodnight, and I'd read till midnight and after.

It was through the library that I first got to know Miss Dove. She didn't teach me English then but I saw her almost every day because she'd come in most lunchtimes. Once she got used to me being there she'd look to see what I was reading. Sometimes she'd make a comment, or ask me what I thought of a book. She seemed to have read everything! Then she started suggesting books to me. It was Miss Dove who got me into Jane Austen. And Kate Mosse. And Margaret Atwood. She was there when I went into school during the summer holiday after Year 11 to get my GCSE results. She knew already that I'd got an A★ in English Literature and the same in Language.

'Well, I don't think there's any doubt what you ought to be doing,' she said. 'I think you should join my advanced English group.'

So I did, and I carried on reading, right up to the Cambridge exam, right through everything until now. Now I've stopped, even though there's plenty on my shelves waiting for me.

Do you read, Adam? Most boys don't, at least not as much as girls. I've not got you down as a Philistine, though. I think you have a sensitive side. I think you'd read. Anyway, you'd better read this diary, because nobody else will.

I wonder what you'll think of me. Looking back over some of the things I've written I can't believe how normal they seem. Chatty, jokey even. 'How could you feel like that?' you say. But I don't, not most of the time. Most of the time I'm depressed as shit and all the time

I'm near to tears. But when I write it's different. It's as if I become somebody else and there's another girl speaking through me. So don't judge me too harshly, Adam, if you think I'm not treating what's happened seriously enough. How would you react in my shoes? It's only the release I feel when I'm writing that's keeping me sane.

TUESDAY

This is scary. After loafing about yesterday and not settling down to anything, I resolved this morning to get a grip. I'm not dead and I'm not going to die (yet). I don't have the guts to kill myself, and besides, I don't want to (yet). So I have no choice but to keep on, and I need to start doing things. That's why I decided to make a trip down into Walbrough. I wish I hadn't.

After my useless visit to the ICC the other day I thought the town would be in a bad way, but it was even worse than I expected. I once saw a movie about the end of the world. There'd been a nuclear war and everybody was dying from the radiation. There was this shot of a city. The buildings were abandoned and the pavements broken and empty. The streets were deserted. There were wrecked cars, and there was litter blowing like ghosts in the wind. Well, when I got into Walbrough the litter was there all right and so were the wrecked cars, but there was something more, something that the movie couldn't convey: the smell! It hit me as soon as I got to where the buildings start.

How to describe it? Well, one day me and Lander were helping Granddad round up the sheep to bring them in from the moor for the winter. Lander was a way off and suddenly he let out a yell and made as if to throw up. He beckoned me over.

'Have you ever smelt anything so gross?' he said.

I hadn't. 'What is it?' I said, and he pointed for me to look over the wall.

All I could see was a dirty grey pile of wool that looked to be mixed up with some slime. Then I examined it more closely. It had been a sheep but a lot of it had turned to liquid. The pinkish bits that were left seemed to be moving and I saw that what remained of the animal's flesh was heaving with maggots. The stink was unbelievable. It took me days to get it out of my nose and mouth and it even clung on in my hair. Well, I'd tell you Walbrough was the same as that but it wasn't; it was worse! However, having come down the hill I was determined to carry on despite the smell, if I could.

There was nobody around, there weren't even any bodies that I could see, and all the shops were shut. Some of the windows had been smashed and various bits and pieces of stock scattered in the road. There were the burnt-out remains of half a dozen cars in the central car park. Along the road two vans were at crazy angles. They looked as though they'd smashed into each other and one of them was on its side. I couldn't see if there was anybody in them, but I'm afraid I didn't look too hard. In the middle of the High Street was a dead animal of some sort. I couldn't make out what, because it was heaving with dogs, tearing at the carcass and snarling. As I watched the struggle one of them, a really big one, backed away tugging something long and elastic in its jaws. When I looked around I could see there were dogs everywhere, slinking along the pavement, hanging about on corners, skulking in doorways. Some were in packs, some on their own. They were a restless, bad-tempered bunch, growling and snapping. I was glad I'd decided against bringing Buster with me, although he'd been keen to come and it would have been comforting to have him beside me.

I could tell without getting out of the Land Rover that the ICC was still closed. The people who'd been hanging around on the steps last week were gone now and there was no one about. There were footmarks on the door, which suggested that somebody had tried to kick it in. There were a lot of them, so whoever it was had persevered but they hadn't broken it down. There was a notice posted. I didn't bother to read it. I didn't care what it said.

I drove round the corner to Newell's Supermarket. I didn't really need anything, but if there was something good left I wanted the option of grabbing it while it was still there. Also I might be able to get some perfume or air freshener to mask the stench of the town.

There was more rubbish in Newell's car park, and two more abandoned vehicles. I parked the Land Rover as close to the front of the store as I could. The plate glass windows were smashed, and although the interior was dark I could see that the store was in chaos.

I opened the door of the Land Rover and the rotting sheep stink hit me harder than ever. It was so gut-churningly gruesome that I could barely take a breath without gagging. I thought I was not going to be able to get out of the car and would have to give the supermarket a miss, but I held my breath and picked my way into the store. I was careful to avoid the broken glass because I had only light shoes and the soles were thin.

The smell inside the store was differently nauseating. There was a heap of mouldy oranges on the floor, and a cloud of green spores erupted when I poked them with my toe. There was a bank of light switches on the wall and I tried them, but nothing worked. I realised that the power in the town must have been off for some time. I wasn't sure exactly what had happened, but it seemed as though after several weeks of the authorities trying to keep things as normal as possible everything had collapsed at once, gone tits up with hardly any warning. For example, there hadn't been time for the store staff to clear the fish and meat counters before they left, with the result that all the surfaces were covered in mounds of glistening grey I-don't-know-what. I didn't go near them. Sticky streams oozed from under the doors of chiller cabinets and freezers. I avoided those, too. I could see that people had been in there raiding, because dry stock had been dragged off the shelves. Packets, tins and jars were scattered in the aisles. Some of the jars had broken and some of the packets were split open, by the fall or by animals. I shuddered and looked around anxiously as the thought of rats came to me. I'm a farm girl and rats go with the territory, but I still hate them.

The raiders had been selective. The section where batteries and small electronic items used to be displayed had been cleaned out, and the off licence section was almost empty too. I went along the food shelves. There were lots of tins and jars but I didn't fancy any of them. I've got plenty at home anyway. I don't need anything, and coming on top of the stench the thought of food was making me feel queasy. I helped myself to some hair products and cosmetics. I found some perfume: Summer Girl. Normally I wouldn't have touched it with a barge pole because it smells like a tart's boudoir, but I splashed it all over me regardless.

I was going along the shelves, being choosy and stowing in my backpack the few things that looked any good, when I heard a noise from the front of the store. I moved away from the end of the aisle and crouched behind a display rack. They were cans of cleaning products and they'd been stacked in tiers. It didn't give much cover but there was no time to find anything better.

The visitors were trying to be quiet but they were not making a very good job of it. One of them looked ill, and as soon as he came inside he flopped down by the door, where he sat with his head propped against the wall. The others left him and made straight for the wine and beer shelves, only one aisle over from me. I kept very still. It seemed as though they might have been there already because they looked and sounded half pissed. I remembered with something approaching panic that I'd left the keys in the Land Rover. However, even though it was right by the door the intruders didn't seem to have paid any attention to it on the way in. I prayed that they'd ignore it on the way out too. If they ever left. They looked to be settling in for a long session. Two of them were on the tiled floor, gulping at bottles. They were clearly embarking on the next stage of a serious drinking spree, although the choice of booze on offer didn't seem to impress one of them. He picked up a bottle and hurled it across the store, swearing. It smashed against the wall. One of the others shouted at him. I could see that the shouter was holding a shotgun.

It looked old and battered, not clean and well-oiled like Granddad's Purdeys, but I had no doubt it would work. I didn't intend to give him a reason to try it and I stayed behind my stack, very still.

One of them wandered to the end of the aisle where there was a stand loaded with gift cards: iTunes, Amazon, MusicMash, Red Letter Days, Deezer.

'Fuck,' he said, 'look at all these.' He grabbed a handful of the cards and stuffed them into his pocket. The gun man started to laugh. 'What's up with you?' the first one said, glaring at him.

'What the fuck are you doing?' said the gun man.

'I'm taking these,' said the first one. He held one up. 'Look at this,' he said. 'A day driving a Ferrari at Brands Hatch. Sharp, eh?'

'You mad bastard,' said the gun man. 'They're worth nowt. They're just plastic. You have to take them to the till to get 'em activated.'

'Well, the tills are there, aren't they?' said the first one, pointing to the check-outs.

'Yes, but they're all empty and shut up,' said the gun man. He laughed pityingly. 'Anyway, where're we going to go to spend 'em?' he said.

'Dim twat,' said the third.

The one with the gift cards was embarrassed. Anger offered a diversion. 'What did you call me?' he said.

'I said you're a dim twat,' the other replied. 'You're a wanker an' all.' He was up for a fight.

They moved towards one another and the gun man stepped aside to give them room. Then he saw me.

'Well, what have we here?' the gun man said. He came

forward and stood over me. The two fighters dropped their fists and turned round. The gun man grabbed me by the hair and pulled me to my feet. He stood back and ran his eyes over me, lingering on my tits and my legs.

'Not bad,' he said. 'Not Miss World, but she'll do.' He turned to the others. 'You sort out your business and I'll do mine,' he said, and winked at me.

The others had lost interest in fighting. They came closer. All three were staring at me now.

'Finders keepers,' said the gun man, warning them off. 'This little girl's mine. You two can have what's left.' Slowly he leant the shotgun against the shelves. He undid his belt, pulled it from its loops and wrapped it around his hand. It was now a weapon. 'Knickers off, love,' he said.

I hesitated.

'Come on,' he said, 'we haven't got all day.'

I'd put on a skirt to come down into the town. I don't know why I'd bothered to dress up like that instead of keeping on the jeans I always wore. Our Mam always expected me and Lander to be smart when we went into town with her so I guess it was habit. It gave me an idea. I put my hands under my skirt and took hold of my knickers. I wiggled my hips as I eased them down and crouched to slip them over my shoes. I made a show of this because I wanted them all to be distracted, and they were. All the time I was staring at the gun man, trying to look smouldering and raunchy, although that was the last thing I felt.

I'd noticed that some of the aerosol spray cans from the display had fallen on the floor. I positioned myself so that as I squatted my skirt belled out and covered one of them. I took it in one hand and hoped it was something nasty. With my other hand I twirled my knickers. They weren't the sort I usually wear, they were a scarlet, lacy pair that I'd got from Victoria's Secret in Manchester one Saturday when I was feeling flush and flighty. Again, I don't know why I'd put them on today but I think something must have been looking after me. The sexy underwear certainly caught the men's interest. Suddenly I tossed the knickers at the gun man. Reflexively he made to catch them and in the second his attention left me I gave him a long burst from the spray can, full in the face. I was taller than him so I got a good angle. He let out a raging howl and his hands flew to his eyes. He stumbled backwards into the shelves and the gun clattered to the floor. I squirted him again.

'Christ! Fuck!' he yelled, his hands rubbing at his eyes. One of the others came at me and I let him have it too. He screamed and dropped to his knees.

The third man seemed paralysed. 'Throw some water on them,' I shouted. He came to life then and rushed towards a shelf of water bottles. Both the others were bent in two, blubbering and wailing. I picked up the gun and ran for the door, chased by their curses: 'Fuck! Christ! Bitch! Cunt!'

As I ran past the man at the door I could see that there was blood round his mouth and nose. He was in very bad shape. Even in my rush to escape I thought I should stop and help him, but I didn't. I got out as fast as I could go.

I hurled the shotgun into the Land Rover and myself

after. My whole body was trembling so much I could hardly start it, and then when I had I couldn't get it into gear. I reversed and hit one of the abandoned cars. There was a thump that jarred my neck and a crunch of metal and glass. I slammed it into forward, floored the pedal and raced out of the car park, crashing the box as I changed up. I glanced at the spray can on the seat beside me. It was black and red. Oven cleaner. *Oh my God, I've blinded them*, I thought.

I'm not a cruel person. I hate seeing people or animals suffer – Lander says I'm too soft for a farm girl – but I was glad about what I did to the two men. They deserved it, and I wished I'd got the third as well. They were all infected, I was sure of that, and the one by the door looked almost dead. Had they infected me? The gun man was the only one who had touched me. He'd pulled my hair, and I'd picked up the gun he'd been holding. But he was the one of the three who'd seemed in best health. Perhaps he was clean. I dreaded another two weeks of anxiously waiting to see if I developed symptoms.

Back at home I put all my clothes in the washing machine on a hot programme. Then I scrubbed my hands till they were nearly raw, showered, and washed my hair. I dressed again and went out to the yard, where I drenched the Land Rover in disinfectant. After that I was exhausted. I made myself a cup of soup and sat on the sofa. I fell asleep before I could drink it, a nervous reaction I think. The last I remember is a silly playground jingle going round and round in my head.

Lost your knickers, you silly mare,
Showing the boys your underwear.
Lost your knickers, you silly cow,
Bet you're in the fam'ly way now.

I wish you'd been there to help me, Adam. I could have done with a bit of extra muscle.

WEDNESDAY

I'm definitely not going into the town again. I don't want to risk repeating what happened in the supermarket. It's shaken me up more than I would have predicted. One holiday Josie was molested by a gang of boys in Blackpool, but nothing like that had ever happened to me before now. She got away by whipping off a shoe and smacking one of the boys with the heel, and the others ran off. She didn't seem fazed by it at all. Whereas my little skirmish had really upset me. I won't go down the hill again until I'm absolutely sure that there's nothing bad going on. Even if I'm not attacked, somebody might see me going back up the hill. They could follow me and find out that I'm here on my own. That thought makes me shudder. The window in our Mam's bedroom gives a good view of most things in the valley, and I've spent a lot of time looking through Granddad's field glasses to see if there's anything moving. I've seen plenty of dogs and other stray animals, but nothing human. Even so, I don't want to make it obvious I'm here. I won't switch on lights at night, I'll use candles and oil lamps instead, and I'll draw the curtains.

LATER

If I'm not going into town I have a problem with the ashes. I know, I'll make something for them. Two boxes. Or perhaps one, with a division down the middle, so they can be together. It will give me something to do. That's why I'm lardy, because I don't do anything. I get up and milk the cows, see to Joey, feed the hens and look for any new eggs, check the sheep. Then there might be a bit of cleaning and tidying, and that's the day taken care of. The rest is mine. I don't have the TV but I can play games and watch moviesticks on my iPad. I'm still not reading, but there's my diary and I spend a couple of hours a day on that. The trouble is, all this involves sitting on my arse. I've always been inclined to put on weight, and I have an ongoing battle with my spare tyre. I look in my bedroom mirror and pinch my stomach, and pull a face. I need to do something energetic, something that will burn off the fat. Or maybe I just need to eat less! Do you like chubby girls, Adam?

FRIDAY

My diary's become so important to me that I feel a kind
of ache if I haven't written anything for a bit. Yesterday
I was grumpy, grumbling at Buster, slapping Bonnie's
rump harder than I needed to, shoving the hens aside.
I didn't realise till bedtime that it was because I hadn't
done my diary. I don't know why not, I just didn't. So this
morning I'm sitting down straight away, before breakfast
even, and writing. Perhaps I'll skip breakfast. That would
be good for me, although I woke up thinking how nice
it would be to have some porridge, made with Bonnie's
lovely creamy milk.

Habit tells me I should do my laundry, but I don't
need to. From what I saw when I was down in the town,
there are so many clothes in the stores in Walbrough that
if I managed to pluck up the courage to go and get them
I could put on something different every day. I expect all
the other valley towns are the same. There'll be even more
in Manchester or Leeds. I think about going over to the
Trafford Centre. H&M, Forever 21, AllSaints, Hollister,
Topshop, Girls Out – I could have my pick. I could just
wear something and throw it away, a proper rich bitch.
There were people at school who would have killed to be
able to do that, but to be honest it doesn't appeal to me. I
like my own stuff, the things I know and have worn before.
For a lot of them I can remember where I bought them,
and when, and who I was with. They're part of my history.

So what's new in the forty-eight hours since I last
wrote? Well, I'm trying to dry Bonnie off. She's been in

milk a long time and I know it should be done because Granddad used to do it, but I'm not sure how. Every day I take a bit less milk from her to encourage her to stop lactating and I think it's working. After that there'll just be Dolly. It will be a relief to have only one cow producing. I have too much of the stuff. I drink a little and Buster loves it, but there's always plenty left over. I could make more cheese, and butter, and yoghurt, but the fridge and freezer are stacked full already. There's rice, semolina, tapioca in the pantry and I've got Gran's recipe book, so I could make some milk puddings. I don't fancy them, though. I used to love them, but now even thinking about them makes me feel like barfing. So I pour a lot of the milk away. I hate doing that and I think how our Mam would have gone ballistic about the waste. I wonder if I could get another freezer up the hill. The problem would be how to get it onto the trailer. I might be able to go down in the tractor and use the bucket to lift it in, and I could unload it and put it in the barn. Then I could store some more.

I don't need another freezer. I have more than enough of everything. I could do absolutely nothing for ages and still have all the food I can eat. It's a life of luxury really. Everything I need without having to work for it. Paradise.

SATURDAY

If there was anybody else left alive I'd know by now, don't you think?

It's not just that the valley's dead, that's only this immediate area, but if there were people left in other places I would surely have seen some sign – a plane or a helicopter or something. I would have heard vehicles, or there would have been a train winding along the line from Leeds to Manchester. Or the TV or the radio would have come on, suddenly blaring and scaring me to death. My mobile would have started up (I still keep it charged), and there'd be pages of notifications, texts, messages and missed calls. But there's been nothing, not even a reply to the voicemail I left for Steve.

I must think about this rationally. Mr Armitage, who used to teach me philosophy and logic so I'd be ready for the Cambridge exam, told me to deal with a big question by breaking it up into smaller and smaller ones, arranging them in order and reaching an inescapable conclusion. So here goes.

Big question: What evidence is there that every other person in the UK is dead?

Smaller question 1: Have I seen anybody in the past week?

Answer: No, just the four guys in the supermarket, and one of those was almost dead. I bet by now the others are too.

Smaller question 2: Do I have any of the usual signs that there are other people alive somewhere else? *Answer:* There's no TV, no radio, no internet and the phones aren't working, so no.

I don't think there's any need to go on. I think the logical conclusion is that without any evidence for the existence of another living person, everybody else has gone. Does that apply to the whole country, to the whole of England, Scotland and Wales? Well, it seems crazy, but it probably must. I can't imagine London being dead, with all the houses and the hotels and offices and government buildings closed and empty, the large stores just vastly bigger versions of Newell's. Imagine not just Walbrough's few thousand, but eight million people dead! God, think how that would smell! But what other reason could there be for there being no sign at all of life elsewhere?

The last few news bulletins I saw were obsessed with how incredibly quickly the Infection was spreading once it had taken hold over here. We already knew that it was rampant on mainland Europe, and that it got there having devastated North Africa and the Middle East. So pretty much every bit of this segment of the big orange was affected before everything went off. The TV news was all about what was happening here, not much about anywhere else, but I remember a dispatch from America that said the Infection was getting serious over there too, that the President and Congress had moved out of Washington to secret locations, and New York and L.A. had practically shut down. But America is vast, huge stretches where there are no people at all. Wouldn't the wildernesses act as isolation corridors? Surely the Infection couldn't have spread everywhere there, could it? And what about the rest of the world? Russia, and China and Australia? What about the islands?

Lander said the Infection can be carried by birds. Birds fly thousands of miles, across lands and oceans. Birds could take it anywhere, and if you touched something an infected bird had landed on you'd get it. There were rumours that some animals might be hosts as well. I don't think the Government wanted that spread; they must have been worried about people turning on farm animals and murdering each other's pets. Are Bonnie and Molly and Dolly carriers? Is Joey? Buster? The cats? I have no way of finding out.

One of the last news reports I saw said that the Russians were accusing the Americans of spreading the virus to destabilise them. The Americans were saying it was terrorists, probably helped by Islamic State, Al-Qaeda, the Kremlin, you name it. Before the TV died the accusations and counter-accusations were turning into threats. America said it would go to any lengths to defend itself and Russia said the same. Did Russia and America finally nuke each other? Did some potty outfit like North Korea decide it was going to do something spectacular? Have I survived the Infection only to perish from radiation?

Anyway, having examined the matter fully, Mr Armitage, here's my judgement:

1. I should have caught the Infection long ago. I ought by now to be dead. Why aren't I? I nursed our Mam

and I deliberately took off my biohazard suit and sat on her bed and held her hand. Lander bawled me out and said I was bound to catch it, but I didn't. Gran and Granddad got it, but not me.

2. No one else is left. If you'd suggested that to me even three months ago I would have said you were terminally stupid. But now I think it could be true. If there were people alive in the USA, or Russia, or China, don't you think they would have come here by now? You might say, why would they? They must know what the situation is, and what could there be here of any use to them? But even so, they'd come to find out what was going on. Wouldn't they, if they could?

So, the reason I haven't caught the Infection is because... I'm immune. There, I've been thinking about it for a while and now I've said it. I'm the only person in the UK, maybe in the whole world, who isn't susceptible to the virus. I could be the last human being left alive. Maybe I ought to be pleased about that but I'm not. It's not a privilege, it's a curse. I am alone, and nothing I can possibly do will make any difference to anything.

Fuck, I get depressed at this time of night. I stay up late, writing rambling rubbish by candlelight and I get morbid. I'm going to bed. But I keep thinking: is there anybody else?

And if not, why me? Why me?

I wish you were real, Adam. I could do with a cuddle, something to take my mind off it all.

SUNDAY

I'm thinking of cutting off my hair. It will be hard because it's my best feature. It's the colour of dark chocolate, wavy and luscious, everybody used to say so. I've always been proud of what Granddad used to call my tresses, and I tried not to be smug when my friends told me how much they envied me. My hair's thick and long... and there's the trouble. It would be a lot easier to have it short. I tie it up but it gets in the way and sometimes it falls down. If I'm busy with something messy and my hands are filthy, that's a problem because I can't tuck it back. It can be dangerous, too. I burn the household waste because if I leave it out it attracts animals. I take one of the wooden pallets from behind the barn, toss it into the old slurry pit, drop the rubbish on top, douse it with petrol and chuck in a match. Yesterday I did that and it went up like a rocket. My hair was loose and it almost caught fire. One side got singed and there was a horrible smell. It scared me. There's also the risk of it catching in something. I remember there was a girl at our school who was practically scalped because her hair got caught in the flywheel of a grinder in her dad's workshop. It ripped it all off and she had to wear a wig.

I feel sorry for women who have to hide their hair. I can remember when I was little asking our Mam why some of the girls I saw in town covered their heads with cloths.

'Their religion makes them do it,' she said.

That didn't seem to me to be a very good reason. 'Why?' I said.

'They're Muslims,' she said.

I spent a lot of time wondering what was under the headscarves, and thinking that it must be something really awful if it had to be kept out of sight. There were Muslim girls at our school, so I don't know why I didn't just come out and ask them, but I didn't. Instead I concocted a fantasy that they were concealing something terrible, like a hole in their heads so you could see right through their skulls into their brains. I had nightmares about it.

Of course I'd grown out of the nightmares by the time I went to St Winifred's. Then I just assumed that a Muslim girl's hair must be dull and boring, if she had any at all. Then, when I was in Year 8, I went into the toilets and found Minal Akram. She was in my form and I knew her quite well but I'd never seen her without her hijab. Now there she was, standing in front of the mirrors with her head bare. I didn't really think she'd be bald but I never expected what I saw. Her hair was beautiful, gorgeously black and glossy. I was astonished.

I said, 'Minal, I never knew your hair was like that. It's lovely. What a pity that you have to keep it covered up.'

She said, 'It's my religion. It's what Muslim women do.'

At the time I was flirting with different faiths, trying them on. Our Mam was vaguely C of E, Gran and Granddad lukewarm Methodists, but none of that impressed me. One problem was that I didn't like the idea of some supreme being watching me all the time, scoring my behaviour and deciding whether I should be rewarded or punished. I had school for that! I'd just got round to considering Islam. I liked its simplicity and compassion and charity, but after my conversation with Minal I dismissed it. I like to think that wasn't just because of vanity.

Until the Infection I washed my hair at least once a week. I can't always do that now, but I try. I love to shampoo it in the bath, and rinse it and put on a bathrobe and sit by the fire brushing it out and drying it. It keeps things normal. Every time I run the bath, though, I wonder what would happen if the solar panels stop working. I suppose it's not so much 'if' as 'when'. It must be ten years since our Dad put them up on the roof to give us free hot water. I have no idea what their lifespan is, but when they do break down I won't know how to fix them. Getting hot water then will be a lot more difficult. At least I've got enough shampoo to last me for the next 400 years.

I know that the sensible thing to do would be to hack off all my hair and shave it back to my scalp. No tangles, no chance of lice, no risk of an accident. Yesterday I sat at the mirror for a long time, winding it in my hands, pulling it back and trying to imagine what I'd look like without it. I might look a wreck. Or maybe it would just look punk. The thing is, I don't want to. It really would be like slamming the door on the past. It would be confirming that things will never again be the same as they were. Of course I know they won't, but as long as I've got my hair I can hope there might someday be something more than this. I can't bring myself to cut it off. Not yet.

MONDAY

Molly is huge. I looked this morning at her vast, rounded flanks. I could see her calf moving inside her. I think that gives me a little time because Granddad said that calves go still before they're born.

I'm really nervous about this. It might be simple, it might all be straightforward. It's not Molly's first so she'll know what's going on. But suppose something goes wrong.

In English we did a Ted Hughes poem with Rudy, about a sheep trying to give birth. The lamb was coming out head first, not feet first like they're supposed to, and Ted Hughes writes how he had to reach inside the sheep and cut the unborn lamb's head off. Then he pushed the stump of its neck back inside her so that he could reach in and get the legs and pull the dead lamb out. It was awful. It made one girl sick and she had to run out of the classroom. I felt a bit churny myself. I think Rudy did it deliberately. He'd sold Ted Hughes to us by saying that he'd written a lot of poems about animals, and we'd already read *Thought Fox* and we all liked that. This one was different and Rudy enjoyed the effect it had on us.

When I looked at Molly I remembered that poem. What if that happens with her calf? I couldn't do what Ted Hughes did, I know I couldn't. Would I have the strength to get the .22 and put Molly out of her misery?

LATER

There was a girl at our school, Tracey Blackburn. She was really slim and we all wanted to be like her. However, she got thinner and thinner until her face was a skull and her arms and legs were sticks. Nobody wanted to be like her then. One day she was rushed into hospital and we were told she had a severe eating disorder. Her blood pressure had tumbled and she'd gone into an anorexic coma. She'd not been eating anything, nothing at all, and when we thought she was eating she wasn't, she was pretending. She almost died.

I don't know how she could do it. Last night I went through my wardrobe and tried on lots of things I haven't worn for a bit. They were all tight! Some of them were very tight!! I got out the dress I wore to the Year 11 prom and it wouldn't do up. Except for when I went down to Walbrough last Monday, what I've been doing is wearing the same old sloppy things day after day and it hadn't really struck me how lardy I was. I got on the bathroom scales and… well, I'm too embarrassed to tell you what they said but I will say it was too much! So this morning I didn't have any breakfast, and I haven't had any lunch, and it's three o'clock and *I'm starving*. How could Tracey not eat, day after day after day? How could she sit in front of a plate of food and only play with it?

Will you still love me, Adam, even though I'm a dough ball?

TUESDAY

I managed to get through to bedtime yesterday without eating anything at all. Aren't you proud of me, Adam? Yeehaa! I expected when I woke up this morning that I'd be starving and ready to eat the first thing I set eyes on, but not so. I feel okay.

I've taken against mirrors. We have so many of them. It never occurred to me before, but we must have been a very vain family. I have two in my room, there are two in the bathroom and another two in our Mam's bedroom and en-suite. (Why don't I sleep in her room? It's nicer than mine, and I could use the en-suite. I might move.) Back to the mirrors; that's six so far. There's one in what was my grandparents' room, two in Lander's room, one on the landing, one in the hall, and a little one in the porch that our Mam would use to check her hair and make-up before she went out. There's another over the mantelpiece in the dining room. I think that's all but I can't promise I haven't missed one. Anyway, that's thirteen mirrors for what were five people. Hang on, fourteen – I'd forgotten the one in the downstairs loo. Fourteen mirrors, just for me. This means that I see myself a lot, and I don't like it. Sometimes I catch the reflection of a movement out of the corner of my eye, and even though it's only me (well it must be, mustn't it, there's no one else here) it makes me jumpy.

This morning, after I'd done the milking and seen to Joey, I went round the house and took down all the mirrors and turned them to the wall, leaving only the one in the bathroom that's on the cabinet.

I was tubby before the Infection, but once it started Gran and our Mam, and me too, forgot everything we knew about a balanced diet. We were eating potatoes a lot because we had plenty and they're easy. We were eating pasta because it's quick and simple. Gran went on a bake-a-thon and made loads of cakes, and we were drinking Bonnie and Dolly's creamy milk and eating their cheese. The night our Mam was taken ill I found a packet of éclairs in the freezer and I ate them all in one go, before they'd properly thawed out. I didn't even offer one to Lander, I just sat in the corner of the barn and guzzled them. I told myself that I was under pressure and I needed the extra energy, as if that would make it all all right and it wouldn't just all turn to blubber. The next day I found a box of chocolates at the back of our Mam's wardrobe. She must have been keeping them for a present for somebody, and I ate all those too. Then I made myself sick. Don't be shocked, I know about bulimia and I'm not bulimic. I hadn't wanted the chocolates but I couldn't stop myself eating them, and once I had I felt an irresistible urge to unload them. It was like I'd blundered into a cycle of behaviour that belonged to somebody else, not to me. I won't do it again, I promise.

On top of all the gorging, I've not been doing enough. On school days I used to walk to Josie's and then with her to the bus stop, and back home up the hill in the evening. I was never into games or PE, but sometimes Josie and I would go for a run round the park, especially if there were any of the boys we fancied playing football. Now after my chores I just sit on my butt.

I'll miss the mirrors because I talk to myself in them. Is that nuts? Often when I passed one I'd wave to myself, or I'd pull a face, and say hi. Sometimes I'd stand in front of one and ask it a question. Sometimes I'd read out a poem: Sylvia Plath, Adrienne Rich, Emily Dickinson, Carol Ann Duffy. I know some off by heart. Elizabeth Barrett Browning wrote one for us, Adam.

How do I love thee? Let me count the ways.
I love thee to the depth and breadth and height
My soul can reach, when feeling out of sight.

Isn't that gorgeous? It makes me go all goose bumpy. I like Keats, too.

My heart aches, and a drowsy numbness pains
My sense, as though of hemlock I had drunk
An hour since and Lethe-wards had sunk.

Isn't lethe a lovely word? Lethe, lethe, lethe. I just love the sound of it. I told Josie that if I ever had a daughter I'd call her Lethe.

She said, 'Well, if you want everybody to know what a mad cow you are, why not?'

I suppose she had a point, but anyway it won't happen now. I don't believe in virgin births.

I like Andrew Marvel, too. Or I like *To His Coy Mistress*, which is the only poem of his I know. We read that with Miss Dove. I wonder what he was like, Andrew

Marvel. Was he as hot as his poem? He was an MP, so probably not.

I've just looked back at this, and all the stuff about eating is a bit embarrassing. It's certainly not sexy. I thought about tearing the page out, but then I thought I'd leave it so that when I've slimmed down we can laugh at it together.

WEDNESDAY

I'm in a bad mood today, so you'd better stay back, Adam. I didn't feel hungry yesterday but I do today, and I always get grumpy when I'm hungry. But I think it's working already. I didn't eat anything at all on Monday, or the day before, and I only drank water, and Mam's scales say I've lost four pounds!

I'm wandering round the house trying to think what to do and I see that the liquid gas tanks are nearly empty. They're for the kitchen cooker and the gas fire in the front room. I'm trying to save them. I'm not using the cooker and I don't need a fire yet, but when they're gone that's it. I'll have to get by without. I saw some in the valley, four big ones outside a factory, but they're too heavy for me to move them on my own. Another job for you, Adam.

Electricity isn't a problem so long as I'm careful. I've got the turbine and the solar panels. They're enough to keep the fridge and freezers running, charge up my iPad and phone and give me some light. Sometimes there's a day when there's no wind for the turbine and it's so overcast and dim that there's little from the panels. Then I just carry on and do my best to conserve the batteries. I use candles and oil lamps at night. I could use electric lights – we've got energy saving bulbs everywhere – but I don't want to draw attention to the house by lighting it up like an ocean liner. I know there's probably nobody out there, but I prefer the candles and lamps, anyway. They're cosy. And romantic.

The taps don't work any more but I can get water from the spring in the yard. I found a whole box of water purifying tablets out the back and I used those for a bit. Then I forgot and nothing happened, so ever since I've been drinking the water straight from the spring. Every day I fill a couple of buckets which I use to flush the loos. There's a septic tank for the drains. Dad used to get it emptied every year, but there's nobody to do that now. I suppose some day it will fill up, but as there's only me now it'll probably be ages before that happens.

I'm not looking forward to the winter. We get lots of cold winds up here, and sometimes we're snowed in. Keeping warm is always an issue in the winter. I must make sure I've got plenty of logs split for the fire.

At this time of year the cows are outside, but from November, when they're inside all the time, I'll have to muck them out. Lander used to do that with a hose (see, he did have his uses!) but I'll have to carry buckets from the spring. I wonder if they really have to come in. The sheep stay out all the year, so why shouldn't the cows? I'll have a word with Bonnie about it. She's the most sensible of them.

Do you really need to know all this? Of course not, I'm just thinking aloud.

THURSDAY

I'm looking through my things, trying to fight the boredom by finding something to do, and I come across my love letters. Five of them. From Federico Garcia Lorca. I start to read them and I think how terrific they are, how much I like them. Well, I should; I wrote them!

It was the Easter holiday in Year 10. The term had been miserable for me because I was being bullied. You'd think I would have got used to it, because it had been happening ever since early in Year 9. There were three girls who were behind it: Donna Dugdale (she was the main one), Tamsin Sharpe and Jessica Parker-West. They were all September birthdays, and so although in the same year group as me they were almost a year older. They were physically much more mature, too. Donna was tall and blonde and very curvy, and Tamsin and Jessica were well developed, too. There were some bystanders and hangers-on, but these three were the ringleaders. They all had rich parents. The Dugdales had a fleet of trucks; you see them often on the motorways, or rather, you did. The Parker-Wests own Medbourne Hall, an up-market hotel and conference centre. I don't know what Tamsin Sharpe's family did, but they were loaded too. These girls seemed special. They got away with things that the rest of us weren't allowed to do, like wearing make-up and jewellery to school. They had the latest phones, tablets, laptops. They were brought to school in cars, Donna sometimes in her dad's Bentley.

Josie and me, on the other hand, came to school on the bus.

They didn't take much notice of the rest of us, so I suppose really I brought it on myself by sticking my head up. There was always an admiring, awe-struck gaggle around them, and for reasons that now embarrass me, Josie and I took to hanging around on the fringes of this flock. One day I mistakenly pushed myself to the front. I can't remember exactly what I said, but I was trying to get Donna's attention to impress her. I mentioned seeing one of her dad's trucks and I referred to his business as haulage.

She gave me a withering look. 'It's not "haulage",' she said with a sneer. 'It's logistics.'

I felt a complete idiot. I suppose I'd seen the word logistics on the trucks but I had no idea what it meant.

The bullying started soon after that. They found out I live on a farm, and whenever I came into a room where they were they'd say things like, 'Phew, can anyone smell cow poo in here?' Or, 'Look, it's the girl from udders feeled!' Or they'd pass me in the corridor and start singing *Old MacDonald Had a Farm*.

It was low-level stuff and I didn't really mind. It went on for the rest of the term, until they found somebody else to plague and it eased off. Then a few months later it started up again, and this time it was nasty.

I'd always been a tubby kid, but as I moved into my teens I got worse. 'Lardy-arse', 'Jelly-belly' and 'Nelly' were their favourites, and when it got too much for me and reduced me to tears, 'Blubber-tub'. They got a damaged chair from somewhere and put it in my place, and when I sat on it and it collapsed they couldn't stop laughing, even though I hurt myself.

I could have put up with the name calling, and the tricks they played on me and the stories they spread. What really got to me was when they took it online. That way it wasn't just our year that knew about it, it was everybody. Somebody got a photo of me and superimposed it on the body of a hippo. There was a supersize porn star called Melissa McStrange and they got a still of her in action and put my face on that too, together with my mobile number. That was awful. I had to change my SIM, but it still got to the stage where I was scared to look at my messages or my pages because of what I might find there. I used to cry myself to sleep every night.

Josie tried to help me. She told them to leave me alone, but then they started on her too, stuff about her having buns in the oven (her dad's a baker – or was), and she had to back off. She encouraged me to go on YouTube. There was this guy who called himself Sweet Cheeks. He had his own channel, where he helped people with their problems. I did look, but he was in America and it was all high school stuff and not really serious: 'A boy I really like is in the football team and I'm a cheerleader but he looks at the other girls and not at me. What can I do to get his attention?' and Sweet Cheeks's reply was, 'Take your clothes off'. I didn't think he'd be able to help me so I never contacted him.

Lander knew there was something wrong, even though he went to a different school. One Sunday evening just before the last week of term he came into my bedroom and found me crying. He asked me why and I told him I wasn't going to that school any more. He pestered and suddenly it all came out and I told him what was happening.

He had a solution straight away. 'You need to distract them,' he said.

'How?' I said.

He thought for a minute. 'Well, you can point them at somebody else instead of you,' he said.

It was tempting, but I didn't know how to do it. And I couldn't bring myself to, it wouldn't be fair to the other person. If I did that I'd be just like the bullies.

'That wouldn't be very nice,' I said.

'Well then, you need to find something else about you for them to talk about, something that's more interesting than your lardiness.' Lander was always one to call a spade a spade.

The answer came to me in bed that night. I needed a boyfriend! He had to be romantic, exotic even, and he had to be somebody Donna and her mates wouldn't know or expect to meet. Suddenly all the details arrived in a rush, and I began to build a story. He was foreign, Italian. He was over here for a visit. Our Mam, Lander and me were going to Scarborough for a few days in the holiday to stay with Auntie Madge and Uncle Ernest. That's where I'd meet him. There would be an intense, whirlwind romance and then we'd have to part. It would be so romantic.

The first thing I needed was some photographs. I spent ages trawling the internet. There were plenty of suitable candidates from model agencies but all the pictures were stamped with watermarks so were no good to me. Eventually I found an unstamped face that would do. There were several shots of him. He was about the right age, seventeen or so, good looking, with floppy hair, a frank gaze and dimples when he smiled. The problem was his hair was fair and his eyes blue and he simply didn't look Italian. Then I had a flash of inspiration. He was only *half* Italian. His father was Italian but his mother was English. That's why he was in Scarborough, visiting her family before going back to Verona (we'd been doing *Romeo and Juliet* at school). It was because of this link that he could speak good English. I printed some of the photographs and I posted one on my iKnowU page with the message that I'd seen this really nice looking boy and I thought he fancied me.

He had to have a name, and I couldn't think of one. Apart from Romeo I could only think of Mercutio and Tybalt and they wouldn't do. I did a Google search and there were millions, so many I couldn't choose. I asked our Mam for some Italian boy's names (I needed them for a project at school, I told her) and she came up with Giovanni, Giuseppe and Lorenzo, none of which I fancied. I went into a bookshop and started browsing the shelves and there I found it, on the spine of a book: Federico Garcia Lorca. *Perfect*, I thought. My boyfriend would be Federico Lorca, Ricci for short. I didn't find out till later that the real Federico Lorca was a famous playwright, and was Spanish anyway!

I'd now got his name and some photos and I started concocting the story online about how we'd met. It had been love at first sight. He had seen me sitting alone in a coffee bar in Scarborough, and asked if he could join 'the lovely English rose'. We talked and talked, and when we parted he asked if he could see me again. I said yes and he kissed my hand.

Several of my friends posted back, intrigued and envious, and a girl called Amber, one of the Dugdale mob, also replied: 'Really?? Tell me more.'

I knew I needed more than a few photos. I needed something concrete to demonstrate that Ricci was real. I told Lander what I'd done. I expected him to tell me I was stupid, but he thought Ricci was a really cool idea.

'If you need something more to show them, when we get home write yourself a love letter from him,' he said.

'Nobody writes love letters any more,' I said.

'Maybe Italians do,' he said.

I didn't wait till we got home. I wrote a love letter that afternoon. I had to do it on my iPad and print it because I would have to show it around and I couldn't risk anybody recognising my handwriting.

My dearest darling Kerryl, I wrote, *How I miss you. Being apart from you breaks my heart. My arms ache for you. I long to see your smile, to bathe in the pools of your wonderful eyes, to hold you under the moon and stroke your beautiful hair...* and so on. Yes, I'm sorry, but I was only fourteen. I wondered whether to make it raunchy and thought not. Ricci is a good Catholic boy and doesn't go in for casual sex. I put the printed letter in an envelope, addressed it to myself at the farm, and posted it. The Scarborough postmark was important.

That night I wrote four more letters. I really enjoyed doing it, although reading them now I'm appalled at how cheesy they are. I looked up some Italian endearments (*cara mia*, *ti penso*, *ti voglio tanto bene!*, *bellissima* and so on) and scattered them in my text. I put each letter in an envelope addressed to me. Then I stamped the envelopes and gave them to Auntie Madge. I asked her to post them to me one at a time, when I phoned her and said so. I told her it was for a project we were doing at school on the Royal Mail and girls were getting people from all over the country to post letters to them. (It's amazing what parents and relatives will believe if you tell them it's educational!)

My scheme worked. The second day back at school I took in the first of my letters. I made a big show of trying to keep it secret and then reluctantly giving in and showing it. Donna Dugdale's crew were like a flock of birds. They rose into the air, circled and when they came down again they were grouped around me, not her.

My hot Italian boyfriend was the main interest in our year group for several weeks. Have you called him? Have you texted him? Has he written? When I felt that interest was beginning to wane I phoned Auntie Madge and asked her to post me another of the letters. Sure enough, it arrived the next day. I passed it around and the whole affair was rekindled. My size was forgotten. The important thing about me now was that I was Ricci's girl.

I'm not sure that Donna Dugdale herself ever really bought it. She wasn't stupid, and she examined the envelopes with their Scarborough postmarks very carefully. I'd got Lander to sign the letters and write the addresses, but I think she was still suspicious.

'How come we only ever see photos of him,' she said, 'and not of the two of you together?'

I explained that we'd been alone, and I'd taken pictures of him on my phone and he of me on his.

'Ever heard of a selfie?' she said. 'And this one, there are palm trees in the background. That's not Scarborough.'

'It was taken in Italy,' I said. 'He messaged it to me.'

Whether she believed me or not, she could do nothing about it. The other girls had all swallowed the bait and were hooked.

I made up stories about Ricci, things he'd told me, things we'd talked about on the phone. I put a PAYG SIM in an old phone of Lander's and texted myself messages from Ricci. I even had him chuck a girl he'd been seeing in Italy for me. It was like a soap.

As the weeks passed the curiosity of my audience waned, and so did their interest in me. They transferred their bitchy attentions to somebody else and I was free. Besides, I was making a determined effort to lose weight and I was keeping to a strict diet. No way was I Miss Sylph, but my efforts were showing and there were now other girls almost as fat as me, one of them being Donna herself!

I met Donna after she'd left at the end of Year 11. She was waiting for her lift and was nice as pie.

'Whatever happened to that Italian hunk of yours?' she said.

'Oh, we split up,' I said. 'It was the distance. We were too far apart.'

Why go into all this? Well, Adam, it's just so you know you're not my first imaginary boyfriend. Ricci beat you to it.

FRIDAY

Something weird has happened. It's so strange I don't know what to make of it. I don't even know whether I should write it down because you might think I'm losing it. Of course, there could be a perfectly reasonable explanation but at this moment I can't think of one. See if you can.

I'd been reading through the first part of my diary, the purple one that I wrote to give you the background to where I am now. I wanted to check that I'd put down everything you need to know. I'd been sitting so long at the table that my back was aching, so I put the diary aside and went out. I thought I'd saddle up Joey and go for a ride. I started by cleaning out his stable and then I fetched him from the paddock and put on his saddle and bridle. He seemed edgy and kept scraping the ground, and I had to work to calm him down. I thought it might be the weather – it's quite close today – or maybe some stray animal had come by and scared him.

I decided to ride round the edges of the fields, circling the whole farm to see how things are going. The grass is long and I was thinking that I would have to decide how to handle the haymaking. It should probably have already been cut by now because the seeds are falling, and that's where the goodness is, in the seeds. Joey and the cows will only eat about half of it, so I won't need all the hay and there's nobody left any more to take the rest. The problems are, which fields to cut, how to do it, and what to do with the stuff I don't need. If you don't maintain fields like this they go back to being moorland, so I'd better cut them all. I can handle the cutting. I can drive the tractor, no problem, I've been doing that since I was twelve, but I've never used the mower or the baler. Granddad and Lander always did that. I'll have to learn. It can't be that hard. Can I shift a couple of hundred bales, load them onto the trailer and stack them in the barn? Well yes, I can. There are forks on the tractor to lift the bales and an elevator for stacking them, but it will be hard work and it will take me a long time. It's not something I'm going to look forward to. All good for fighting the flab, though.

I rode round the top field, turned Joey, encouraged him into a canter and headed for the low stone wall separating it from the bottom field. He took it easily. He's a great horse and he was enjoying being ridden again.

I was keeping alert. There are loads of animals that have gone feral and they can be threatening. They must have been let out when their owners got ill, or maybe they broke loose: rams, pigs, cows, bulls, goats, dogs. A farm further along the hill kept alpacas, and I saw one of those ambling around the other day. It looked comical, with its dozy expression and silly haircut, but I know they can bite. The countryside's turning into a sort of safari park. The animals leave you alone, apart from the dogs. The dogs are different. Half starved and wild, they go around in packs and they're scary. I've only seen a few up here but I don't let Buster run out like he used to.

I digress (again). I'm just putting off writing about this strange thing that happened. I know I have to tell you, but I'm worried because I think you might not believe me, and you'll think I'm mental.

Deep breath. I was trotting across the bottom field, keeping Joey near the edge so that we didn't trample down the grass, and then I saw it: the gate from the field onto the lane was *swinging wide open*!

'Is that all?' you say. 'What's the big deal about that?' Well, the big, fucking huge, enormous deal is that this gate is always kept locked. Always always always. Locked with a padlock and a chain, through hoops so it can't be slid off. It's been like that for as long as I can remember. Granddad kept it locked to stop walkers going into the field for picnics because he didn't like the mess they left. This time, though, the gate was wide wide open. More than that, the chain and padlock were gone, although the hoops for the wire were in place.

'Maybe it's been unlocked for some time and you just haven't noticed,' you say. 'Maybe Lander unlocked it before he left,' you say.

Stop trying to be smart, Adam, because you don't know what you're talking about. It's nearly three weeks since Lander went and it can't have been open all that time. I *know* the gate was shut and locked because last week when I went into Walbrough I took the Land Rover down the field track and came out through this gate. I came back the same way and chained it up again. And yes, even though I was freaked out by what had happened in the supermarket I am *sure* I locked it behind me. I can remember stopping and doing it, because my hands were shaking so much I could barely fit the key into the lock. I was careful to fasten it properly because

I was worried that the men might be following me. I remember too that when I got back to the farm I didn't put the key where it normally lives in the kitchen with the others, I put it in the ammo box in the Land Rover so it would be handy when I needed it again.

I headed Joey straight back to the farm, opened the Land Rover and looked in the box. Empty. So who opened the gate? And how did they know where to look for the key? And what have they done with the padlock and chain? And given that the Land Rover was open with its key in the ignition, why didn't they just nick that?

In a way it's creepy, but actually I'm puzzled rather than scared. I'm also a bit cheered. Might it mean that I'm not the only one left? That somebody else is still alive? That I have company? Ah, but what company?

Granddad always used to lock the doors every night when we went to bed. I haven't been bothering with that. Tonight I shall.

SATURDAY

I wish you'd been here last night, Adam, beside me in my bed. Not for that! (Although it would have been nice.) No, I wish you'd been here because I heard noises. I know what you think; it was my imagination running wild after discovering the open gate. But it wasn't. I know the usual nocturnal noises. The countryside isn't as quiet at night as townies think. There's always a lot going on, and since so many animals have been roaming around loose the disturbances have been more frequent. They wake me up, but they don't bother me.

Last night, though, was different. It was too rhythmical and deliberate for it to be stray animals. Buster could hear it too, and he was making that low-level, under-the-breath growling he does when he's worried about something.

I was scared. I got up and went to the window, hiding behind the curtain in case anyone was there. There was a moon, not full but bright enough to light the yard. I watched for a long time but I couldn't see anything. I went back to bed but I didn't sleep. I just lay there, listening for more of the noises and thinking about the gate.

This morning the sun is shining. I've been out to the barn and looked around the yard and there's no sign of anything amiss. In the broad daylight last night's noises seem unreal.

How to describe them? Well, it's hard because they weren't really like anything, except somehow they seemed human. It was almost as if someone was chanting my name rhythmically – Kerryl, Kerryl, Kerryl – but very quiet and very low, not clear enough for me to hear it properly.

Am I having hallucinations? Am I going bonkers? It wasn't you, Adam, was it?

LATER

Forceps used to say that we were very lucky girls because we went to one of the best schools in the north of England. If she was right and St Winifred's Girls' School really was one of the best, then God help the others. Although other people must have thought it was good too. When I went to Cambridge for my interview, Dr Smith said, 'Ah, St Winifred's,' in the sort of tone that suggested that not only had she heard of it but that she thought well of it. Of course, other girls had gone from there to Cambridge in the past, so perhaps she did. It got rated outstanding in so many inspections that the inspectors stopped coming.

When I told my family that Girton had offered me a deferred place to give me time to 'broaden my experience' Lander said, 'It's because you're a thick farm girl. Will a year be enough?' We had a fight, but a friendly one, not serious.

Well, my experience certainly is broader now.

If I'd gone to Cambridge, what would I have done? Miss Dove wanted me to become a writer. She said I have a talent for description and story telling. I was co-editor of the school magazine. We changed its name from 'The St Winifred's Magazine' to 'Winefride' (the Saint's original Celtic name) and gave it a feminist slant, and we published a couple of my own stories. But I don't think fiction really is me. I would have liked to have been a journalist, a correspondent. Perhaps if the Infection had come later I might have been in Africa, in Senegal where it first broke out. I could have described it, what it did, maybe given everybody a warning. If governments had been persuaded sooner to take it seriously perhaps people would have survived and not all died.

I might have been a lawyer. There was a courtroom drama on TV that I used to like. It was called *My Learned Friend* and it was about these two gay guys who shared chambers in one of the London Inns. When they worked together they always won their cases but sometimes they ended up on opposite sides and then they were constantly trying to put one over on each other. I've still got some episodes on moviesticks.

So yes, I would have liked to have been a barrister. I like the idea of standing up in court and defending the poor innocent girl who's accused of something she didn't do. It's plain to everybody that she's guilty, except to me. I believe in her innocence and at the last minute, just as the case is swinging away from me, I discover this vital piece of evidence which proves she couldn't have done it and shows how wrong everybody else is. Besides, I rather fancy the gown and the jabot. (That's the name for the ribbon thing they wear at their throats. Did you know?) Of course, I'd have had to cut my hair to get the barrister's wig on, so it might not have worked out for me after all. I wouldn't have wanted to be a judge, though. I don't think the judge's wig suits a woman.

I would have been a good barrister. Granddad always said I could argue for England! I told our careers teacher, Miss Sleuth (truly, I swear it, Daisy Sleuth she was called, honestly), and she said that for a barrister far more important than being up for an argument was to be stubborn and determined, and I was both those things. I'm still trying to figure out whether it was a compliment.

I told Lander I was thinking about being a barrister. He said, 'It's easy, but the pay's rubbish.'

I said, 'Don't be daft, barristers get paid a fortune.'

He said, 'Don't you believe it. Go down to Costa Coffee and you'll see loads of staff with 'barista' on their shirts, and they're all on living wage.' Then he fell about laughing. He thinks he's so funny.

All this rambling! I can't help it. It takes my mind off the spooky stuff like the gate and the noises. The only explanation I can come up with is that it really was me that left the gate open. I was so flustered after my narrow escape in the supermarket that I didn't lock it properly and my memory's playing tricks on me. I've almost persuaded myself of that, but it only deals with half the problem. Where's the key? Where's the padlock and the chain? And I still can't explain the noises.

LATER STILL

I go across to the barn for the afternoon milking. Bonnie and Dolly are already waiting outside to be let in. Molly's been in all day. Her calf is due any time now, and she spends all her time lying in her stall, except today she's standing up. I think that's a sign it might be soon. I go over to her and rub her neck and make soothing noises and she makes that hollow sighing noise that cows do. I wish I felt confident about this.

I get the other two in. Bonnie's really jumpy. That's unusual, she's generally so placid, but I put it down to the fact that I've been taking less milk from her, and perhaps her udders are over full and that's causing her discomfort. Perhaps it would be kind to take a bit more, but I really do want her to give up.

I'm just getting her into position when I catch a movement out of the corner of my eye. A cat? A rat? No, bigger than those, but nothing clear at all. It's more a change in the light than a shape. It's nothing. I get the stool and settle into the milking. Then I'm aware of it again, the edge of a shadow curling round the door. I jump up, knocking over the milk, startling the cows with the clattering bucket, and I run outside. I look down the length of the barn and catch it rounding the far corner, elusive as a wisp of smoke. I run to the end of the building. Nothing. No sign of anybody or anything. I call, shout to come out, but my words die on the wind.

I go back into the barn, shut the door and put the bar across. My pulse is racing and I lean against the wall till I feel calmer. I stay still for a long time, listening for any sound, but all I hear is the wind. The cows stare at me patiently.

There are no more disturbances and I finish the milking. Were there any to begin with? Did I see anything at all? Was it just a trick of the light, passing clouds, the effects of a sleepless night? Then I have an idea: Bryst. Perhaps it's Bryst come back to see how his son is, to get him. I go to the corner of the yard by the gate and shout his name, Bryst, over and over again. Rooks billow and caw in the trees down the lane, but there's no other response. I shiver, although it's not cold.

I'm sure I saw something. When I come over to milk tomorrow I'm bringing a shotgun with me. The cows don't like Buster, Molly in particular is fidgety when he's around, so I've been leaving him in the house because of her calf, but tomorrow he comes.

Perhaps it was you, Adam. Perhaps instead of shouting for Bryst I should be calling your name: Adam. Adam. Adam.

SUNDAY

I've written before how much I was dreading Molly's calving. I know that most of the time cows calve on their own, but I was scared stiff there might be a complication. It's not just the sheep poem. I can remember that once when one of our other cows gave birth Granddad had to pull the calf out with a rope. Suppose Molly's were to come out back feet first. That's not unusual, I know, but the cow often needs help with it. Suppose the calf died inside her. What would I do? There's no vet to phone.

I looked at some of Granddad's old books on stock management and they made me feel worse. They talk about scary things like an undilated cervix, uterine inertia, and there are photos showing people using things called 'calving chains'. We don't have one of those and I don't think I'd be able to use it even if we had. I'm strong but I can't heave a cow around. I wish I'd looked up all this stuff on the internet before it went down. Videos on YouTube would be a lot more help than fuzzy photos in old books, most of them in black and white. I wish I'd paid more attention to how Granddad handled a difficult calving, instead of just burying myself in my books or my iPad.

But Molly didn't need me anyway. She managed it all on her own, good girl. I slept like a log and heard nothing during the night – probably a reaction to my broken sleep the night before – and I went over for the milking, shotgun in my hand. Buster was at my side, in guard dog mode and wagging his tail, pleased to be needed.

I could sense something was different before I got to the door. Molly was resting in her stall and beside her was her calf! It's lovely – tiny, shiny, coffee coloured and perfect. You'd love it, Adam. It stood on its spindly, wobbly legs and looked at me with big, innocent eyes. Molly licked it. Bonnie and Dolly were leaning over the gate, for all the world like a pair of friends visiting the maternity ward.

I did the milking, feeling huge relief. Joy, too, at this new being, this demonstration that the world is not coming to an end, that despite everything life is going on. It may not be human life, but it is life.

I have to admit, though, that the calf is a problem; or rather he will be, because it is a 'he'. He looks sweet as a doughnut now but he could be a handful when he's older. Little male calves grow up into bulls, and the last thing I want is a rampant, randy bull to cope with. Granddad would castrate it but I don't know how to do that, I wouldn't know where to start. Well, I would know where to start but not how to start, if you see what I mean. Anyway, I don't think I could bring myself to do it.

I don't want Molly's calf, but I don't want it to be harmed either. I'll keep it for now. Molly will look after it, and at least I won't have to milk her.

LATER

I've spent a long time today just sitting on the milking stool in the barn and looking at Molly and the calf. It made me think. What would I have done if there had been complications and Molly had been in terrible, endless pain? It would have been obvious what was the right thing to do, but could I have done it?

Another thought is what would happen if it wasn't a cow in trouble but me, if I needed a doctor? I don't mean the Infection, I'm sure now I'm not going to get that, but there are other things. I dreamt a few nights ago that I found a lump in my breast (all right, I don't put everything in the diary, not at first anyway). I had to get up and check myself. Of course, there was nothing there, but I couldn't get back to sleep again. Suppose I did find one. Or I got something else. Or I had an accident, like Dad did. He bled to death when there were loads of people around. With nobody here I wouldn't stand a chance. And what about the shadow I saw in the barn? Suppose it's someone – or something! – that means me harm.

Back in the kitchen I write myself a list of things to do or avoid to keep me out of trouble. This is it (with annotations). If you can think of anything I've missed, feel free to suggest it.

- Don't walk around outside in the dark. (The Baxters' eldest came home late one night drunk from a party and fell into the slurry pit. He didn't drown, but it was very nasty.)
- Always put things away – don't leave tools or kitchen stuff around, and especially not on the ground. (Charley McMichael's mum left a kitchen knife on the floor beside her chair after she'd been peeling apples and walked on it and cut her little toe off.)
- Make sure that everything electrical is switched off when it's not in use. Check wires and plugs regularly.

Don't touch any of the supply equipment without throwing the isolator. (Granddad got a heck of a shock one day off the regulator in the shed. He said he might have been killed if he'd not been wearing rubber boots.)

- Don't leave candles or fires burning unattended. (We've got smoke alarms, but who would hear them?)

- Make sure ladders are securely fixed before climbing them. (Obvious.)

- When using tools or machinery concentrate on what you're doing and don't daydream. (Obvious again, but daydreaming is my problem – it sort of goes with digressing.)

- Lock the doors at night and never leave the house without a loaded gun.

There must be lots more, but these are the ones that come to me first and I'll start with them. I skewer my list and fix it to the kitchen pinboard.

I worry that I'm relying on guns. Carrying a shotgun around with me feels strange. I never touched one before – I hated them in fact. I'm still not keen, but a gun gives me a feeling of comfort. It's not just the open gate or the night noises or the whatever-it-was in the barn (no repeats of the latter, I'm glad to say) that have made me edgy. I'm also scared of the dogs. There seem to be more of them every day, and they're getting bolder. I often see them skulking around the edge of the yard or chasing and fighting in the fields. They growl and bare their teeth, but so far they haven't come near me. I know that one day one of them will, and then we'll see if I've got the balls to pull the trigger. Oh, I wish you were here, Adam. I do so wish you were here.

MONDAY

I get up late and I spend some time with Molly and her calf (any ideas for a name for it?), and suddenly I'm at a loss. What shall I do next? I have nothing to add to the diary because I haven't done anything. I don't want to read, or watch moviesticks, or play games on my iPad. I don't want to go for a ride, although Joey would like it. There's no cleaning to be done. I don't need any clothes washing or anything ironing. What I really want to do, the thing that would be top of my list if I could choose anything, is to talk to somebody: Josie, Miss Dove, our Mam, Gran, Granddad, Lander even.

It's not that I don't use my voice. I talk all the time. I talk to Buster, Joey, the cows, even the hens. I used to talk to my own reflection in the mirrors until I turned them round. I talk all the time to you, Adam. What I don't get is to hear anybody reply. I don't have conversations. The closest I come are the movies and shows on my moviesticks that I play and play and play. I've got about thirty and I know practically all of them off by heart, so that I talk along with the characters. Sometimes I play more than one part, using different voices. I've got quite good at this, particularly for some of the older ones: *Friends*, *The Office*, *The Simpsons* (Granddad loved them, Gran hated them), *Batman*, *Star Wars*, *Twilight*, the High School Musicals. If I'd known what was going to happen I'd have got a whole lot more moviesticks and recorded everything I could.

A terrible, hollow feeling comes over me. I may never ever hear a living voice again. I didn't know that loneliness could feel like this. It's a hurt, a physical pain that I can't locate because it comes from everywhere, while being deep inside me.

It's some time before I realise that I'm crying. Then I get cross with myself. 'Snap out of it, you silly bitch,' I tell myself. 'You are alive when everyone else is dead,' I say. 'Count your blessings and stop wingeing.'

Then inspiration strikes. It's been a while since the supermarket incident. There can't possibly be anyone still around in Walbrough. I'm sure it will be safe by now. I'll go and find some moviesticks. I'll saddle up Joey and ride him down to the town. Joey will get some exercise, so will I, and if I'm on Joey I'll be able to get away quickly if there's a problem.

Every TV has a slot to take a moviestick, and when I was a kid lots of stores sold pre-recorded ones. At some stage people stopped using them because they found it easier to watch movies and shows online, and you could get absolutely everything on Netflix, Amazon Prime and the others. There was a second-hand market for the sticks, though, and I've seen them on market stalls and in charity shops. I might try those. Perhaps the vandals haven't hit the charity shops as hard as the other places because they'd not expect to find much of value in them. I can check out some of the clothing stores, too, maybe get some new outfits. If there's nobody around.

I change out of my scruffy jeans into smart ones. I seriously think about wearing a skirt because that saved me last time, but it wouldn't be as easy on Joey. Then I get Lander's air pistol from his bedroom. I've scanned through the binoculars and not seen anything down there, but you never know. The air pistol is easier to carry than a shotgun and it looks like a proper automatic. It wouldn't do much damage, although a pellet from it would sting and it might be enough to scare somebody off. But as Granddad used to say, 'A gun's no substitute for being careful', so I'll have to keep my eyes open.

LATER

Another disaster only just averted. What is it about me?

Joey seemed happy to be out and was eager to go. I made him wait while I locked the front door. I wouldn't have bothered but while I was upstairs changing I heard a noise downstairs. At least, *I think* I did. I was singing along with my iPod so I can't be sure. 'Catch the Rain' by Far Sighted, since you ask. Do you like them? They used to be my favourite band, although I'm going off them a bit now. I wonder if they survived. I reckon stars and celebs must have, don't you? I mean, with all their money they must have been able to buy things to protect them.

Anyway, back to the noise. It was quite loud and sounded like a chair scraping on the kitchen floor. I came downstairs with my heart pounding, holding the gun out in front of me like they do in the movies, and found... nobody! There was no one in any of the rooms and no signs of entry. All the doors and windows were shut and locked. Buster must have heard it too, though, because he was in the middle of the kitchen, hair bristling, growling softly. It was probably only another dog in the yard, but it was the fourth thing that had made me feel queasy: the gate, the noise in the night, the shadow in the barn and now this. So I took the time to look around the yard carefully before I went out, and to lock the door behind me.

Despite telling myself to keep calm, my spine tingled as we came down the lane to the open gate. Except it wasn't open any more. Had I shut it? I'm not sure. I didn't think I had but it was closed now. Perhaps I pushed it to. Or the wind took it. I couldn't remember. Something as simple as that and I couldn't fucking remember! It's not as if there was a lot of other stuff to fill my head. I think I must be going crazy.

As I'd expected, Walbrough was deserted. There was even more mess, more litter, more rubbish and I think more broken windows, but there were no people and, strangely, no dogs. The smell was still there but not as bad as before. I took Joey along Canal Street towards Chez Annette. That's where my prom dress came from. They usually had something nice in there, and it being expensive was no longer a problem. The front of the shop had been caved in, like all the others, and stock thrown about and walked on, but there still looked to be plenty of good stuff inside. There were some very classy bags on a shelf but I couldn't see any point in taking them. What would I use them for? I started searching the rails. There was a really nice skirt, aquamarine with splashes of orangey reddish circles. I glanced around – you can't be too careful – and slipped out of my jeans. The skirt wouldn't do up! Even though the label said it was my size!! Must be a mistake. I tried another. A bit better but not ideal. I took off my shirt and stood in front of the only mirror that wasn't broken in my bra and knickers, and took a good, honest look. I'm too fat. I turned sideways on. No point pretending, I am. (I'm only putting this down, Adam, so that later when I'm skinny we can look back on it and laugh.)

Right, I thought, *I've been eating less but it hasn't worked. Now I've got to get serious.* I grabbed the nice skirt, and half a dozen others in a size down from my normal one, and a couple of dresses and some tops, and I stuffed them in plastic bags. I put on my jeans and T-shirt and stamped out of the shop, promising that I would starve myself until I could get into the things I'd chosen. I climbed back onto Joey, and whispered in his ear an apology for the extra load I'd become.

Quite close to the centre of town is Almond Street. It's a row of newish, detached houses set back from the road, homes favoured by successful small businessmen or middle managers commuting to Manchester. I thought they were the sort of places that might still have some moviesticks around somewhere. Joey took a bit of persuading to go up the path to the first one and kept shying back. Somebody'd already called there because the door was wide open and the doorframe was splintered, so I wasn't holding out much hope. Still, it wouldn't hurt to look.

I slid off Joey and walked towards the door, holding out the air pistol. I stepped over the broken glass in the doorway, and almost threw up. The smell was unbelievable. I took another crunching step and froze. There was a horrible growling, and the biggest dog I've ever seen was between me and the door. It was huge, black and ugly. It went for me. I didn't think, I just pointed Lander's air pistol at it and fired. I snatched the trigger so much you would have thought it was a certain miss, but I must have hit it somewhere because it yowled and ran off, yelping like a puppy. I charged out, scrambled onto Joey and urged him away. I didn't slow his gallop till we were well out of the town and on the track towards home. Then I reined him in to a walk and took several long, deep breaths. My heart was racing and the blood pounded in my head. Oh my! That. Was. A. Fucking. Big. Dog.

After a few minutes I began to calm down. Wouldn't it have been a thing, to survive the Infection that wiped out the whole world, only to be killed by a poxy dog! Miss Dove would have called that anomalous. It's from a Greek word meaning uneven, she said. She told us lots of tragedies were based on anomalous behaviour: the loyal hero Macbeth killing his king, selfish Lear giving everything away, Othello murdering the woman he loves more than anything else in the world, and the whole scene in Elsinore. I don't want any anomalies, thank you.

I am not going back to that shitty town again! Not ever. It's a death trap. The houses contain decomposing bodies (and possibly dogs), and that's why they smell so frightful. They must be hotbeds of germs and disease. And there are too many things hanging about waiting for a chance to attack you.

There is another reason that I don't want to go back. I felt awkward going into that house in Almond Street. It doesn't seem right to help yourself from what were people's homes. I know that whoever lived there doesn't need their possessions any more, but picking over their stuff seems disrespectful. I wouldn't like the idea of snoopers raking through my belongings and taking what they fancy, even when I'm dead. Raiding the stores is different. That's just like shoplifting, and we've all done that. Haven't we?

TUESDAY

I woke this morning with my bedclothes damp, my chest tight and my whole body wired. It felt like somebody'd wrapped me tightly in wet towels. I think I'd been crying in my sleep, because my cheeks were wet and there was a big dribble stain on my pillow. I went to the bathroom and examined my face in a mirror. I looked awful. My eyes were puffy and red, and I had a smear of dried snot on my cheek that made it look as if it had been varnished. I couldn't remember what I'd been dreaming but I was so aching with loss that I began to well up again. I wrote so glibly the other day about everybody being dead and me the only person left. Then I felt detached, as if the Kerryl who was doing the writing was not me but another girl, someone in a story. Now I've collided with reality, and I feel alternating waves of misery and panic. They are gone: all my family, all my friends, everybody I knew. I will never see, hear, touch any of them again. I may never see another living soul. I am alone. Can I go on? How can I go on? What's the point? I felt wretched, bleeding.

I looked out of the window. The farm was surrounded by a mist so dense I could barely see the edge of the barn a few metres across the yard. There was no way through it, no way out of it. It echoed how I felt: blind, imprisoned, trapped in a landscape without features or landmarks. In a fog like that you could walk for hours and only go in circles.

According to Miss Dove, John Ruskin (he was a big-shot honcho of the Romantic Movement) had a term for when a writer uses nature to parallel a character's emotions, like the way the storm in *King Lear* is in sympathy with the King's inner turmoil. He called it 'the pathetic fallacy'. I think that's a stupid way to look at it. Okay, I accept that the weather isn't caused by how a human being feels (duh) but that's not the point. A writer creates the world of their fiction and it's up to them to say what happens in it, so how can that be fallacy? Unless Ruskin's saying that all fiction's fallacy. I suppose you could argue that, but what is fiction? Where does reality stop and imagination begin? What's the difference? The imagined is real for the person who's doing the imagining, and for some people what seems real to them is actually only imagined. One of Gran's friends, Mrs Kippax, had dementia. We'd go to see her in the home and on a bad day she'd sit rigid in her chair, face twisted and eyes staring, shouting and railing at nothing. Whatever she was seeing was real enough to her. Ruskin uses the word 'pathetic' too. For me that means either he thought it was a cheap device, or he had a very low opinion of creative writers. Or both. Anyway, I get the last laugh, Mr Ruskin. You're dead. There's nobody left to read you except me, and I shan't bother. So much for you. Besides, you're wrong. There are lots of times when the weather or a natural scene chimes in with my mood, and this was one of them. The vapid, enshrouding fog caught my emotional state exactly.

Reluctantly I dressed and went over to the barn to see to the cows. Molly and her calf were fine. He's got great big eyelashes and a cute, bewildered expression, as if he doesn't know what to make of all this newness around him. He's gorgeous. I wish I knew what to do with him. I milked Bonnie and Dolly but the yield was way down. Perhaps soon both the cows will be dry. I'll be pleased. I have no use for the milk. Dairy products make me fat, so I end up pouring it away.

I went back to the house. The mist hadn't lifted at all and the claustrophobia was getting to me. I grabbed my jacket, whistled for Buster (always up for a walk) and set off up the hill. Cloud like this is quite common when the valley warms up after rain, although mostly it goes quite quickly and here at the farm it's usually below us. This morning, though, it seemed to be everywhere and lingering. I hoped that by climbing the hill I could get above it and into the sunshine.

I walked out of the yard past bales of honey-sweet smelling haylage. There are a lot of them, shiny and black like enormous stubs of licorice, stacked three high. Our land produces more hay than our few cows need, and Granddad used to bale the rest and sell it. There's no one to buy it now. I think I might just get a knife and slash through the plastic, letting out the luscious fodder for whatever comes around to enjoy.

The path up to the moor is paved with flat slabs of stone. It's an old packhorse track, made in the days before the valley roads when ponies would fetch and carry fleeces and rolls of cloth between the upland dwellings. The paving has been smoothed by centuries of use, and in places there are twin grooves worn by the iron-rimmed wheels of narrow carts.

The mist soon thinned and I emerged above it, as I'd expected. I kept on walking, getting higher all the time, and as the sunlight filled me my spirits rose. Buster seemed glad to be out of the murk too, and he ran about sniffing and investigating. At one point he disturbed a pheasant that startled us both, exploding suddenly from the heather in squawking protest. When he was younger Buster would have chased it but now he doesn't bother, and he watched it flap away with disdain.

I was heating up, and I took off my jacket and dropped it to pick up on the way back. No one was going to nick it, were they? I wished I'd put on shorts instead of jeans. At the top of the hill where it bends over onto the moor proper I stopped for a breather. The sky up here was bright blue. There were no signs of human life, apart from the line of wind turbines on the opposite hill. The sun splashed gold down the shafts and on the blades, still uselessly turning. The valley was a white-topped basin and looked as though it had been filled with mashed potato. This was what it would have looked like if, like scores of others, it had been dammed and flooded. Just hills and a desolate lake, with no hint of the lives that had been played out below.

On the way up the hill Buster had been shooting off in elliptical runs, overlapping search patterns with me always at the centre. Now he walked by my side. I wondered if he'd smelt or heard something that made him cautious, but he seemed happy to go on. I scanned the moor around us, on the lookout for feral animals. All seemed well. Perhaps he was just taking a break.

I hadn't set out for the Bride Stones but that was where I ended up. The old rocks looked mellow and less sinister than usual in the sunlight. I sat down on one, the

Bride Stone itself, where girls would wait, hoping for a vision of their true love. Buster flopped down alongside me. How many girls before me had been in this very spot? Had any of them ever seen anything? I peered into the distance, screwing my eyes against the glare. Buster's nose twitched and his paws flickered as he hunted in his sleep.

I took off my trainers and put my feet in the peaty water. It was startlingly cold but wonderful after the hot climb. I lay back, my head on my hands, and let the sun bathe me. The stone was flat and smooth, hard but not uncomfortable. Far away a sheep bleated, and nearer a curlew called. Somewhere high above a skylark sang, its beaded bubbles of sound tumbling to earth.

The sun was really hot now, and the cool water inviting. Even though I knew there was nobody to see me I glanced around to check. Then I unbuttoned my shirt, slipped it off, and undid my bra. The fresh air felt good. I stood up, dropped my jeans and wriggled out of my briefs. I took off the band holding my hair and shook it down. I spread out my arms, letting the sun stroke me while I revolved slowly on the stone. Not for a long time, not since I was a young girl, had I been naked in the open air and the sensation was wonderful – liberating and erotic. A light puff of air brushed me, delicate as a feather. I squatted on the rock and lowered myself into the pool.

The water came up to my knees and I gasped from the chill. I took a couple of steps in, then I crouched and launched myself forward. It was only just deep enough for swimming. I did one circuit, a slow breast stroke, then climbed back onto the stone, shivering while I dried myself with my shirt. The cold water had hardened my nipples and I caressed them, working them gently with the palms of my hands.

Suddenly my rising enjoyment froze and I felt a rush of adrenaline; I was being watched! I know it sounds ridiculous, but I was sure of it. I untangled my wet shirt and put it on, bending over and keeping my legs together. Then I scrambled into my jeans, struggling a bit because my legs were wet. I did up my zip and buttons and looked around. I could see no one, but there are a lot of places to hide, in the bracken or behind the rocks. Hurriedly I stuffed my feet into my trainers and put my bra and briefs in my pockets.

Buster looked up sleepily, stretched and wagged his tail. He didn't seem at all bothered. He can pick up people approaching long before I can, but he hadn't reacted. Does that mean there was no one there? I was certain there had been. Knowing you're being looked at is a sort of sixth sense. I don't know if boys can feel it, but it's something all girls pick up. It's what tells you when the boy on the bus or the man in the pub is checking you out, even when he's behind your back. You just know it. That's what I had felt. Had I imagined it? It was so strong. Was it just my over-active imagination again? My heart was thumping as I hurried back to the farm.

I'm not going to write any more diary today. I need some space to think about things. Despite Buster's lack of response, I am certain that this morning up at the Bride Stones I was not alone. Was it my true love? Was it you, Adam?

WEDNESDAY

Okay, Adam, I agree; leaving the farm doesn't work. I just scare myself. I'm best staying here. Nice of you to point that out to me now! I came to the same conclusion myself last night while I was watching an ancient *Strictly* on the PVR. The doors were locked and I'd lit a fire, because although it's only August the evenings can be chilly. I'd made myself some nettle tea. I didn't use honey like I prefer, but sweetener. I don't have much of that, so it will have to be honey or sugar when I run out, because sure as shit I am not going down to the shops again.

Right: doors locked, old feel-good show on the TV, log fire, room lit by candles, sprawled on the sofa with a mug of something hot and sweet, and Buster asleep with his head in my lap. Time to take stock. I've been concentrating too much on the minuses. I may be all on my own and I'm certainly missing people a lot, but on the plus side there's nobody to answer to or to try to please. The only demands on me are those made by the animals, or ones I make myself. I should be content. I'm free.

On my way back from the Bride Stones I came round the far side of the shed and saw the words Lander had scrawled on the blackboard, rain-rinsed but still legible: Welcome to Paradise Farm. It set me thinking about one of the lessons on *Paradise Lost* we'd had with Miss Dove. Jocasta Short, who was always a bit full of herself, said that she thought that Milton's paradise sounded boring, and if she'd been Eve, or Adam, she'd have been only too glad to get out of there.

Miss Dove went round the group and asked each of us for our own definition of paradise, what the word meant for us personally. There was a range of answers. Monica Woodbridge said that paradise for her would be having a life of luxury, with everything you could possibly want, like being a celeb. Miss Dove sighed and moved on. Minal Akram said that the Islamic view of paradise was the state of being closest to God. Miss Dove said that could describe Milton's paradise too. Somebody else said that paradise for them would be a place where there was no evil and people were always kind and good to each other. When it came to my turn I said that complete freedom would do it for me. My paradise would be the freedom to do anything I wanted without ever having to ask for leave or permission, and to have no need to please anybody but myself. Miss Dove said that a complete lack of responsibility to or for other people sounded like extreme selfishness, which would be the opposite of what most people thought of as paradise. We argued.

We had English again after break, this time with Rudy. When I came into the classroom he said, 'Ah, the Paradise Girl.' It seems that Miss Dove had told him about our discussion over coffee. After that he'd often use it. 'What does Miss Paradise think?' he'd say. Or, 'Paradise Girl, would you mind collecting up the essays?' I didn't like it. He said it with a sort of sneer that I thought was creepy and it made me feel awkward.

I can see now that Miss Dove was right. I am my own boss now. I can please myself. I can do exactly what I like and I don't have to do anything I don't want to. I can get up and go to bed when I like, think what I like, say what I like, wear what I like. I can walk around all day naked, like Eve, if I want to. There's nobody to tell me to do anything, and nobody expects anything of me. I have the paradise I described. But this isn't paradise at all. You see, I left the main thing out. Milton wrote 'Solitude sometimes is best society', but he was wrong. The main thing that turns an ordinary place into paradise, as the biblical Adam well knew, is having someone to share it with. Without that it's not paradise at all; it's hell. And that's where I am.

THURSDAY

I didn't feel well when I woke up. There was a rawness at the back of my throat and I had the snivels. My head felt thick and I had no energy. The Infection? Of course, that was the first thing that occurred to me too. However, I was sure it was not that. My joints weren't achy, I didn't have a temperature and I certainly didn't have diarrhoea – the opposite if anything. Besides, how could I possibly have become infected? There's nobody left to infect me.

I would have stayed in bed if I could, but the bloody animals needed seeing to, didn't they? I milked Bonnie and Dolly and let them out to pasture, Molly and her calf too. Then I opened up the hens. I didn't look for eggs. To be honest, I couldn't give a toss if they lay or not. I've got loads of eggs in the fridge and bowls of them in the pantry and I'm not eating them. In fact, I'm not eating anything.

When I'd done with the animals I boiled some water, put in it a splash of lemon juice and a slug of Granddad's rum and took it to bed. I planned to stay there for the rest of the day. I've not had anything to eat and I hardly had anything yesterday and I'm not hungry. If this goes on I might soon get into those clothes I took from Chez Annette.

LATER

My throat was sore, and even though I was comfortable in bed I didn't sleep. Things turned over in my head and I got to thinking about hobs. When I was a little girl Gran would tell me stories about them.

'Hobs,' she used to say, 'are small, like dwarves. They're covered in shaggy hair and have huge feet. They live in hob holes and have got super strength.'

Hobs used to fascinate me, but they scared me too.

'No need to be afraid,' Gran would say. 'A hob won't harm you. It will help you if you treat it right.'

'Where do they come from? Where do they live?' I asked.

'Well,' she said, 'nobody knows where they come from, but a hob finds a farm that it fancies and makes that its home. Then, once it's settled in, it will work in secret to help the farmer.'

She seemed to believe this, because if there was a problem, like a sick sheep or a cow with mastitis, Gran would say, 'We could do with a hob now', and Granddad would say things like, 'This looks like a job for a hob.'

It's true there were times when problems that had seemed serious suddenly evaporated. Like when our Dad was all set up to finish the hay. It had been cut and tedded and was ready to be baled and stored, and the tractor wouldn't start. He said something on it was seized up and it needed new parts, which would have to be ordered. It would be out of action for several days, by which time rain was forecast and the hay would be ruined. And then, just like that, the tractor started. Our Dad hadn't done anything to it; the seized part had freed itself. The baling was done and the hay got in. Gran said it must have been a hob.

'Mm, a hob with a City & Guilds in Agricultural Engineering,' Dad said. He didn't believe in hobs, said all that stuff was country rubbish fancied by people who spent too much time on their own.

You were never to let on you knew the hob was there. Gran told a story of a farm in the Dales where a hob saved the harvest and the farmer thanked it by leaving a leather jerkin out for it. The hob took offence and from then on it went from helping to causing mischief.

'Why, Gran?' I said. 'They were only being nice to it.'

'Ah, but the hob didn't see it like that,' she said. 'Hobs are proud. A hob's a spirit, and it belongs to no one. It does what it does because it does what it does. If you thank it, even worse if you try to reward it, it thinks you're treating it like something you own or employ, and it takes offence.'

I believed in hobs when I was a kid. I'd always be wary when I was out on my own, especially if it was dark. If anything mysteriously nice happened, like the time I found a litter of puppies in the barn, I'd know it was a hob that had done it, but I'd be careful to avoid appearing grateful or thanking it. When I got older I agreed with our Dad; hobs are just stories. Or are they? Could it be a hob that left the gate open? Did a hob help Molly with her calf? Was it the shadow of a hob I saw in the barn?

Don't be stupid, Kerryl. Get a grip. A hob would be useful now, though. Gran said that some hobs were supposed to have extra special powers and could cure children of whooping cough and worse. I could do with one of those hobs. My throat feels as though it's been sandpapered.

LATER STILL

I slept for a long time. In the afternoon I went down and did my chores, and then I came straight back to bed. I think I'm feeling a bit better, but I don't have any energy. I don't want to read or use my iPad, and I'm only writing this because I get withdrawal symptoms if I don't.

FRIDAY

I spend the whole day sliding in and out of sleep. I don't dream of anything, not even of you, Adam (although I'd like to).

When I wake up it's pitch dark and I reach out for the matches to light a candle. Buster watches me, standing at the end of my bed with his tail thumping my mattress. 'Sorry, old sport,' I say. 'We're not going for a walk. I'm staying here and so are you.' He understands, because he sighs and lies down on the rug, his chin on his paws.

I leave the candle burning for comfort. Having slept all through the day I'm wakeful now, and I lie for a long time listening for any sounds outside. It's a thick, late summer night – hot and heavy. I open the window. Unusually for up here, there's no wind. If that lasts it will be a concern because my wind turbine won't work and I'll be struggling for electricity. It won't, though. A very still period like this is always followed pretty quickly by high winds and rain.

I hear an owl hooting and somewhere a dog yelping, but not the distant planes and trains and traffic I would normally have expected on a night like this.

I conjure up an image of Adam and begin to touch myself. (You're not to read that bit, and if you do you're to forget it immediately!)

SATURDAY

For the last couple of days I've been getting up for just long enough to milk Dolly and feed Buster. I've slept most of the time, with occasional vivid dreams. I've drunk a lot of water and a little milk, but I've eaten nothing.

My throat feels better, but when I got out of bed I was very wobbly. I had a cup of milky coffee. Then I made myself a slice of toast, but I couldn't eat it. Too scratchy.

Now I'm at the kitchen table writing this. My headache has gone and so has the fever. I got so hot in my own bed that I had to throw my duvet on the floor and go and lie on Lander's. My bedclothes must be really smelly, because even Buster's abandoned my room! I'll try to wash and dry them today.

I have my slice of toast beside me and I've only taken one small bite from it. I don't want it. I won't have anything else to eat today. I pinch my midriff. Definitely thinner but my tummy still shows through my PJs. When I have a bit more energy I'll try on some of my old clothes, the ones I'd pushed to the back of my cupboard, and see if they fit me. I won't risk the new ones yet because I'll be so disappointed if I haven't reached my target.

What I need is a table where I can record my progress towards the weight I want to be. I turn to the back of my diary and rule three columns. I head them:

Date	Weight	– (or +!)

I fill in the first few lines from memory. From now on I'll weigh myself at least once every day and write down the result in this table. Then I can easily check how much I'm losing, and if I'm not losing I can do something about it.

I look up from my notebook and gaze out of the kitchen window at the side of the hill that rises above the farm. In the early hours the weather broke and rain lashed the bedroom windows. It's stopped now, and been replaced by another dense mist. It's as if the farm has been packed in cotton wool. Or put in a white plastic box and the lid closed. I hate it, but at least it's an excuse not to go out. I'm not going up to the Bride Stones this time!

Tomorrow is August 31st (at least, I think it is) and that's my birthday. I hope I'm properly better for it. Not that there's anyone to celebrate with, apart from Buster. And of course you, Adam.

It's just as I turn my head away from the window and go back to my notebook that a movement catches my eye. I look up, and see something on the path. It's a man! Even as I try to focus the mist wraps the figure and hides it from me.

I get up and rush to the window, leaning forward and straining into the white haze. Was there someone there? Did I see him? Did I really see him? My head's spinning. Tiny, multi-coloured dots swirl in front of my eyes. I feel dizzy. I grip the sill. Then the cloud parts once more and

I see it – him – again. He's on the path no more than fifty metres away. He stands with his thumbs hooked in the pockets of his jeans and he's looking at the house, and at me. He's there for no more than a few seconds before the mist takes him again.

I stand at the window for ages waiting for the mist to part, but it doesn't. My heart thumps and my legs are trembling. Who was it? Did he see me? Am I in danger? Where is he now? I'm frozen, expecting to hear some movement in the yard or a rap on the door. The man had been young, and he wore a black T-shirt and jeans. He'd had a bag hooked over his shoulder. He looked well built and fit. In the glimpse I had of him he looked friendly, not threatening. Despite that I was nervous.

I come away from the window. My fingers are aching from gripping the sill so tightly. My dressing gown has slid off my shoulder and I am freezing. I ease it back on and go to the cupboard. I'm not a great drinker but I need a slug of vodka. This is medicine, not pleasure. While I'm trying to pour it with dithering hands I feel Buster's wet nose snuffle my leg. It occurs to me how strange that is. Usually if anybody he doesn't know comes within a hundred metres of the farm Buster will go to the door and bark, and if he feels especially put out he'll growl. But he's not done any of that. He's just stayed in a lazy, doggy heap on the mat beside the boiler cupboard, the warmest place in the house. That means either that he hasn't registered the stranger (impossible; Buster's got the sharpest ears and nose of any dog I've ever known) or the visitor is somebody he knows. Also impossible.

LATER

I keep going to the window. Gradually the mist thins, then it clears completely, but I see nobody out there. Should I go out and search? I get dressed and put on my boots. What if the mysterious stranger is still close, hiding in a nook in the yard, waiting to jump me when I go out? I get one of Granddad's shotguns and slide a cartridge into each barrel. I don't know if I'm shaking so much because I'm scared, or still cold, or it's the hangover from the 'flu I've just had. God help me if I have to aim at anything.

I unlock the door and ease back the bolt, making as little noise as I can. Then I change my mind and lock it again. I go from room to room, looking out of every window. Then I do the same upstairs. Doing this I can see the whole of the area around the house: the yard, the front terrace and both sides. Obviously I wouldn't be able to see anybody behind the barn or in one of the sheds, but everything close is visible. I try to persuade Buster to come with me but he isn't bothered. I spend a long time at each window, keeping myself concealed so I won't be spotted. I see nothing. Then I go round the house and do all the rooms again. Still nothing.

I go upstairs and sit on my bed in an agony of indecision. Part of me is elated that there's another human being close by, another person who's survived the Infection. Another part of me is more cautious. The person I saw was male, young and strong looking. That's both exciting and worrying. He's not done anything to suggest he might mean me harm, but there would be little I could do to stop him if he did. Should I hide? Or should I go out and try to make contact?

Time passes and I wait. In the afternoon I go downstairs to write this.

I drink a glass of water. Sooner or later I'll have to go out. I should already have been to milk Dolly. She'll be all right, she's been giving less and less anyway. I'll have to see to her tomorrow morning. I'll have to go out then, cross the yard to the barn, whatever the risk.

Of course, there's one thing I've pushed to the back of my mind but now I must face it. The person I saw was tall and he looked tanned and fit, and he had curly, fair hair. Was it you, Adam? Have you come to see me for my birthday?

SUNDAY (MY BIRTHDAY)

Today I am eighteen. Or I think I am. A couple of weeks ago I let the battery in my phone run out and for some reason it wouldn't start up again. I had to do a reset and it lost all its data, including the date and time. My tablet got screwed up at the same time. So I may have missed a day and I can't be sure, but it's near enough. Anyway nobody's going to remind me, or turn up to my party on the wrong day!

Eighteen. An adult. Old enough to serve on a jury. Old enough to vote, if there was anyone to vote for. I think I'll vote for Buster. I pat him and give him a dog biscuit. He thinks being a politician is a good idea.

It took me ages to get to sleep last night. I was thinking about the guy on the path. This morning I wanted to lie in, but I could hear Dolly complaining and I had to get up to go and relieve her. I took the shotgun and eased the door open. I had a good look around and all seemed clear, so I ran across to the barn and dived inside. It was only then that I thought I should have checked before I burst in. I should have done what they do in the movies: position myself beside the door with my back to the wall, swing round, kick the door open and stand in the doorway holding out my gun. Lander used to go on about how stupid that was. 'Imagine,' he'd say, 'standing in the doorway like that, against the light where you'd make the best possible target!' Anyway, it didn't matter. The barn was empty. I got Dolly in and she looked accusingly at me. 'Where were you yesterday?'

she was saying. She was fine, though. So were the others. Molly's calf is already growing, and looking really fit.

After I'd done the milking I went back to the kitchen. There was an envelope with my name on the table. Nothing mysterious this time. It's a birthday card I've written for myself. Well, I've got to have at least one! Even though I know what it looks like and what it says inside, I open it and stand it on the table.

HAPPY BIRTHDAY, KERRYL
YOU'RE THE ONLY GIRL IN THE WORLD
ALL MY LOVE
ADAM
XXXXXXXXXXXX

I cook a birthday breakfast for Buster and me: tomatoes, beans, eggs and some tinned ham which I fry. Even though I'm off meat I hope it will taste like bacon. It does a bit, but once I've loaded my plate I don't want it. The look and smell of the food makes me feel sick. I give it to Buster and he finishes it in about three seconds. Then he goes to sleep on the rug, alternately snoring and farting. I loaf on the couch and read some magazines. I've read them all before, every word, front to back and back again to the front, and they're getting really tatty. It's tempting to risk another trip into town to see if I can find something more recent, but not today. I've decided I'm not going to do anything today that isn't essential, so when I get bored with the magazines I watch some old episodes of *Carla's Secret* on my iPad, until it runs out. Then I pick up my diary and start writing again.

I've almost finished the purple one, the account of how things got to be like this.

LATER

I've got writer's cramp. I drop my pen and shake my fingers. I push the notebook aside and stretch. I don't fancy coffee and I'm short of tea, so I make some nettle tea and put a spoonful of honey in it. I know, honey! But I can't slim on my birthday, can I? Anyway, I didn't eat the breakfast.

I sit in the window, watching the rain swirl across the fields. I'm bored. I look for my iPad to play a game or watch a moviestick but I can't find it. I was using it earlier, I'm sure. I look in the kitchen and under the cushions on the couch but it's not there. Where did I have it last? Perhaps I left it upstairs. I'll get it later.

It's still raining. I wonder if I might see again the figure I saw yesterday. I keep looking, hoping I will, scared that I might, but the hillside is empty.

I do the afternoon milking and give Dolly and Bonnie some cow cake in honour of the day. I go to the stable and give Joey some oats. I spend some time with him, rubbing his muzzle and patting his neck. He whinnies a bit and paws the ground. I think he's lonely, too. A horse like Joey needs exercise, and my 'flu means I haven't ridden him for several days. I'll take him out tomorrow. I'll go up to the Stones and gallop him across the moor.

I go back inside. The evening's come on early because of the bad weather, and I draw the curtains and light a fire. It takes me a while to get it to burn properly.

The chimney's getting smoky. I can't remember when it was last swept. I watched the sweep do it once and I think I know how to do it. I just need the kit. They called the sweep Sooty Morgan. Perhaps his address is in Granddad's notebook. If I can find it, I could go to his house and borrow his brushes. But that would mean leaving the farm again.

I make some more tea and open a tin of Dundee cake I've been saving. I've got some candles, too, and I arrange eighteen of them around the top. Buster ambles into the kitchen and looks hopeful. I give him a handful of dog biscuits and he wolfs them. I don't think he would have appreciated candles, although he does like cake. I light them and take the cake into the front room. I blow out the candles and wish. I can't tell you what I wish because that would stop it coming true, but you can probably guess. I cut a piece of the cake and take a bite but I don't like it. It tastes like sweet sawdust. It makes me feel ill. I go to the sink and spit it out, on the verge of retching. I throw the cake in the bin.

I didn't know loneliness could be like this. Before the Infection I had the reputation of being quite a solitary person. I had a lot of friends but only one of them, Josie, was what you could call close. With full days at school and Lander, Mam, Gran and Granddad at home it was a relief to be on my own. I used to spend hours reading in my bedroom and resented being dragged out to do something on the farm. But being alone is different from being lonely. Loneliness hurts. Yes, it does. It's a physical pain in every crack and cranny of your being. It's a hurt that can't be eased or subdued, that no tonic will relieve.

Sometimes it gnaws and sometimes it tears. There may be moments when you're distracted by something else, but it never goes away and it will come back stronger than ever, seizing you by the throat and demanding attention. I ache for the sound of a voice, the touch of another person. I think I would go completely mad were it not for Buster. And of course you, Adam.

It's because I'm lonely that I've looked out of the windows today, like, 500 times. By the 350th time my mood has swung from dreading seeing somebody out there to desperately wishing I would. Oh, where are you, man on the path?

I lie on the sofa and close my eyes. None of the things I could do appeals. I don't want to read, listen to music, watch moviesticks. Anyway, I still haven't found my iPad. I throw one of the cushions at the wall.

'It's my fucking birthday,' I shout, 'and I'm all on my own and I'm miserable and I'm bored.'

There's silence. Just the crackling of the fire and the ticking of the clock that I still wind religiously every day. I sink back on the remaining cushions. Buster regards me anxiously. I close my eyes.

Perhaps I dozed off, I'm not sure, but suddenly it was later and a noise made me jump. Now I'd better warn you, this is weird. It's so very weird it seems mental to write it down. But I'm not going crazy, it did happen. The sound that woke me was familiar to me but strange, a sound I know so very well but haven't heard for a long time. It was my mobile phone. It vibrated and it chimed. That's the alert to notify me that I have a text!

I was flabbergasted. I couldn't understand it. Then it dawned on me what it meant, and my heart leapt. I rushed to the window expecting to see the town below lit up, houses ablaze, street lights burning, life back to normal, but it was as dark as ever. I flicked on the TV, the radio. The TV was dead, the radio just noise. Nothing had changed. I was trying to understand what was going on when my phone chimed again, the reminder that the text hadn't been viewed. It was only then that I looked at it. The screen was startlingly bright and there was a single message. It said,

TXT ME.

I cradled the phone in my hands as if it was an injured bird. What does it mean? It must be evidence that someone else is out there. Who? Is it the man I saw yesterday? It can't be, it has to be somebody who knows me well enough to have my number. Does the sender also know it's my birthday? Is this a birthday message? I stare at the thing. The lack of information is infuriating. There are just those two words, **TXT ME.** There's no sender ID. I tap the Who? key and see the words 'new contact'. Big help!

My mind is a maelstrom. I want to acknowledge this contact, to reply, but there's no number listed so how can I? Do the obvious, Mr Armitage would say, so I do. I touch the 'reply' arrow. Then I key in my message: **WHO R U?** My fingers are trembling so much it takes me several goes to hit the right letters.

I press 'send'. I expect it to fail, there's no one to send it to, no network to send it on. There's a whooshing noise while the message pad spins. Then

226

it morphs into a smiley face and shows the notice, 'message sent'.

I place the phone carefully on the table and wait. I watch it expectantly. All the time I think I'll see the stupid bouncing ball that will tell me the message has failed, but I don't; just the words 'message sent'.

MONDAY

Nothing more happened last night. I waited for hours by the phone but it was dead. When I at last went to bed I put it under my pillow, desperate not to miss a message, but it stayed silent. I kept looking at it to check the battery hadn't run down. It was fine, just dumb.

I woke up this morning still thinking about the mysterious contact. In the daylight it somehow seemed less dramatic than it had last night. I checked the phone several times to make sure I hadn't dreamt it. It was exactly as before.

TXT ME.

and my reply

WHO R U?

The reply looked rather stroppy, challenging. Had I been too abrupt? Had the texter taken offence? Don't be daft, Kerryl. Whoever it was had bothered to text you, so do you think that's going to put them off?

I went to let the hens out of their run and that was when I got another shock. There were none there. They were all gone. I looked in the coop, expecting they'd be huddled together inside, but that was empty too. Nothing. No hens, no chicks, no eggs, nada. Okay, maybe I've not been looking after them as well as I should, what with not being well and all, but there was plenty for them to eat and a warm, safe, dry place for them to go.

My first thought was a fox had got in. That had happened before. I was about seven, and I still remember it. I walked into the field and found Gran in tears, holding her head in her hands. There was blood everywhere. It looked like something from a Tarantino movie. The fox had started to eat two of the hens, and the rest had been dismembered, every single one of them. Bits of chicken, savaged and barely recognisable, were scattered round the run: feathers, flesh, sinews, feet, heads. That's the trouble with a fox, Granddad said, it doesn't just take what it wants to eat, it kills the lot. This morning it was different; there was nothing left at all.

I looked in the area around the run and the coop and couldn't see anything amiss. The wire netting was sound and the doors were still securely fastened. I looked for signs of digging, because Granddad told me once that sometimes a badger will try to tunnel its way into a hen run, but there was no sign of that either.

Could somebody have stolen them? When? Why? Who? Is it the person I saw on Friday? Or whoever it was who texted me last night? Might they be the same? Don't be ridiculous. *If* there was anyone else around, why on earth would they take my hens? Hens are plentiful, there are thousands of them running free. I feel sad. The hens were Gran's. She liked them and so did I, poor gentle, dumb, clucking things. Now I feel I've let her, and them, down. I hope they're not dead. I feel a lump in my throat.

I stand in the doorway to the run, take a deep breath, and summon up the spirit of Mr Armitage. The question is, what do I do now?

The possibilities seem to be:

Option 1: Catch a few wild hens and a cockerel and restock the run.

Downside: If I did that I'd feel compelled to watch it day and night to make sure that whatever has happened today doesn't happen again.

Option 2: Do without keeping my own hens, and when I want poultry for food go and shoot a wild one, or a pheasant or a grouse, because there are plenty of all of them about.

Downside: I wouldn't have eggs. Does that matter? I used to eat them a lot but I can't remember when I last had one, and I've got hundreds of them. Buster likes them, though.

There's a third option: go veggie. Part of me thinks that would be a good idea because it would avoid killing stuff. Granddad used to snap the hen's necks. He did it swiftly, just a quick flick, and he said they didn't feel anything, but it was awful. He'd drop them on the ground and their legs would twitch and their feet scrabble, as if they didn't know they were dead and were trying to carry on. It's not only the killing that's horrible, it's the plucking and gutting. Ugh!!!

I leave the hen run door flapping open – no point closing it now – and go back to the house. On the way I scan the fields and the hill, looking for stray hens and wondering if I might see my watcher again. There's Joey in his paddock and the cows are peacefully grazing. There are a few ragged looking sheep on the edge of the moor, and the inevitable mangy dog hanging around on the fringes of the yard. Nothing that looks unusual.

In the kitchen I take out my phone and stare at it, willing it into life. It's mockingly unresponsive. **TXT ME.** What does it mean? I don't understand. I feel nervous, apprehensive. If this person can reach me by text, why don't they call me? Why don't they talk to me? They have my number, so why can't I hear their voice?

I can't settle to anything. I go and see Joey. He trots across his paddock to me and I rub his nose.

'Did you see what happened to the hens?' I ask him.

His big brown eyes gaze at me from under their long lashes. It's as if he's saying that he does know and he would tell me, if only he could.

I milk Dolly and give Molly and her calf the rest of the cow cake. The calf's not up to eating it yet but seems to enjoy licking it. Bonnie and Dolly look on forlornly. I don't have enough for them. My supplies are running low. 'Nursing mothers and children only,' I tell them. There's a feed merchant along the valley where I'm sure there'd be some. However, restocking cow cake is not on my list of priorities at the moment. Sorry, gals.

Out in the yard I look at the spot on the track where the guy I saw was standing. There must be rational explanations for all the odd things that have been going on: the gate, the noises, the strange feelings, the sighting, the text, the hens. I am as certain as I can be that I am the only person alive around here, but I know nothing of anywhere else. The major services have gone down, but that doesn't mean no one's left in other places. Perhaps there are a lot of people unaffected by the Infection but we just can't communicate with each other. Perhaps some of them are looking around, searching for others.

The big mystery isn't that somebody else might have survived, but how a text message could appear on my phone when, as far as I can tell, the mobile network is dead and has been for weeks. Wearily I go back into the house. I take my phone from the table and rouse it. The two texts are still there.

There are no answers to my questions. I lie down on the sofa and fall asleep with the mobile on my chest.

TUESDAY

Buster woke me by licking my face. For a second or two I couldn't work out what was happening, there was just this wet mess and his tongue going right into my ear. I pushed him away. His breath was foul. Memo: clean his teeth.

My eyes were prickly and my mouth dry. It was still dark and I turned over to go back to sleep, but Buster started licking me again and wouldn't leave me alone. I shoved him away, more roughly this time, and he started whining. I swore at him and sat up. It was pitch black and I reached out to the switch for the standard lamp beside the sofa. Nothing happened, it wouldn't work. I groped my way towards the light switch on the wall. That didn't work either. We keep a torch in the top drawer of the sideboard and I shuffled towards that, stubbing my toe on a chair leg and cursing. The torch was feeble, but it gave enough light for me to light a candle and find my trainers.

None of the light switches worked. I opened the door to the yard. There was a strong wind and the turbine should have been pushing out plenty of power. The torch beam was just bright enough to pick out the pole at the end of the yard, and to show the blades stationary. Perhaps it had jammed – it did that once before – but there should have been power in the batteries. I was still fuzzy from sleep, but I grabbed my coat and shuffled over to the barn, where the inverter and the rest of the stuff for the electrical system are fitted. I shone the torch on the meters. They were all on zero! There was no power. There was nothing coming off the mains (obviously), nothing from the solar panels (it was the middle of the night), nothing from the turbine (I'd just seen that it wasn't going round), and the fourth display told me that the batteries were flat. Just then there was a beep, warning me that the back-up that keeps the meters working and remembers the power management settings was low too.

I went back to the house and lit some more candles. I have plenty, and I put extras in the hallway and up the stairs, around the kitchen and in the front room.

I'm sitting at the kitchen table now, writing this and trying to figure out what's gone wrong and what to do about it. When did I last check the meters and the electrics? I didn't. It was always Granddad's or Lander's job and I never thought to do it. It's been overcast for the past few days, so the solar panels won't have been doing much. Was the turbine working yesterday? I didn't notice. I'm so used to it being there I don't see it any more. It could have stopped generating days ago and as long as there was power in the batteries I wouldn't have noticed.

I can't do anything till daylight, but I don't feel like going to bed. Buster pads after me to the kitchen, making hopeful, attention-seeking noises in his throat. I open a tin of Dog Star (beef in jelly, his favourite) and tip it into his bowl, dodging his wild tail. I wince as I stand up. My back's stiff from sleeping on the sofa and I do a few stretches. I've brought the bathroom scales downstairs and I step on them. I've gone down again. I write the new number in the back of my diary. I'm pleased with the progress I am making, but there's still a way to go yet. I return to the table to await the dawn.

I remember my phone and retrieve it from where it's slipped down between the sofa cushions. Yesterday's message thread has another entry.

TXT ME

and **WHO R U?**

are now followed by **????**.

The timing is 2.34am, an hour ago.

My hands tremble. Is that a response to my question? Does it mean my message was received? Am I having an actual conversation with somebody? A row of question marks; perhaps it's just an error message.

I tap the 'reply' arrow and begin to key in. I've just started when there's a red slash across the screen followed by the notice 'Your device is running on reserve power and will now close down' and the whole thing dies. I scream in anger and frustration, and come close to hurling the fucking thing away. I have a booster, but of course it's empty. I can't charge the phone until daylight and the solar panels start working, or I get the turbine going again. There's somebody out there who has not only sent me a message but now responded to mine, and I can't contact them. I scream again. Buster looks anxious.

There's nothing to do but wait. I go back to the kitchen. I can't even make a cup of tea. Hang on a minute, I can. We've got a paraffin stove in the cupboard under the stairs. Do I have any paraffin? Don't know. Can I be bothered looking? No. I open a packet of peanut butter cookies, take a bite out of one and toss the rest in the bin. I don't like them any more. Buster looks at me as if I've just destroyed the *Mona Lisa*. He loves peanut butter cookies (well, actually he loves all cookies) but if I gave them to him he'd inhale the lot and make himself sick.

How bad a problem do I have? If I can't fix the turbine I'll be dependent for power on at least a bright day, if not a sunny one. And winter's coming, when there'll be less daylight. I suppose all I really need electricity for now is to run the fridge and freezers and to charge up my phone and iPad, and as I still haven't found my iPad that means just my phone.

Doesn't the dawn take a long time to arrive when you're waiting for it? I remember all those schooldays, when morning seemed to hurtle in at warp speed, and way before I was ready it was time to get up. Now, waiting for and wanting the sunrise, it takes forever to arrive. At last the sky lightens enough for me to go out into the yard and investigate.

LATER

Right, report.

I think the turbine may just be stuck. When it did that before, Granddad got a ladder and levered the blades free with a tommy bar. There's a further problem, though, because our ladder got nicked from the barn about a year ago and we never replaced it. We have a shorter one but it won't do. If the turbine had stopped with one of the blades aligned with the pole, i.e. at six o'clock, I could have just about got to it, but it's stuck with one blade at four o'clock, another at eight o'clock and the top one at twelve. I can't get anywhere near them.

It's daylight now and the panels are charging the batteries, but I don't yet have enough power to boil a kettle. There's warm water in the tank so I can take a shower and I go up to the bathroom for a long one. I stand in front of the mirror and look at myself. I'm moderately pleased. I'm definitely losing weight. I've not been eating much at all. I'm not really hungry, either, and when I do feel hungry and try to eat, as soon as I taste it I don't want it. But that's a good thing, isn't it? It means I'm getting somewhere.

LATER STILL

While I was in the shower I had an idea. I think it's a good one. There's an elevator in the barn that Granddad used to lift hay bales up into the loft for storage. If I hook it up to the tractor I can back it under one of the turbine blades. I might then be able to climb up it and reach the blade. It's totally off the rails safety-wise – Lander would say it has A&E written all over it – but it's worth a try. It's sunny today so I have enough power. That gives me a breathing space, time to think. It would be daft to rush into anything.

It also means I now have enough juice to get my phone going.

WEDNESDAY

I managed yesterday to get my phone charged up again. There were no more messages. I'd asked the sender to say who they were but all I'd got back were the question marks. What does that mean? It means that he/she doesn't want to say who they are. Why not? Why are they being so mysterious? Maybe I have to make the next move. I tap in

MY NAME IS KERRYL

and hit 'send'. There's the whoosh, the spin, the smiley face and 'message sent'. Again I can't believe it. Sent where? How? Who to? (Oh all right, to whom?)

I wait and stare at the screen, desperate for it to come to life but it doesn't. It's agony. The closest I've come before to this feeling of excited frustration was when I had a date with this really hot guy and we'd arranged to meet under the market clock and I was there first and he was late, only a few minutes but it seemed like hours and I thought he wasn't coming. Of course, the person I'm texting could be hundreds of miles away, thousands, maybe on a different continent. That's it. They're in a different time zone and that's why replies are slow coming.

I open a game on my phone but the screen's too small for it to be interesting. I need to find my iPad. I search the whole house, even our Mam's room and Gran and Granddad's, although I know I haven't been in there. I check the barn, though God knows why I would have taken it over there. Anyway, I hadn't. It's

238

gone. Surely it can't be far away. I must just have put it down somewhere and forgotten. I'm definitely losing my marbles, as Gran used to say. I expect I'll suddenly come across it when I'm looking for something else, but I wish I could find it. I miss it.

LATER

I've checked out the bale elevator. It's an adjustable, trough-shaped ramp, with a chain conveyor fitted with spikes running up the centre. When it's working the spikes catch on the bales and pull them up. It seems firm enough and should be easy to climb. I'll have to watch the spikes, though, because they're savage and if I were to slip I could end up with a nasty cut. I was tempted to have a go right away, but I was tired so I decided to leave it till later. I was early in bed last night and despite everything that's happening I slept well. In the past I didn't allow Buster to sleep with me, mainly because he always wants to be right in the middle of the bed and I have to arrange myself around him, but since Gran and Granddad went I've been letting him sleep at my feet – on them really. He spends the nights gradually easing himself up the bed a millimetre at a time, like some big hairy quantum experiment, so that by morning he's in a good position to lick my face. It's comforting feeling him there, makes me feel less alone. But I'm not alone now. Am I?

LATER STILL

I thought about staining this page with blood, just to highlight the drama! It certainly gets a row of scowly faces, all of them in pain. Writing's not easy but I can still manage it, so here goes.

I succeeded in hooking the elevator to the tractor. That was hard. The elevator was too heavy for me to pull, and it took me three goes to get the tractor into the right position to fix the coupling. Then I towed it out and backed it up to the turbine. That wasn't as difficult as I'd expected, and I got it right underneath the blade that was at four o'clock. The only problem was that the ground around the bottom of the turbine was uneven and I had to shore up the elevator with flat stones to get it level and stop it wobbling. When I was happy that it was firm I climbed up. Hairy, or what? The base was solid but the sloping bit (the trough) that takes the bales swayed about. There was nothing firm to stand on because of the spikes. Besides, the thing is made for hay bales, not for a human, and it protested. It creaked and wobbled about and I thought I was going to fall off. I was wetting myself. I'm not good with heights.

I managed to wedge myself near the top of the trough, with my knees braced against the sides and in a position where I could reach the blade. I stretched out and the elevator lurched scarily. I wasn't helped by Buster deciding at just that moment that he'd climb up too and help me. I thought he was going to have us both off and I had to shoo him away. He watched the rest of the performance from the edge of the yard, looking rejected and upset.

I caught hold of the turbine blade and tried to move it. Although it did give a little, it wouldn't go round. It was well and truly stuck. My thigh muscles were aching from pushing against the trough. I gave the blade a big push and the elevator lurched. I flung out my arm to steady myself and caught my hand on one of the bale spikes. I screeched in pain and watched with horror the blood running down my arm.

I spent the next half hour getting myself down from the top of the elevator and washing and sterilising my hand. The gash really stung and I think it probably needs stitches, but there's no chance of that. I cleaned it as thoroughly as I could and applied pressure. After a while the bleeding stopped and I rummaged in the first aid box to find some germicide. There were no butterfly plasters but there were some bandages. Have you ever tried to bandage your own hand? Definitely a two-person job. Even Buster couldn't help, although he offered. I don't think dog lick is much use as an antiseptic.

I'm now writing this while I calm myself down and wait for the throbbing in my hand to stop. Luckily it's my right hand that's hurt and I'm left handed. As soon as it settles down I'll change. My T-shirt and jeans look as though I've just come off a shift in an abattoir.

Maybe what's preventing the turbine going round is a problem with the hub. The hub has a cover and if I take it off I might be able to see if there's anything jamming the works. It would make sense to leave it for today and let my hand heal a bit, but I've got this far and I want to resolve the situation. I want to get the thing going, or I want to know for sure that it will never work again. If it's that, I'll have to make plans to manage without it.

EVEN LATER STILL

It took quite a long time for my hand to feel better enough for me to have another go on the elevator. When it did I went back to the shed to get a selection of tools. I was so busy thinking about the turbine hub and hoping I'd cleaned my wound enough and that my hand wouldn't become infected that I forgot to take the shotgun with me. I left it leaning in a corner by the sink, where I'd put it when I came in. One of my safety rules, remember? Never leave the house without a loaded gun. Well, this time I did.

Driving the tractor one handed was a bit of a challenge and it took me a while to move the elevator forward from its original position. Then I backed it until the slopey bit (hope you don't have trouble with these technical terms, Adam) was leaning on the turbine pillar. I wedged it in place by using stones to stop the wheels moving and womping them with a sledge hammer, again one handed. I tell you, if I go on like this I'll be a contender for Miss Universe! Anyway, the elevator was much more stable in its new position because the pillar stopped it swaying.

When I was happy that it was firm I crawled up the trough again. This time I'd thought to use some old rubble sacks to cover the chain and spikes. It didn't make the spikes completely safe but it gave some protection.

I got to the top and stood up on the wobbly ramp, hooking my right arm around the pillar to steady myself. I could see straight away what the problem was. The rotor shaft was snagged with baler twine, a lot of it. If you don't know – and I suppose that if you're a townie,

Adam, you might not – baler twine is a thin cord used to tie up bales of hay. When Granddad was a boy it was made from hemp and the bales were tied by hand. Now it's spun from strands of plastic and a machine compacts the hay and ties it up like a parcel. Except sometimes it gets it wrong. It misfeeds, and then instead of you getting a tight pack the thing falls apart. Other times you'll pick up a bale and it collapses. In both cases, and in several others, you're left with lengths of redundant loose twine. In Granddad's eyes it was a major crime to leave this lying on the ground. He was always meticulous about picking it up and he insisted that we did too because it can foul machinery or choke a grazing animal. So where did all this on the turbine come from?

I got a spanner from my tool belt to loosen the nuts that secure the housing. It was hard trying to keep my balance on the unsteady ramp while undoing the fixings with my good hand and holding on to the elevator with my other arm, but I did it. I even managed to catch the housing as it came away and stop it falling to the ground.

Next I got a cutter and started to hack away at the twine. It was wound round and round and round the hub, several metres of it, effectively jamming it tight. I don't think that could happen by chance. I suppose if one end had got caught on the spinning shaft it might have done it, but how could it get up there in the first place? It looked more as if the job had been done deliberately to sabotage the thing, but that was nonsense. How could anybody get up there without me seeing them? And even if they could, why would they? I'd made several cuts and the twine was coming away when disaster struck. The wind had been buffeting me while I'd been working and the turbine began to move. Immediately the shaft broke free. I was astounded at the power of the blades, there was no way I could stop them. One of them struck the elevator, the whole thing swayed, rocked off its support and I lost my grip. Part slipping, part falling, I landed hard on the ground on my left foot. Pain shot through my ankle and up my leg and I collapsed, cursing and shrieking. I barely noticed that the turbine was now whirling like crazy above me.

I lay on the ground, teeth clenched and sobbing, waiting for the pain to ease. I sat up and tried to assess the damage. I didn't think I'd broken anything, but it really hurt. I was wondering how I could make it to the house when I saw something in the corner of the yard. At first I thought it was another dog, but as it came closer I saw that it was a worse problem than that. A large boar was snuffling along the barn wall. Either it was a wild one or an exotic domestic breed, because it had tusks. At first it didn't notice me, then it did.

I froze. I know boars are dangerous. Granddad always used to say that he'd rather face a bull than a boar any day. It stared at me with cold, piggy eyes. It was massive, bigger than a man. The tusks were huge and its ears flopped over its eyes. Its hide was covered in spiky black hair. It gave an arrogant snort and trotted towards me. It didn't at that stage look threatening but I couldn't be sure. I had a screwdriver and the twine cutter, but what use would they be? Besides, I had a bad hand and I didn't think I could stand up. The boar stopped a metre or so away to take stock. Then it lowered its head. I picked up a stone and flung it at the animal. It shied away and the stone glanced its flank. It looked affronted, grunted and came for me.

Suddenly all hell broke loose. A snarling, barking, furious whirlwind called Buster hit the boar like an express train. He ran round it, snapping at its flanks. The boar looked pained at the distraction and turned away from me. Buster sank his teeth into one of its back legs. It squealed, twisted and caught the dog with one of its tusks. Buster yelped in pain and bit again. The boar made to fight back, thought better of it and ran away, snorting and squalling. Buster chased it to the edge of the field, snapping at its heels. Then he came back to me. I couldn't stop trembling and Buster was sure that the best way to help was to lick me. I hadn't the will or the energy to push him away, and I lay on my side until he'd finished, when he settled down beside me, whining gently. I ruffled his ears and stroked his nose with my good hand and he snuggled closer. I patted him and he yelped, and it was then I saw the damage that the boar's tusk had done. There was a nasty, weeping tear in his flank, just above his rump. It needed seeing to.

Somehow I got across the yard to the house, Buster limping along with me. Once in the kitchen I dragged a chair to the sink and flopped onto it. It clearly hurt Buster to have his wound touched, but he seemed to know I was trying to help him, and he sat mostly still while I bathed it and put on some of the cream I'd used on my hand. As soon as I let him go he started licking it off, but I couldn't stop that. I reckoned that it might do him good from the inside too. I limped to the freezer and got an ice tray, which I tipped out into a tea towel to make an ice pack for my ankle. All through the whole operation I was in a storm of pain. Every movement was agony, which didn't slacken until I'd been sitting with my leg raised and the ice pack on my ankle for some time. Buster went to check his bowl, which I took as a good sign.

For the rest of the day I've been using one of Granddad's sticks to get about. It would have been easier with two but I can't manage a stick in my bad hand. I must look a proper sight and sound worse, a snivelling, drivelling wreck. I don't bother trying to hold back my sobs and yelps of pain, or to wipe my running nose. There's no one here to impress.

I'm feeling better now. I'm writing this in bed. I have a bad hand. I have a bad leg (my ankle's wrapped in a cold, damp towel). I have a very affectionate dog (lying as close to me as he can possibly get). We're both of us feeling very, very sorry for ourselves, but it could all have been so much worse. My ankle could easily have been broken and it's not, and that's a mercy (Gran used to say that, I'm not sure what she meant). I could have hit my head when I fell, and knocked myself out. I could have been lying in the yard unconscious when the boar came. Buster could have been shut inside. If he hadn't gone for the boar I'm sure it would have attacked me, and if he hadn't had the guts to keep on fighting it even when he'd been gored it could have killed us both. Thanks to him I got off lightly.

My hand's a worry, though. I think I managed to clean it all right, I certainly applied industrial quantities of antiseptic to it, but if everything had been normal Mam or Gran would have been pestering me to go along to the clinic for an anti-tetanus jab. No chance of that now. I'll just have to wait, and trust to luck.

There is one good thing that's come out of this; I now have a working turbine. Before I came to bed I was able to hobble over to check the read-outs and all is well, power is being generated, the batteries are charged up. Then I hauled myself up the stairs, but before I did I locked and chained the door to the yard.

THURSDAY

I didn't write this down yesterday even though it shook me up. My hand and my ankle were enough to think about. Also it's crazy and you, my beloved Adam, might think I've jumped totally off the bus. You probably do anyway – I've been telling you about some weird shit – but this was stranger than anything yet.

When Buster chased the boar away from me there was a second when it turned round, as if it was going to take him on, before it veered away and ran off. In that instant it didn't look at Buster, it looked straight at me. It had a really sad expression, disappointed and hurt. Obvious question: how can a boar's face show an expression? Not so obvious answer: it was not the face of a boar that looked back at me; the face was human.

There you are. I told you that you'd think I'm a nutter. Is it because I'm lonely and starved of people that I had this creepy hallucination? Or is it because I'm not eating? I know that since I went off food I've been having peculiar dreams. Perhaps this was just another one of those, except wide awake and so scarier. Perhaps the animal really was a person. Perhaps there are some people the Infection doesn't kill and they are morphed into other creatures. Now come on, Kerryl, get down out of that tree! Not a bad idea for a story, though. I might write it one day.

LATER

I didn't think it would be so easy to stop eating. Now I can understand how Tracey Blackburn did it. People who say that dieting's hard are wrong. It's the simplest thing in the world. You just stop stuffing food into your mouth.

The first couple of days after I decided to fast I didn't want to eat. The next few days I was starving and would have hoovered up anything in sight (that must be how Buster feels all the time!). That was tough. I was thinking about food every waking minute. It took a lot of will power to stop myself bingeing. Then one morning I woke up and out of habit my first thought was breakfast and then I thought, *I don't want anything. In fact, not only do I not want food, but if I do try to eat something it will make me sick.* It's been like that ever since. It's as if eating was a habit, like smoking, and I've got out of it. I can't fill in my weight table because I can't balance on the scales on one foot, but I certainly *feel* thinner. I pinch my stomach and the fat roll seems to have more or less gone. I bet a lot of my clothes fit me now. Maybe not my prom dress yet, because I worked hard to get really svelte when I wore that, but soon.

I've been here in bed since yesterday and that's where I am now, reading, dropping off, reading again, and in between writing this. Buster's been sleeping at my feet, except at one point early this morning when he tried to sleep on my bad foot and I hit the roof. He's been downstairs several times and I think he's checking his bowl. I'm pretty sure he's not into dieting and so I'll have to go down soon and refill it.

Getting upstairs yesterday was a real performance. I sat on the bottom step, held the mug of tea I'd made myself in one hand and used the other hand and my good leg to hutch me up to the next stair. I did this, one tread at a time, until I got to the top. Buster was keen to help me but didn't know how, so he just got in the way and at one point he almost knocked the mug out of my hand with his tail. I shouted at him and he went away. He spent the next hour curled up in the corner of my bedroom, sulking. It would have been funny if my leg hadn't hurt so much. It would have made a great clip for *You're the Star*. If there'd been anybody around to video it, or to watch it. *You're the Star* was one of Gran's favourite TV shows. It was a half-hour collection of home-made phone or camera clips of people (and animals, and children) having disasters, falling down, bumping into each other, knocking things over and generally doing silly things. She used to look forward to it all week.

Why bother going upstairs? you say. Why not sleep on the sofa, like before?

I'm not really sure. It's a bunch of things. For one, sleeping on the sofa gives me a bad back, and I can spread out in my own bed. More than that, I just feel safer upstairs. I don't know what I'm afraid of, and I can't explain why being upstairs makes me feel less threatened, but it does.

LATER STILL

I fell asleep again. I expect it's shock that's making me sleep so much. I woke up and Buster was whining. I assumed he was hungry, so I got out of bed to go down and feed him. 'I must teach you how to work a tin opener,' I told him. 'Then you can feed yourself.' Then I thought, *No, not a good idea. You're a lovely dog but let's face it, you are greedy, so I don't think self service would work.*

250

I felt really wobbly. Going down the stairs was easier than coming up yesterday because I didn't have anything to carry, and I swung on the handrail, hopping on my good foot. I got down all right but I felt dizzy when I reached the bottom and had to cling to the stair post while my head cleared. Why am I so weak?

I hobbled into the kitchen to get the dog food from the dresser. I fed Buster and thought it would be a good idea to take a few cans and an opener upstairs, to save me coming down every time he needed feeding, except I didn't think I could bear the smell of the dog food in my bedroom. I could feed him on the landing, but that would mean I'd have to get out of bed anyway.

I was wrestling with this problem when I caught sight of my phone where I'd left it on charge. At that very second the screen sprang to life and there was the buzz of the vibrator and the chimes for an incoming message. I jumped and dropped the pack of dog food.

There was the message I'd sent yesterday before all the fuss with the turbine:

MY NAME IS KERRYL

Under it was a reply:

I KNOW

FRIDAY

I'm in bed again, but I haven't been sleeping. I couldn't get to sleep at all last night. I tried reading to take my mind off things, but I couldn't concentrate. Every couple of minutes the realisation would beat in my head – somebody knows my name! somebody knows my name! somebody knows my name! – and when that happened I'd be seized by a fit of trembling. At first I couldn't believe what I saw on the screen. I thought it must be some fault with the phone, or perhaps a virus. Do phones get viruses? A phone's a kind of computer, so I suppose it could.

When I first read the message I took the same energetic and decisive action I had after the first one: I sat down and looked at it for a long time and wondered what the fuck was going on. Then I hobbled round the house and made sure (again!) that all the doors were locked. Then I climbed back upstairs.

Now I've decided I'm not happy lying in bed. Between ourselves I've been here for so long my bum is getting sore. Also I've changed my mind about being upstairs and decided that I feel more vulnerable up here than I do sleeping in the front room. I know that in theory I could stand at the top of the stairs and if anyone tried to come up I could whack them with something heavy, but downstairs I have a better idea of what's going on. So I'm going to get dressed and go down.

LATER

I've put on jeans (no trouble at *all* doing up the waist – in fact I'm having to wear a belt!). I've also put on one of Lander's shirts, nice and loose in case I have to move quickly. My ankle feels better but I couldn't run yet. I can hobble, so long as I don't lean on it too hard. I've drawn all the curtains. I hate that, it's like living in a cave, but the idea of somebody out there peeping in at me gives me the creeps.

Okay, I'm scared but lolling around here in a shaking heap won't achieve anything. I must be rational. Summon Mr Armitage's training again and set out the situation logically.

1. Somebody is able to send me text messages and to receive them from me.
2. This is despite the fact that the whole mobile phone network seems to be down, along with everything else that could communicate.
3. The sender knows my name. (Well, of course they do because I told them, but they say they knew already – or do they just want me to think that?)
4. The number of individuals who know/knew my name must be limited to a hundred at the most: family, friends, some of the girls and teachers at school, a few people in the town, the tutors at Cambridge who interviewed me and dealt with my application.
5. As far as I know all those people are dead. Of course I can't be certain. Maybe someone's survived. I have.
6. Only a minority of those who know/knew my name would have known where I live.

So the big question is, does whoever it is who knows my name also know where I am? I have to face that possibility. That's why I'm scared. But why should I be? Why should I think of them as a threat? Well, what they've done so far doesn't fill me with confidence. If they're friendly, why not send me a full text introducing themselves properly, instead of two-word messages that seem designed to freak me out? Why not call me and talk? *Why not just come round and knock on the fucking door?* It's as if they're deliberately trying to spook me.

The use of the 's' word does bring up another possibility, and I hesitate to mention it. All these weird things that have happened – the gate, the shadows, the hens, the man on the path, the turbine and the text messages – are being caused by something supernatural.

There, I've said it. It's been in my head for a while but I've not admitted it in case you think I'm a complete fruit cake and go right off me. I don't believe in ghosts, or I didn't. Gran did. She was sure she kept seeing a strange woman in old-fashioned clothes around the farm. Lander and Granddad pooh-poohed it. I'm not sure what Mam thought. I don't think she could make up her mind, and neither can I now. The figure I saw on the path didn't *look* like a ghost. I don't mean that it should be something in a long white shroud, but he looked so, well, *solid*. And he was fit. I think of ghosts as being ancient and flakey. This guy was young, and a hunk. Another thing is my mobile. I've never heard of a ghost sending text messages, have you? Here, now, in broad daylight, the idea of poltergeists or spirits or hobs is ridiculous. But in the dark, when the house feels desolate and the wind whistles outside, it seems perfectly possible. It's scary, even though I leave candles burning all night (breaking my own safety rules).

I've loaded Granddad's two shotguns and hidden them (one's on the floor under the sofa in the front room and the other's behind the coats in the hall, in case you're looking). I keep Lander's air pistol close at hand, wherever I am. His .22 is in the cupboard, and that's loaded too.

I wish you were real, Adam. I could just do with a useful bloke around at the moment. Not to defend me, you great lunk – what do you think I am? – but to fight alongside me, if it comes to it.

LATER STILL

Of course, there's yet another explanation for the texts. It's that the sender is Lander. That must have occurred to you, too. He knows my number, and I wouldn't put it past him to be able to figure out some way to make texts work on my phone. He's gone off somewhere for reasons only Lander would know, and he's decided to get in touch.

However, I don't think so. Make no mistake, Lander would love the idea of freaking me out, but I don't think he'd go to these lengths. I don't know where Lander is or what's happened to him, but he's not the texter. How can I be so certain? Well, this won't seem very convincing to you unless you're one yourself, but it's the twin thing. We're not identical, but for the first nine months of our lives we shared the cramped living space of our Mam's womb, and since then we've rarely been apart for more than a few hours. Since as long as I can remember I've always had a rough idea what Lander was up to. If Lander was close, I would know it. If he was trying to contact me, I would know it. It's not Lander.

I ponder what to do. I can't spend whatever's left of my life surrounded by guns and with the curtains drawn and the doors locked. I have things to do. In the long term I need to work out how I'm going to start building myself a life, because I can't go on like this, moping about, seeing things, living from one day to another without any clear plan for the future. There are some jobs that need doing straight away. I have to put the cover back on the turbine, do something about the hay, make the yard safe from stray creatures, look after the animals. The animals! Oh shit!! The cows!!! Joey!!!! In all this mess I've forgotten them. I haven't done the fucking milking!!!!!

EVEN LATER THAN THAT

As soon as I remembered the animals I dropped my diary. I got my bad foot into a boot. That hurt. I picked up one of the shotguns and called for Buster. Then I limped across the yard to the barn, feeling hugely guilty and expecting the worst. I couldn't understand why Dolly hadn't been making a fuss. Usually when a cow needs milking it bellows enough to crack the windows, but I've heard nothing. I noticed that Buster was limping too, probably out of sympathy, and he wasn't running about like he usually does. He keeps worrying at his back, where the boar got him. I've put a bandage on it to try to stop him licking off the antiseptic ointment and he looks a dufus, quite comical in fact. The wound must have been bothering him and I promised him I'd have a look at it after the milking.

I opened the barn door expecting, well, I didn't know what, but I was prepared for some sort of trouble. However, everything was normal. The cows were in the barn, Molly and her calf in their usual stall, Bonnie and Dolly in theirs. They watched me with only a casual interest. There was fresh straw on the floor and they looked totally happy. I grabbed a bucket and the milking stool and started massaging Dolly's teats, but there was nothing there. It seemed that my neglect had forced her to run dry – or she'd been milked already. I went to the cooler. There was milk in there, fresh and still warm. Somebody had been in the barn. Somebody had done the milking.

My blood literally ran cold. I didn't really understand what that cliché meant before, but I do now. It's the feeling that your spinal cord has been flash frozen. I took the gun and limped round the end of the barn to the paddock. Joey was there, calmly nibbling grass. He didn't even come over to me when I leant on the fence. It was obvious he wanted nothing. Buster whined. He couldn't understand it either.

Is this the work of a hob, you ask? Hob my arse! I stamped back to the house, as well as I could stamp with a bad foot. I was fed up with all this creepy stuff. Whoever was doing this and the texter were one and the same, I was convinced of it. I was going to take him on, whoever he is. I was going to challenge him. How do I know it's a 'him'? I just do.

I took off my boots. I stuffed Lander's air pistol in my waistband (with just a momentary feeling of satisfaction that it fitted so easily). I sat down and took out my phone. Underneath the last message I entered a new text:

WHERE R U?

SATURDAY

I was too wired to sleep last night. This morning I'm wrung out, dizzy when I stand up. I feel as though I've been hollowed out. See what you've done to me, Adam.

This is what happened. This isn't for you because you were there so you know, but it has to go down in the diary, for the record. All right?

Okay. Last night. I came in from the barn and warmed myself a can of soup. It tasted watery and I only had a couple of spoonfuls. Nothing else appealed, so I went through to the front room and curled up on the sofa. I spent ages there, listening to my music and waiting to see if there was any reply to my text. Buster wheezed on the rug beside me, and made occasional whimpering noises in his sleep. At last, it must have been well after midnight, I forced myself to go upstairs (yes, I'm sleeping – or trying to – upstairs again, and yes, I know, I'm pathetic because I keep changing my mind). I fancied a bath, so I ran the tub. There was a flask of Eau d'Amour on the window sill. It was Mam's favourite and I haven't been using it because the scent of it makes me think of her and that upsets me. Besides, it was expensive and nowhere in Walbrough was posh enough to stock it so I don't know whether I could ever get any more. Then I thought, *Oh, what the hell. Here's to you, Mam*, and I tipped in a generous slug.

I lay in the silky water for ages. My ankle and hand are better but they still hurt a bit, and I flexed them in the warm suds. It was so calm and cosy lying there in the candlelight, my Bluetooth playing quietly in the background. It seemed so normal, like it had always been. I could imagine Mam and Gran downstairs watching the TV, Granddad reading his paper, Lander in his room on his computer. Perhaps they really were there, and as long as I stayed here and didn't look at them they would remain. I closed my eyes. When I opened them again the bath was stone cold. I clambered out, shivering, and wrapped myself in a towel. My playlist had finished and the house was silent.

I took a candle into our Mam's room and turned her big mirror around (you remember I faced all the mirrors to the wall because catching sudden sight of reflections spooked me?). The girl I saw was like a creature in a vampire movie. My arms and shoulders were boney. My eyes were sunken and had dark rings around them. Panda eyes, Lander would call them. My lips had been sore for a couple of days but I was surprised to see how dry and cracked they were. I bared my teeth. My gums were red and bleeding. What was wrong with me? I bent towards the mirror to get a better look, and that was when I saw a figure. It was at the end of the landing, beside the door to Gran's room. For a nanosecond I thought it was Lander back. It was wearing a T-shirt and skinny jeans, and looked fit. The face and hair were in shadow. It looked at me and I clutched my towel round me. Then I turned, and it had gone!

I ran to the top of the stairs and peered down into the gloomy hall. I listened. The grandfather clock ticked and Buster snored in the corner of my room. Apart from that there was no sound. Buster. He'd not reacted at all.

Usually if a stranger comes near he growls and his hair bristles, but he was sleeping like a baby.

Had I been dreaming, still dozy from my bath? The figure looked so solid. And when I went where it had been, where it had stood and watched me, I thought I could smell a man's cologne. It was one I knew, one that Lander sometimes used – Boss or Armani or something like that. There must have been someone there.

Of course, I couldn't sleep. The strange thing is that I wasn't scared, not at all, but I was wired up. What had happened? Who had I seen? Was it you, Adam? Who else could it have been? But how did you get into the house, through locked doors? Where are you now? Are you watching me?

All these questions and more made such a clamour in my head that rest was out of the question. So this morning I feel like a zombie. Perhaps I am a zombie, one of the undead caught in the daylight. Perhaps I did get the Infection and my corpse has been reanimated. Eek!

LATER

There's another problem and it worries me, a lot. I thought Buster hadn't been himself and I took a look at his shoulder. I've been putting it off because of my hand, and when I did examine it I felt guilty because it's clearly been hurting him and he couldn't tell me. He whimpered while I was seeing to him, but he stayed still and let me take off the dressing, bathe his wound with disinfectant and water, and apply more ointment and a new bandage. When I'd finished he licked my hand, his way of saying thank you, and I rubbed his ears. Then he went to lie down again.

I'm concerned for him. The gash looks infected. It smells bad. It's swollen, and when I pressed it puss came out. I've used loads of antiseptic on it but God knows where that tusk had been. I could go down into the town and raid the chemist for antibiotics. Except I don't know what to get, or how much to give him. He needs a vet. Please please please let Buster be all right. I can't bear the thought of him in pain, or of being without him. 'I'm sorry, old friend,' I told him. 'I'll look after you better, I promise.' I think he understood.

Later still

OMG. I've had a reply. I was trying to tidy up a bit, part of my plan to take control of my life and get busy, when my phone vibrated. It was in my jeans pocket and it made me jump.

The text I sent yesterday was

WHERE R U?

It was meant to be a challenge, to force the texter out into the open. The reply throws it right back at me. It's one word.

CLOSE

SUNDAY

If whoever's sending these texts meant to give me yet another sleepless night, they surely managed it! The text coming right after the apparition (was it?) on the landing, I couldn't clear my head of either.

I tried all sorts: reciting poetry in my head, reliving visits I'd made to places, imagining the walk up to the Bride Stones, but none of it worked. I'd distract myself for a few minutes but then the thoughts would push back. Finally I gave in and got up. I picked up a candle, and because I'd been thinking about him I wandered into Lander's bedroom.

I wish I'd found his message sooner. I can't think how I missed it, but how did he think I'd know it was there? He could have left something to alert me. That's typical of Lander, expecting everyone else to be in step with him and able to read his mind.

I've been in his room a few times since he left, to tidy up and to put away the clothes I'd washed, and I don't know why I didn't see it then – thinking about something else, I suppose. To be fair to Lander, the message was pretty obvious: a memory card taped among the posters on his wall with a big arrow in red felt pen and a large 'K'.

I powered up his computer and mounted the card. It contained a single text file. I opened it. What I saw explains a lot: why Lander went away, why he was so strange before he did, why he was so mad about me going into his bedroom. I read it on screen. Then I printed a copy. Here it is.

Hi Kes

I was going to say that if you're reading this it means you've not caught the Infection and you're still in the land of the living. Then I thought that sounds naff, and I can hear you saying, fucking duh. I have some stuff to tell you. You're going to find it weird, but I haven't time to explain properly so you'll just have to trust me and go with it.

When the Infection came it just didn't make sense that everybody who was exposed to it died. The virus is a parasite and can only live a limited time outside a human body. How could it carry on if it killed all its hosts? It was against all the rules of evolution and survival. Well, I wasn't the only one who thought that. I went on the dark net and found accounts from quite a few people who claimed to have caught the Infection and got over it. The trouble is, most of them seemed complete nutters. Not all, though. There was this guy called Anton, in Belarus, who ran a forum. He did a regular blog and I signed up as a follower. He had over a hundred of them. They seemed just like you and me. They'd all been mega-exposed to the Infection and all their family and friends had caught it and died, but for some reason they'd not. They called themselves The Selected, no kidding, and they thought they were special. They seemed to be clustered in southern Asia: Kazakhstan, Afghanistan, Nepal, places like that. They swapped news of where they'd been, what they'd been doing, why they thought they hadn't been got by the bugs. Their reasons went from being super-holy and chosen by God, to bathing in special rivers, to eating weird food. Some of them were completely gaga. There was one guy who only ate berries, and another who made pills out of yak dung! It was a hoot. A few of us started a sub-net to share the crazy stories.

Somebody suggested that the survivors should all get together to found a new civilisation, but nobody could agree where, or figure out how to arrange it or how to get past the ban on travel. Then something started to happen. To cut a long one short, it seems it wasn't that these people had escaped the Infection, just that they'd caught it in a different way. One of the guys in the group is a doctor and he explained it best. He said the intention of the virus, if you could call it that, is to find a human host, occupy its brain and live there. The human provides food for it and transports it so it can spread to others. That's what's supposed to happen in the second stage of the Infection, after the fever and the cramps. The problem (for the virus) is that most people die before it can get itself lodged in their brains. So if you shiver and cramp up and shit your insides out and die, then the virus has fucked itself and has nowhere to go. If you don't get those symptoms, or if you do and you survive, then it can move in upstairs. But that's rare. According to the doctor, that's why it's evolved to mutate like it does and to be so easy to transmit, because it needs lots of goes before it finds somebody who lasts long enough for it to be able to move on to the next phase. Now there's a new strain, where the initial symptoms are a lot milder, not much more than a cold, and you get over them and it's easier for the virus to settle in your head. He and some others are working on a treatment, a way to wipe out the virus without frying your brain. He thinks they're on track.

I wanted to know how you'd know if it was happening to you and the virus was living in your brain.

265

Then Anton started writing about it on his blog. He said he'd been infected but had got through. At first he thought he was back to normal, but then he started seeing people who weren't there. Alongside this he was doing things and forgetting he'd done them, so that he thought there was some other dude there with him. He figured this out because as an experiment he listed every single thing he did as he did it, throughout the day. When he read it back there were things on his list that he had no memory of doing, none at all, and when he'd discovered them he'd thought they'd been done by somebody else. It was like he'd become two people. The same thing was happening to other dudes and they all found it tough to deal with. One loony-tune said the virus was aliens come to take us over and this was how they were doing it, by occupying our minds. Another said he was going to top himself and he must have because he didn't post any more. Anton stayed quite clear and calm throughout, even when things got bad for him. He said that his head was full of all these imaginary dudes, more every day. He could see them and hear them, but they weren't real. He proved it by making videos of him having conversations with them, but there was nothing there, only him talking in an empty room. Then the site went down and I couldn't follow Anton any more.

I started to see things myself, guys I used to hang out with who couldn't possibly have been there (e.g. Bryan Fry and his dad, who were drowned when their boat turned over a couple of years ago). I found that things were being changed round in my room. I accused you of doing it and we had a row. Remember? After that I fixed the lock on my door so I could keep you out but stuff still got moved around

266

so it could only have been me. What clinched it was when I saw our Mam walking across the yard, two days after she'd died. Ghosts are rubbish, so I knew it must be the virus that had got into me.

I got scared then. Before Anton's site closed one guy posted how he was regularly visited by a dude who called himself The Master, and he ordered him to kill his father and somehow he couldn't refuse and he did it. I wondered what would happen if one of the people I was seeing ordered me to kill you. Or Granddad, or Gran. Or if I just lost it and went on a rampage. I couldn't risk that, so I've decided to go away. If I can I'll get to Anton's group and see who's left. And I'll try to find the guys who've been working on the treatment. Then I'll come back for you. That's a promise, so keep out of trouble!

I hope this stuff doesn't happen to you. All the people posting on the site were blokes, so perhaps chicks don't get it in the same way. I hope it's like that. Anyway, that's all. I can't remember ever writing so much before! Pity it's not a school essay. Fucking A★, eh?

Keep safe. L.

P.S. I've taken my iPad. You can have my computer. I've cleaned off all the porn. Just kidding!

So that's why Lander went: to protect me, to protect the rest of us. That's typical of him. Tears were in my eyes by the time I'd finished reading. I want to hug him. I want him back.

MONDAY

There were no texts yesterday and there've been none so far today. I keep checking but there's nothing since that single word.

CLOSE

It hasn't wobbled me as much as you might expect. You'd think it would totally freak me out, the idea that some monosyllabic stranger was stalking me and was near, wouldn't you? Because that's what it is, stalking, isn't it? I'm okay with it, though, because I know that the texter isn't threatening. I thought he was at first, and I still keep the doors locked and the curtains drawn, and I still make sure there's a firearm close by, but I'm positive he doesn't mean me any harm. If he'd wanted to hurt me he could have by now, he's had lots of chances. He could have smashed a window and got in, or jumped me on the way across to the barn. And what about the other night? He was only a few feet away and I had nothing but a towel. He could have done what he wanted. Why didn't he? Because he's Adam, and Adam is my friend. That's why I'm not scared.

There's one thing that does bother me, though. What if there is no Adam? What if my brain's infected and all the weird things that have happened – the field gate, the hens, the shadow in the barn, the watcher on the path and on the landing – are either in my head or things I've done myself? The problem with that is there are some things on my list of the weird and creepy that I couldn't possibly have done. For example, there's no way I could have got downstairs on my own with a bad ankle, hobbled across the yard, milked the cows, put some fresh straw down and then gone back to bed again and forgotten all about ever doing it. For those couple of days it was torture to put any weight at all on that leg, and walking was sheer agony. So believe me, if I'd done all that I would have known! Then there was the damage to the turbine. How could I have done that? If it was Adam who did it, he's no friend, he's a bastard! Sorry, Adam, if you read this and it wasn't you. But if it was you, you deserve it!

LATER

I've been looking at the texts again. I took the word 'close' to mean 'near'. However, it could be 'close' meaning 'close down' or 'end'. Perhaps Adam is telling me that the exchange of texts is over. Perhaps it's a sign-off. This makes me feel let down and crappy, like I've been dumped.

LATER STILL

This afternoon I've been napping on the sofa in the front room. I don't seem to have any energy. I don't want to do anything and even writing my diary is an effort. I suppose I ought to eat something but I don't feel hungry. When I got up this morning I weighed myself. I've lost almost thirty pounds since my top weight before the Infection started! Thirty pounds!! I came down and tried to drink some milk, but it tasted horrible, greasy and sour, and it made me gag. The only thing I do fancy is chocolate, but I don't have any and I don't intend to go down the hill to

269

look for some. Tonight I'll make myself eat something. Promise.

EVEN LATER

I wake up and Josie and Miss Dove are sitting in the armchairs in the front room. They look really well. Miss Dove's hair is in a French plait and she's wearing a powder blue top with a greenish scarf, the colour of her eyes. Josie is in her school uniform. She has pink cheeks and a red nose. I want to hug them both but I can't get up.

'You're all right,' I say, 'you've survived.'

Miss Dove smiles at me – she really does have the most fabulous smile. 'Yes,' she says, 'we have, and I can see that you're all right too, although you look a bit pale.'

'I'm fine,' I say. 'It's great you're here.' It doesn't occur to me to ask how they got in through locked doors.

'We came to tell you about school,' says Miss Dove.

'We're all going back,' says Josie.

'But it's still the holiday,' I say.

'No matter,' says Miss Dove. 'The Governors have said we should go back now because the school closed early, before the end of term.'

'We start on Monday,' says Josie. 'Isn't it great?'

'Yes,' I say, 'it's fantastic.' It really is. I can't wait. 'What about the other girls?' I say. 'What's happened to them?'

'They're all fine too,' says Josie.

'We'll all be back together again on Monday,' says Miss Dove.

Miss Dove and Josie get up. Miss Dove bends over and kisses me on the forehead. Her hair brushes my face and I smell her perfume. Josie puts her arms round my neck. She smells of the bakery. 'See you, Kes,' she says. 'Take care.'

They go out through the door to the hall and close it behind them. I sit there and touch my forehead where Miss Dove kissed it. My fingers come away carrying a trace of her scarlet lipstick.

EVEN LATER STILL

When I wake up again I'm cold. The curtains are closed but I can see it's still dark. I stand up and stretch, and have to grab the back of a chair to steady myself. I don't seem to be able to get up nowadays without feeling giddy. I go through to the kitchen and stare at the fridge. There's nothing in it apart from milk, a bit of cheese and the remains of a loaf. None of it appeals, although some toast might be okay. I pull out the loaf. It's covered in green blobs. I bin it. I look in the pantry. There are lots of tins: beans, stewed meat, soup, rice pudding, peaches, plums, pears, tomatoes, sardines, sweetcorn. I can't face any of it.

I pick up my phone. Does what Josie and Miss Dove said mean that everything is back to normal? I go through the usual trials but nothing works. I can't connect to the internet. The TV screen stays blank, all the channels dead.

There's no further message on my phone. Did 'close' mean 'end'? What are you playing at, Adam? I text again. **R U STILL THERE? WTF'S GOING ON?**

There's no reply. I didn't expect there would be. I put some food down for Buster but he doesn't seem interested in eating either. He doesn't get up, just looks at me and

271

wags his tail, feebly. His dressing will need changing but I don't want to disturb him now. I'll do it in the morning.

I lie on the sofa, drifting in and out of sleep. I don't worry about the milking and seeing to Joey. Someone will have done it.

Sometime later I'm suddenly awake. I'm freezing cold. I look at my phone. There's another message, although I hadn't heard the alert.

I SAW U SKINNY DIPPING. NICE!!

Oh no! Jesus! Fuck! I feel myself blushing and my hands tremble. I *was* being watched. He was there! He was looking at me, ogling me like a peeping Tom. I tremble so much that I drop the phone and it thumps on the carpet. I roll onto my back and stare at the ceiling. My teeth and fists clench and I feel a surge of anger. Who does this prick think he is? How dare he? Then another emotion kicks in. I realise that I don't actually mind that much what he did. In fact, when I think about it it's like a scene from one of the Greek myths we read with Miss Dove: the nymph, naked on the rock, and the mortal looking at her from behind one of the Stones. It's a bit of a turn on. If I'd known at the time that he was gawping at me I'd have given him more of a show!

TUESDAY

OMG, what a dream. If it was a dream. I'm not sure what it was. All I know is that I woke up with my sheets in a complete tangle. I'm hot and wet. I mean not only sweaty wet, but wet down there, too. My lips feel swollen, my breasts are tender and I feel as though something's hit me between the legs. At the same time I feel easy, as though a weight's been lifted off me. I lie there for a long time enjoying the memory of my dream. If this is what being ravished feels like, I like it.

When I came upstairs last night for some reason Buster didn't come with me. He usually does but all he wants to do at the moment is lie down by the boiler cupboard and sleep. I put an extra blanket down for him and he seemed to like that. I think his wound's really bothering him. I wish he could tell me where it hurts and what makes it feel better. I lit a candle on the landing in case Buster wanted to come upstairs in the night. Then I stripped off and lay in bed, thinking about the latest text.

I SAW U SKINNY DIPPING

At some point I dropped off. I don't know how long I slept, but suddenly I was wide awake again. There was something different about my room, although I couldn't see what. I rolled over in bed and touched something warm. I shrieked and leapt out, calling for Buster and ready to run downstairs. Then I heard this voice. It was deep and musical, calming and reassuring. 'Come here,' it said. 'Don't be afraid. Sit here.'

They were invitations, but at the same time they were commands. I had to do what the voice said, there

273

was no choice. I grabbed the sheets to cover me and sat on the edge of the bed, ready to take off at any moment.

'How's your ankle?' said the voice.

I swallowed. 'All right, thank you,' I said. 'It's getting better.'

'I'll take a look,' said the voice.

He rolled off the bed and knelt at my feet. It was a single movement, fluid and athletic. There was enough light from the candle still burning on the landing for me to be able to see the top of his head, the blond curls. He was on one knee, and was wearing nothing except for a pair of white briefs. He took my foot and flexed it gently. His fingers were firm and his hands were strong, but also tender. I watched the muscles of his shoulders rippling under his skin. He began to massage my ankle between his thumb and his fingers. What he was doing ought to have hurt but it didn't, it felt wonderful. He ran his hand up my calf to my knee. His hand was smooth and soft, but solid. I felt myself flush. I was breathing faster.

He stood up and I saw the bulge in his trunks. *OMG*, I thought, *I think this is it*. He stooped, put one arm under my knees and the other round my shoulders, and picked me up as if I weighed nothing. He laid me on the bed, gently, spreading me like something sweet and special. He lay beside me, his head propped on one arm.

'I'm Adam,' he said.

'I know,' I murmured.

Gently he put his hand flat between my breasts. 'Your heart's racing,' he said, 'and you're trembling. There's nothing to be afraid of.'

He leant over and kissed me on the nose. 'You're very beautiful,' he said. Before I could make the protest that any well brought-up, modest girl should his mouth was on mine. His tongue flickered on my lips. I parted them and I answered his tongue with mine. He eased himself on top of me and my hands wrapped round him, feeling the strength in his shoulders. One of his hands buried itself in my hair. His other hand stroked my thigh. His knee rose smoothly between my legs and I settled onto it. My body was like a bow string. I knew that this, whatever he was going to do, was what I wanted, and that I wanted it more than I had ever wanted anything before.

The whole night wasn't so gentle. Once we got going we twisted and writhed, locked our limbs round each other and wrestled. At one stage I felt as though I was being electrocuted and I flung myself back and yelled. Then I felt him jerk, and shudder all over, and we were still. We were both panting and wringing wet. For a while he lay on me, heavy, while our breathing and the throbbing of our pulses eased and I felt his hair, his back, his bum. He rose on his elbows and gave me one more kiss, long and slow, as he withdrew from me. I had never felt happier, or more relaxed. Everything was marvellous and my world was rimmed with gold. I gently nibbled his ear and he gave a contented sigh. I felt drowsy, and slowly we sank into sleep.

When I awoke I felt for him. I wanted him again. I wanted to talk to him. I had so many questions. But he wasn't there. I felt a rush of disappointment. I had felt his body against mine only seconds before I woke up, I was sure of it. I called, 'Adam.' There was no answer. He had gone as quickly and mysteriously as he had arrived.

I waited for a long time, drifting – asleep, awake, asleep, awake – feeling my body where he'd touched me, yearning for him to come back. Late morning I got up and had a shower. I dried myself and put on a little make-up and one of the dresses I took from Chez Annette, because he might return at any time. Then I went downstairs and made some tea. I put out two cups. Does he take milk? Sugar? For the first time in weeks I was hungry. I spread some crispbreads with jam. I was just starting on one when I noticed something was missing. Where was Buster?

I called, expecting to see him padding round the door, his claws clicking on the tiles. He didn't come. I called again. Maybe he was locked in somewhere. If so I should have heard him whining, but the house was silent.

Perhaps he went out with Adam. How did Adam leave when the house was locked? I'm thinking about this as I go to the front door, and there's Buster. He's lying on the doormat. He looks to be asleep. I squat down to stroke him. He's cold and stiff. His usually wet nose is dry. He's dead.

I let out a howl of misery. MY BEST FRIEND IS DEAD. With trembling fingers I check him over, looking for damage, but there's no obvious indication of what's killed him. It can only be the tusk wound. It must have been worse than it looked, worse than I thought. I lie on the floor in my pretty dress and put my arms round his neck and I weep. I haven't been looking after him. I'm a selfish bitch. I've been so wrapped up in myself, my moods, my own hurts, the texts, Adam, that I didn't give him the care he needed, the care he deserved. While I was busy upstairs with Mr Universe, my dog was down here dying.

When I've finished crying I'm angry. I spread a towel over him and go looking for my phone. It's on the dresser, where I left it last night. There's my text,

R U STILL THERE?

and his sexy answer,

I SAW U SKINNY DIPPING. NICE!!

I grab the thing and hammer in my message, my nails beating the screen.

WOT HAVE U DUN TO MY DOG?

The reply comes almost at once. **???? NOTHING. NOT ME.**

I send, **THEN WHO? WOTS HAPNING? I WANT ANSWERS.**

There's a slight pause, then the reply. **MEET ME, I'LL XPLAIN.**

I hesitate. Meet him? I so desperately want to see him, to hold him again, and there's the promise of an explanation. At last I'll know what all this is about. I send,

WHEN? WHERE?

There's another pause. Then,

BRIDE STONES. TOMORROW. NOON. B READY.

WEDNESDAY

He told me to meet him 'tomorrow' but it might as well have been light years. The time passes so slowly. I can't face using my own bed with its rumpled sheets and the smell of him, so I sleep downstairs on the sofa again, or rather I try to. Several times I get up and go to where Buster lies under his towel in the hall. Every time I look at him I cry. I can't believe he's dead. I keep expecting him to look up and wag his tail and slurp me with his big, sloppy tongue.

The Bride Stones. Shall I go? I must, but why there? Why not here? Perhaps there's a reason he's selected that place. Does he know its romantic associations? Does he know it's a place for lovers? **B READY** the message said. Ready for what? I feel a delicate quiver of anticipation that this is the place Adam has chosen for us to meet again.

Eventually I can't put up with lying on the sofa any more and I get up. It's 5.30; six and a half hours to go. I scramble into a pair of old jeans and a sweatshirt, then I go across to the shed to get the wheelbarrow. I don't bother any more with the gun or locking the door; I know I'm safe. I bring the wheelbarrow back to the house and somehow manage to get Buster's body into it. I try to be gentle with him, but it's hard because he's heavy. All the time I'm alternately crying and cursing.

When I've got Buster in the barrow I wheel him round behind the barn. The rest of the pallets that Lander and Granddad had fetched up from the town are stacked against the wall, next to the old pit. I throw four or five of them in. Then I get the barrow to the edge and roll Buster on top of them. I go to the barn, fill a bucket with diesel from the tank and splash it all over Buster and the pallets. I hate doing it. I can hardly see through my tears, and as the oily liquid soaks his coat I have to keep telling myself that he's dead and he can't feel it. I wish I could manage a better send off for him. He was a good dog.

I go upstairs and run a deep bath, thanking our Dad yet again for installing the solar panels all those years ago. While it's filling I scrub the diesel off my hands. Then I wash my hair and wrap it in a towel. I tip plenty of Eau d'Amour into the bath and wallow. I shave my legs, my armpits and my bikini line. I get out of the bath, towel myself dry and rub myself all over with that really expensive lotion Gran and Granddad gave me for Christmas. I dry my hair, adding some Screengirl and brushing it till it shines. I take the tweezers and pluck my eyebrows. I apply some foundation to my face, just a little, and a little blusher. I dab a trace of gold on my eyelids and run some eyeliner round them. I eyebrow pencil my brows and stiffen my lashes with mascara. Finally, I put on some lipstick, pouting and blotting.

I stand in front of the mirror and check myself out. Do I look good enough for him? I've lost a lot of weight. Am I too skinny now? Am I still curvy? I'm pleased that my skin looks smooth. When our Mam went on her diet she lost so much weight that her skin sagged, so it looked like it belonged to somebody else and she'd just slipped it on for now. I'm young enough for my skin still to be elastic and there's no sign of sags.

I'm still sad about Buster but I'm excited about what might happen at the Bride Stones.

My phone sounds. Another message.

R U READY?

I text, **ALMOST.**

At once the reply comes back, **CAN'T WAIT TO C U. COME 2 ME.**

My hands are shaking as I text the reply. **B PATIENT. I'LL B THERE. XXX.**

I've decided that if I'm meeting a mysterious someone at the Bride Stones I'm going to dress for it. I put on my best underwear, including suspenders and stockings (when did I last wear those?). Then I get into my prom dress. It fits me easily now. I take another look in the mirror. Do I feel ready for my wedding? Do I look like a bride? It's an odd wedding where the bride doesn't know the groom, like one of those arranged marriages that Minal's sister had. I do know the groom, though. He's Adam. He's my Heathcliff and I'm his Cathy, and we will come together on these moors, just like they did.

There's one more thing. In a box on our Mam's dressing table is her wedding ring. I slipped it off her hand before they took her away and it's been in the box ever since. I put it on my finger, the third on my left hand. It fits me. Now I am a bride.

Downstairs I put on some flats and a rather smart gabardine that our Mam bought just before everything fell apart. I tie on a headscarf, tuck in my hair, take a box of matches from the kitchen and go round to the back of the barn where Buster lies on the pallets. The matches won't take in the wind, but I crouch behind the wall where I can light a paper spill. I toss it on the pyre and it explodes in a tower of flame. I jump back and watch it for a few moments. I'd meant to say a few words for Buster, but the flames leap and blacken his hair and I can't bear to look any more, so I come away. Buster used to be Lander's, but then he was mine and he knew I thought he was the best dog in the world.

Back at the house I check my make-up to be sure it hasn't smudged. I pick up a pair of beige heels and put them in a bag. I'm writing this last entry. Then I'll put my diaries in the bag too, and go to the Bride Stones.

After

SURVEY AND RECONNAISSANCE UNIT (SRU) NW14, based in York, was nearing the end of its tour of duty. The six-person crew had been tasked to scour a segment of West Yorkshire, and for the past five days had been working their way through the string of towns along the Calder Valley. The status of each had to be recorded, every street videoed, major buildings photographed. The aim was to find out what remained of the life that had been before the Infection, and to report back to the clear-up and reconstruction teams. They had not been told specifically to look for survivors, although the possibility of finding someone who had escaped the plague was always in their minds. Hope of that receded after each day of fruitless searching.

The driver, Sandy Lisle, sighed as she brought their vehicle, a specially equipped Toyota Avatar, to a stop in the last town on their list. They'd been at it since four that morning, done two towns and this was their final call. With luck they'd be finished by noon and on the road back to York, to a long bath, a good meal and some leave. She rolled her shoulders to loosen the knots and looked at the desolation that surrounded them.

'My God, what a hole. Where are we?'

Jackson Pollard, seated behind her, read from the briefing sheet. 'Walbrough. Market town and civil parish. Former mill town, now a commuter area for

Manchester, Bradford and Leeds. Local employment mainly light engineering, services and agriculture; major employer Lamb's Sweets and Confectionery. Three primary schools, one secondary. Pre-Infection Population 12,002.'

'Any flags or alerts?' said the unit commander, Charlene Adams.

'None I can see.'

'All right. This is the last one. Let's get suited up and go. Maggie and Jacko, you take blue sector. Chris and Mahmood, you take yellow.' She handed them pads which showed Walbrough divided into coloured sections. 'Sandy, you stay here with me. When the others get back we'll do green. It's the usual drill, folks: check in every fifteen minutes, look out for stray animals, and if you come across any dogs that look as though they might have rabies, shoot them. Don't enter any buildings, even if the object of your dreams is beckoning you from a bedroom window. Wear your suits and hoods at all times, and if by any remote chance you do find any humans alive, avoid contact. No heroics. Remember, we're here to look and report on what we see. If there is anybody still alive, they'll have managed on their own until now and a few more hours won't hurt them. Any questions?'

Pollard raised a finger.

'What is it, Jacko?' Charlene asked, although she knew what his answer would be.

'Do we have to do this?' Jackson had a whiny voice that irritated Charlene. 'We've spent the last three weeks going all along this God forsaken valley. We've stopped at every smelly little town and village. We've been down every

283

street and examined every rat hole and dog kennel, and look what we've found. Broken windows, smashed doors, burnt buildings, looted shops, starved animals and rotting corpses. This place is just like all the other dumps we've been to, worse if anything. I mean, look at it. I say we drive round, take some video and get our arses back to base.'

Charlene sighed. This was Jackson's standard speech at every stop they'd made for the past week. 'You know that's not on, Jackson. If we're ever to get things back and running again, we have to do this. The authorities need to know the situation on the ground, otherwise how can the reconstruction begin? We're all tired, but we're going to do as good a job here in Walbrough as we did on the day we came out of the arks and started this work. We'll do a proper survey, and then we'll go home. Anybody else?'

Nobody spoke.

'Very well, then, off you go. And remember, take care. These streets may not be inhabited, but they are still dangerous.'

The pairs checked each other's suits and hoods, and tested their communicators. One took the video camera and an emergency kit, the other an automatic weapon, and they started out across the square.

Charlene watched them go, then climbed into the front seat of the Avatar beside Sandy. 'Do you think he'll do it?'

Sandy laughed. 'Who, Jacko? Fuck no. He's a lazy bastard. He'll cut more corners than a blind tailor. He'll go out of sight, smoke a vape or two and then come back. You should have sent me with him.'

Charlene shook her head. 'Maggie's with him. She's all right. She'll keep him up to the mark. Besides, I want you here. We need to talk.'

Sandy groaned inwardly. She thought she knew what it would be about. However, she was wrong, Charlene didn't want to talk about their 'relationship'. Instead she said, 'You know, Jacko's right. All this is pointless. Everything's smashed up. There's nobody here. Same with the other RSUs. Every night we check in and the reports are identical. Mess, stink, squalor, damage, death, decay. Nobody and nothing has survived. All the places are the same. We might as well just drive away and leave them to rot. Look at that.'

Sandy peered through the windshield at the desolate square. The doors of the surrounding shops had been broken, their windows smashed and the raided contents dragged out. There were rags that had once been clothes, there were split cartons, smashed bottles, a fridge, a mattress, two vacuum cleaners, a TV. Everything was covered in mud, grit and slime. It was the same everywhere the unit had been. As the Infection had taken hold, order had broken down. Those who had not at first been smitten had taken comfort from the surrounding horror by indulging in a bonanza: free food, free goods, free booze, free everything. There had been arguments, fights, fatalities as people tried to grab what they could. Then, one by one, they all started to feel the probing fingers of death. They went to their homes and locked the doors, to sweat, to vomit, to cramp, to bleed and to die.

'Do you think there's nobody left to find, then?' said Sandy. 'Do you think everyone's dead?'

Charlene watched a starved dog limp round the corner of what had been a market stall. Its back was arched and its shrivelled hide stretched like a drum skin over its ribs. It sniffed at something it had found and bared its teeth. No, she didn't think they'd find anyone. Jackson's view came from laziness, not reason, but she agreed with him. However, she recoiled from the bleakness of that message so she said, 'Well, we got through it, didn't we?'

Sandy leant towards the windscreen and rubbed at a smudge with her thumb. 'We survived because we were sent into the arks. If we'd not, we'd be as dead as they are.' She pointed to a confused heap of rags against the wall.

Charlene raised her binoculars and saw that it was, had been, two people. They were wound together. Male? Female? One of each? Had they fallen while fighting? Or were they lovers who, on the threshold of death, had locked each other in a final embrace? Impossible to say. They were questions that, like many others, would never be satisfied because nobody who knew the answers had lived to report them. Those who had been sent into the arks – a network of sealed pods originally constructed to protect key personnel in the event of biological warfare – had gone in with orders to maintain a strict silence, so that their existence would remain secret. There had been no contact with the outside world so they knew nothing. All they could do was emerge when the tests said it was safe, to search, investigate, and start the long process of rebuilding a ravaged civilisation.

Time passed. At one stage Sandy lowered the window to get some air, but the sickening stench forced her to close it again. She was hot and uncomfortable in her bio suit. She undid the zip. It was against standing orders, but Charlene wouldn't mind.

She rested her head in the angle formed by the headrest and the side window. Both the women dozed. They were exhausted, the whole unit was. They did the overnight watch in pairs, taking turns, which meant that one night in three they got no sleep. Poppers would fight the fatigue for just so long, then they ceased to have an effect. They'd passed that point a week ago.

'The simulations were wrong, weren't they?' Sandy said.

'Not half,' said Charlene. She laughed but without humour. 'Remember Operation Dinosaur?' she said.

'Do I just?' said Sandy. 'Building shelters out of sticks, lighting fires with a flint and steel? They were supposed to train us for Armageddon, but nobody foresaw anything like this,' she said. 'This is paradise, or it will be.'

Charlene was shocked. 'Paradise? You think?'

'Yes, I do,' said Sandy. 'Just consider: there were 4,000 people sent into the arks. That means that now the Infection's over there'll be 4,000 people living in a country built to support sixty-five million. Okay, there was a lot of looting and things were smashed up, but that's only in the town centres. There's plenty of stuff in storage. There's enough tinned and packaged food to keep us for a century. There's ample space to grow crops, and fresh meat running wild, there for the taking. There's clothing, furniture, electronic equipment, together with all the spare parts we'd ever need to last our lifetimes and beyond. There are complete factories that just need starting up again. All

4,000 of us could drive flash cars and live in mansions. We'll have to clear up the mess and get the basic infrastructure working first, but it's all still there. We'll have everything we want. In the end it will be paradise.'

Charlene didn't look convinced. She gazed out of the window. 'I suppose that depends on what it is that you do want.'

Sandy gave her long look. 'What's bothering you?' she said.

Charlene turned to her friend. 'Why do you think we were given places in the arks? Why did they choose us?'

'It was a random draw,' said Sandy. 'They said so.'

Charlene snorted. 'Random draw my fanny. Look at the people who were in our ark, and in all the others too. What do you notice? I'll tell you. We're all young adults. I haven't seen anybody under twenty-five or over thirty. Is that random?' Sandy shrugged. 'What's your specialism?'

'You know this. Before the Infection I'd just completed my medical training. I'm a doctor.'

'And what's mine?'

'You have a PhD in metallurgy.'

'And Mahmood?'

'Software systems developer.'

'Jacko?'

'I'm not sure. Some kind of engineer, I think. What's your point?'

'My point is that between us we cover a wide range of skills, and we're all highly qualified in our specialist areas.'

'All right, we were chosen for our expertise,' said Sandy. 'What's wrong with that?'

'Nothing,' said Charlene. 'In fact it's essential if we're going to try to get things going again, but there's something else. What do you notice about our unit?'

'A bunch of idle wasters?' Sandy shook her head. 'I don't know what you're getting at.'

'Yes, you do,' said Charlene. 'You, me, Maggie, Chris, Jacko and Mahmood. Four women and two men. In the arks the ratio was the same, about twice as many females as males. If there were 4,000 of us allocated places, that's getting on for 3,000 women to not much more than 1,000 men. Do you think that proportion came about as the result of a random draw?' Sandy didn't answer. 'No,' Charlene went on, 'neither do I. We've been saved so we can rebuild the population. A thousand Adams and 3,000 Eves. The men will be required to work and to fertilise the women, and the women will be required to breed, and to breed, and to breed. Again and again and again. We'll be machines in a baby factory. That's a funny paradise.'

Sandy was silent while she took this in. Then she laughed.

'What's the matter?' said Charlene.

'They obviously didn't know. We should have told them. We're gay.'

'Do you think they'd care?' Charlene said. 'So long as we each produce a baby a year they won't give a shit whether we're gay or straight. And if we don't produce they'll have no use for us.'

IT WAS OVER TWO HOURS before the two reconnaissance pairs returned, arriving within a few minutes of each other. Charlene and Sandy put on their hoods and slid out of the Avatar so they could spray the others.

'Anything?' said Charlene when they were all back in the vehicle.

'What do you think?' said Jackson, and stared out of the window.

'Use the correct form to report,' Charlene snapped. Then she added more gently, 'Come on, Jacko, we're all tired.'

Jackson, who had bristled at the first reproof, relaxed. 'All right, sorry.' Charlene held out the voice recorder and nodded for him to speak. 'Reconnaissance report, Jackson Pollard and Maggie Phillips, town of Walbrough, West Yorks. Blue sector. All streets surveyed and videoed, file WB4512. No signs of recent human activity. All shops have been entered and show evidence of random looting. No mains water or electrical power. Roads and railway intact, although some roads are currently blocked by vehicles. Some fire damage, but most buildings appear sound. Town Hall and Health Centre are intact. Contact posters left on each street. No survivors seen.'

He handed the recorder to Mahmood. Apart from the different names and sector, his report was the same.

'Can we go now?' Jackson said.

Charlene shook her head. 'We haven't done green sector. That was for Sandy and me.'

Jackson groaned and, for the first time so did the others. Charlene could smell mutiny. Would they miss anything by not doing the green sector? No.

'All right, you win. Let's get out of here.'

Everybody cheered. Charlene nodded to Sandy, who started the Avatar and gunned it across the square, scattering some evil looking gulls.

'Stop!' shouted Mahmood. 'Just a minute!'

Sandy braked the Avatar.

'What is it?' said Charlene. 'This is not the time to need a pee.'

'No,' said Mahmood, sounding excited. 'Look up there. Isn't that smoke?' He was pointing to a small group of buildings on the flank of the hill, high above them.

'Yes, it is,' said Chris.

'Must be a fire,' said Mahmood.

'No shit, Sherlock,' said Jackson.

'Hang on,' said Charlene, 'somebody might be trying to signal.' She got out her iPad and studied it for a moment, glancing up at the column of smoke, which was growing as they watched and was now thick and black. 'It's this farm,' she said, pointing to a spot on the map.

Sandy leaned over. 'Looks like it.'

'We'd better take a look.'

Jackson howled. 'Jesus no, please. You know what it'll be. A fault in solar panels or a turbine, or the sun burning through some glass. We've seen it all before.'

Charlene turned and gave him a scathing look. 'Well, Mr Clever, you might not have noticed but there's been no sun today. There hasn't been any wind, either. It's been dull and still, a bit like you, so there's no chance a turbine would have been turning, solar panels wouldn't have been doing much and the glass option's out, as well.' She looked back towards the smoke and raised her field glasses. 'Anyway, I can see the smoke's coming from behind an outbuilding.'

Mahmood was looking at his iPad. 'There may be a problem. It looks as though that place the smoke's coming from is red flagged.'

Charlene spread her fingers and enlarged her own map. There was a red marker on the edge of the town that she hadn't noticed before. 'Yes, it is.'

'What's that mean?' said Maggie.

'It means it's to be left alone, we're not to go near it,' said Jackson.

'Correct,' said Charlene. 'A yellow flag designates an object of scientific study. A red flag an object of *special* scientific study. This is a red.'

'So we leave it,' said Jackson.

'But why the fire?' said Sandy. 'There must be somebody up there to have lit it. Perhaps they've seen us and are trying to signal. Perhaps they need help.'

Charlene made a decision. 'We're going to take a look,' she said. Jackson moaned.

'I don't know how to get up there,' said Sandy. 'You'll have to direct me.'

Charlene returned to her map. 'Okay, go out of the square and back the way we came. A few hundred metres along there's a road on the right, opposite the park, then a lane on the left.'

Half way up the hill they took a wrong turn and found themselves facing a gate. The farm was across the other side of the field. The smoke was still billowing from behind it.

'Across?' said Sandy.

'Better not,' said Charlene. 'We don't know the terrain, and there's no need to take a risk. Don't want to find ourselves in a hidden ditch. The track goes round the side of the field, let's stay on it.'

'Look,' said Jackson, pointing. In the paddock beside the farm was a large brown stallion. He looked sleek and well fed.

'That horse has been cared for,' said Charlene. 'Come on, I think we might have something here.' Her heart started to beat faster. Were they going to find somebody alive at last, after all their searching? Would her unit be the first to locate survivors?

The track led them round the back of the farmhouse into a yard. The smoke was thicker here. No one said anything but they were all on edge. What went on at a site of special scientific study? What was being studied? Who was studying? What would they find? There was no clue outside the building. The door to the house was shut.

'Right,' said Charlene, 'we do this by the book. Suits and hoods tight, tool up, communicators on. Sandy, you stay here, video everything and open up a communications channel to HQ, tell them where we are and that we're investigating because we think there's an emergency. Keep the engine running in case we need to get out fast. Jackson and Maggie, one each side of the yard. Maggie cover the barn, Jackson the house door. Have your weapons ready but don't wave them about. We want to be alert but not threatening. Chris, round the back of the barn and check out the fire. Mahmood, go to the front. Don't show yourself, just look and tell me what's going on. If anything looks iffy, no heroics. Get the hell out!'

They climbed out of the Avatar. Charlene took a loud hailer from its clip. 'Attention, attention please.' The metallic voice rattled around the yard and bounced off the hill above the house. 'We are a reconnaissance unit sent by the Provisional Directorate for the North of England. We have seen your signal and are here to help you.'

They waited, breath held, pulses raised. Nothing happened. The house door stayed shut, smoke drifted idly across the yard. In the distance a curlew called. Charlene raised the loud hailer again.

'Please show yourselves. We are here to help you, and the Government requires you to co-operate with us.'

Charlene looked at her watch and timed two minutes.

'Anything from HQ?' she said.

Sandy shook her head. 'No contact. The signal's been patchy all along the valley and there's nothing here. I can't get through.'

Charlene was uncomfortable. A red flag was a red flag. They probably oughtn't to be there at all, and they certainly should go no further without proper authorisation. On the other hand, they might be about to encounter somebody who had survived the Infection without the shelter of an ark, and that person might need help. There was a crackle in her earpiece. 'Chris, what you got?'

'Not much. No one here. The fire's still burning. It's quite a big one and it's clearly been lit deliberately. Lots of timber and stuff, all piled up, like a beacon.'

'A beacon?'

'Yes, you know. Like the ones they had when we were kids, to signal special occasions. They'd build them on hill tops.'

'You're sure it's human generated, not just a heap of old stuff that's somehow caught fire?'

'Sure. It's mostly pallets, and petrol's been used as a starter, I can smell it. Something's in the fire. It's a dead animal, maybe a large dog. I think somebody's built a pyre to burn the body.'

'Jesus,' muttered Jackson. 'It's like finding life from space.'

'Let's hope not,' said Charlene. 'Mahmood, anything from you?'

'No, boss. The door this side's shut and there's grass all round it. It doesn't look as though it's been used in a while.'

Charlene thought for a moment, then gave her orders. 'Okay, that's good. Chris, take some pictures, then come round here. Keep to the wall, don't make yourself a target. Mahmood, come back. You and me will take a look at the house.'

Sandy gave her a warning look. 'I know,' said Charlene, 'red flag. Orders. But what if we just went away and there was somebody in there in desperate need.' She tried the house door. Locked. 'Right. I'll go in with Mahmood. The rest of you wait out here, side arms at the ready but not obvious. Remember, if there is someone here it's because they're immune. We're not, so wear face masks and don't handle anything without gloves. Sandy, keep trying to raise HQ. If you get through tell them what's going on and request authorisation to investigate. Oh, and ask for back-up. Jacko,' she said, 'time to show us how strong you are. Get Thumper.'

Jackson took the heavy ram from the back of the Avatar. He lined himself up, swung it back and crashed it into the door. It held firm. 'It's a good one,' he said.

'Again,' said Charlene.

The doorframe splintered, and on the third blow it gave. They were in.

'Careful now,' said Charlene, 'it could be booby trapped.' She led the way in.

Charlene didn't know what she'd expected to see, but it was nothing like what she found. Everywhere they'd been they'd seen mess and destruction, decomposition and decay. But here everything was so ordinary. The place was clean, tidy and well stocked. The kitchen was modern, with a stainless steel fridge, cooker and microwave. Clean dishes were stacked on shelves. Saucepans hung from hooks on the wall. On a draining rack beside the sink were a single plate, mug and knife. A large pantry contained provisions for a siege: tins, cleaning materials, toilet rolls, containers full of rice, flour, dried peas and beans, pasta, jams, sauces. Charlene flicked the switch on the wall. The lights came on.

'Mm, everything seems to be working.'

She opened the fridge. It was empty except for milk and a large bowl of eggs.

They went through to the hall. There was a grandfather clock which was going, a rack with three or four coats. Charlene picked one up and sniffed the collar. There was a long, brown hair on the shoulder. The other coats seemed a similar size. Next to the coat rack was a sturdy looking cupboard, with a key in the door. Charlene opened it. There were two shotguns, a .22 rifle and an air pistol, all clean and oiled. Every slot was full, all the guns present. On the bottom of the cupboard were boxes of ammunition.

'Well,' said Charlene, 'this seems pretty organised. I wonder where she is.'

'She?'

'Yes. There's only one person living here. A young woman.'

'How do you know that?'

'Single place setting on the kitchen drainer means one person. The coats on the rack are women's. I recognise the perfume on them. It's Bitch. That's a young person's fragrance, not something an old lady would buy.'

Mahmood was impressed.

'You check out the rest of the downstairs,' said Charlene. 'I'll do the bedrooms.'

'Be careful, boss. Don't you want me to cover you?'

Charlene smiled. 'No, I'll be all right. I don't think we've got anything to worry about.' She ran lightly up the steps.

'WHO IS HE?' said Charlene.

'I don't know,' said Sandy. 'He waved ID but it's a foreign name and I didn't get it. Says he's from the Department of Information, whatever that is. You'd better go see him. He seems seriously pissed off.'

Sandy had managed to raise HQ and had reported their location and what they were doing. As Charlene had instructed, she'd asked for authorisation to investigate the site but the duty officer had clearly been out of his depth. He told her he didn't have the authority to agree to what she'd requested, but he would refer it up. Meanwhile he'd arrange for back-up. So Charlene had decided to go ahead anyway, and they'd continued searching the house and its surroundings, trying to get some clue to its mysterious occupant.

'Okay, better see what he wants,' Charlene said. 'What's he like?'

'A serious hunk,' said Sandy. 'Tall, good looking, fair hair, muscles. Almost enough to make me turn.'

'Almost.' They laughed.

'Seriously, though, if they want to use us for baby farming he can be my first mate.'

'You think? What we get will be out of a test tube.'

Charlene led the way downstairs. The young man was in the front room, standing beside the mantelpiece and looking at the urn and the white boxes. He was casually dressed in a check shirt and black chinos. His face was tanned and his hair a nest of blond curls. His eyes were a dazzling blue. The only thing about him that looked official was the leather document case under his arm. He was not wearing white gloves, or a face mask.

'They're ashes,' said Charlene, taking off her own mask. 'From cremations.'

'Yes,' said the young man. 'I know that.'

He was probably not much more than twenty, Charlene thought. There was a hint of middle Europe in his accent. Also a hint of chubbiness in his face. It was okay now, but give him a year or two...

He gave Charlene a hard stare. 'And you are?'

Charlene showed him her ID and the young man studied it carefully. He gave a grunt of what might have been disapproval and handed it back.

'Likewise,' she said.

The young man took out his wallet. He'd meant it to be a quick flash and fold, but Charlene stayed him while she read the words beside the photo.

Przemysław Adamski
Field Agent
Department of Information

'Right,' she said. 'Introductions over, what can I do for you?'

Przemysław Adamski put his document case on the table and folded his arms. 'You can start by telling me why are you here,' he said.

The young man's manner was hostile but Charlene answered calmly. 'I am in command of a survey and reconnaissance unit, from York. There are six of us. We've been along the whole of this valley. We were on the point of leaving Walbrough when we saw smoke coming from up here. We came to investigate. We think someone's living here and was trying to signal.'

'You need to go,' said the young man. The women didn't move. 'Now.'

Charlene resented his attitude. She was a unit commander. Who did this guy think he was? 'What do you mean, go? A young woman has been living here, recently, and we need to locate her.'

'No you don't,' said the young man. 'You shouldn't be here at all. It's a Site of Special Scientific Study.' He unzipped his document case, flipped open a tablet computer and read from the screen. '"Sites of particular interest or importance are designated by red or yellow flags. Such sites must not be approached or entered without special authorisation from the Department of Information." This place is red flagged. You have no right to be here.' He snapped the pad shut. 'Well?'

'Standing orders,' said Charlene. 'Yes, I have some of those, too.' She looked at the ceiling and recited. '"The task of a Survey and Reconnaissance Unit is to carry out thorough searches of given areas. All premises and property are to be evaluated and assessed. Units must pay special attention to the possibility of finding survivors, and in the event survivors are located must be prepared to take whatever action the Unit Commander considers appropriate to preserve life." This is our designated area. We've found a survivor. I think the appropriate action is to provide her with assistance.'

The two faced each other for a few seconds. The young man gave ground first and his expression softened.

He let out a huge sigh. 'Cock up,' he said. 'Left hands not knowing what the right hands are doing. We need to get you away, though, before Kerryl returns.'

'Who?'

'Kerryl. The girl who lives here.'

'There is no one here,' said Sandy. 'The place was like this when we arrived.'

'Except the door wasn't smashed in,' the young man said, icily.

'Look, Mr Adamski,' said Charlene, 'we seem to have got off to a bad start. Of course we'll leave if that's what's required, but why do we have to do that before this Kerryl comes back? She probably hasn't seen a living soul for weeks. We should stay and help her.'

The young man sat down at the table and motioned to the women to do the same. 'Call me Adam,' he said. 'Mr Adamski's too formal and most people find my given name unpronounceable.' Charlene and Sandy sat.

'The person who lives here is a young woman called Kerryl Shaw,' Adam said. 'You need to understand that she's very special, unique even. Not because she's survived exposure to the Infection, several thousand people have done that, but because we can find out from her things we can't learn from anybody else. How much do you know about the virus?'

'Mutating organism, strain I/452,' said Sandy. 'Deadly, easily caught and easily transmitted. Causes severe symptoms which usually result in death. I thought it was universally fatal, but you seem to be saying different.'

'It is usually fatal,' said Adam, 'but not invariably. In the last few months we've learnt a lot more about it and how it has been developed to spread through the body. The Infection has two stages. The first is the one everybody knows: a high fever followed by severe cramps, diarrhoea and haemorrhaging. Most people don't get beyond this stage, but a few do and they move on to phase two. By this time the other symptoms have receded, therefore the subject may now appear normal. However, they're not; the virus is still in them. It's migrated to the brain, where it lives on and reproduces.'

Charlene shuddered, cringing at the notion of some alien thing, a parasite, dwelling in a person's head. 'This is what's happened to Kerryl? She's got to phase two?'

'Yes, she has. And she's got there without apparently going through the symptoms of the first stage.'

'And that's what makes her special?'

'Oh yes. It means the virus may be evolving and adapting. But there's something else that makes Kerryl special. She's a twin.'

'What, you mean there's somebody else here too?'

'Not here,' said Adam. 'Her twin brother is called Lander Shaw. He was arrested six weeks ago for attempting to travel illegally, and taken to a DoI centre near Oxford. At first we thought he was just like the rest of the survivors. Then he told us about Kerryl, and we realised we had a unique opportunity. You see, all we could do up to then was study the other survivors by observing them, interviewing them, scanning their brains, putting them through tests. That's helpful but it can't tell us how they might react in the real world. With Kerryl and Lander it's different. They aren't identical twins but their DNA is extremely close. And they've had very similar upbringings. The bonus is that they were together when the Infection spread, so they were likely have been exposed to the virus at the same time and it will be at the same stage in both of them. That means we can scan Lander's brain and spot any changes that take place, and we can observe Kerryl to establish how these changes affect her day-to-day behaviour, her ability to look after herself, to solve problems and live a normal life.'

'So you've been spying on her,' said Sandy.

'We've been *studying* her,' Adam insisted. 'A scientific investigation. The original plan was to watch her remotely and we planted cameras in the house. We hid them in the mirrors, but she must have realised something was amiss because she turned them all round and we couldn't use them. So I've been observing her directly.'

'Without her knowing?'

'That was the intention. I've tried to keep out of sight, but a couple of times she might have seen me.'

There was a long silence. Then Charlene shook her head. 'I can't believe you've been doing this. I can't believe you've been happy just to watch this young woman… how old is she? Twenty?'

'Eighteen.'

'Just to watch her struggling, trying to manage on her own, thinking she's the only person left. How could you do that without stepping in to help her? What sort of a creature are you?' She was gratified to see that Adam at least had the grace to look uncomfortable.

'It's a scientific study,' he said. 'So we can learn how

the virus affects people and how we can help everybody. Besides, I have looked after her. I've made sure she's been all right. For example, she had a bad fall and hurt her ankle. Luckily it wasn't broken, but if it had been I would have been here to deal with it. While she was laid up I did things for her, like milking her cows.'

Charlene wasn't impressed. 'I don't think milking a few cows cuts it. Being here all on her own must have been a nightmare. If it were me I'd have gone mad.'

'That's why we've been setting her challenges.'

'Challenges?'

Tasks designed to enable us to assess her rationality and her response to problems. They also keep her occupied.'

'What sort of tasks?'

'Some of them have been very simple. I left a gate open that she would have expected to be locked, to see how she dealt with a phenomenon that had no obvious explanation. Then we removed her hens to test her reaction to a disturbance in her routine. Others were more complicated. We wanted to know how she would deal with a major survival issue, so we created a fault in her wind turbine.'

'I don't believe this!' Sandy exploded. 'Spooked her with a gate? Took her hens away? Messed with her turbine? Who are you? Don't you think this poor girl has suffered enough without you playing tricks on her?'

'They were not tricks,' Adam insisted stiffly. 'They were tests, so we could study her responses. Kerryl and her brother are extraordinary. They are giving us insights into the effects of the virus that we wouldn't otherwise have. It's vital that we learn everything we can from them.'

Charlene and Sandy made no response. They could see what he was saying, but they were not going to agree with him.

'You really must go now,' he said, 'before she comes back. I can cover the damage to the door, but it would cause a major trauma if she found her house full of strangers.'

Charlene got up to leave. 'A few minutes ago, when you were telling us about the virus, you didn't say it had developed to progress through the body. You said it had *been* developed.'

'Yes,' said Adam. 'Our people think that this virus was grown in a lab somewhere.'

'You mean it was created by humans?' said Charlene.

Adam nodded. 'We think so.'

'Why? As a bio weapon?'

'Maybe. We're not sure why, it could have been innocent, but it seems it was probably an experiment that somehow went out of control and got loose into the population.'

The two women looked at him in stunned silence. 'My God,' said Sandy.

'One more thing,' said Charlene. 'You'd better have this. We found it in the kitchen. I don't expect there's anything on it, the phone system hasn't worked in ages. Anyway, we can't open it.' She put Kerryl's mobile on the table in front of Adam.

'There's a password,' he said. He tapped the screen a few times and the phone came to life. He studied it and a look of disbelief spread across his face. 'Holy shit!' He took an iPad from his case and put it next to the phone. 'Look at these. What do you see?'

Charlene and Sandy peered at the two devices. 'They're text messages,' said Charlene. 'How can that be? Who can she have been texting? And who's been texting her?'

'Exactly,' said Adam. 'Who? Look at the two threads.'

Both screens looked identical, one just a larger version of the other. 'They're the same,' said Sandy.

'No, they're not. Look again.'

Sandy peered at the screens. Then she got it. The messages that were marked 'sent' on the iPad were marked 'received' on the phone, and vice versa. She didn't understand. 'You mean these two things have been sending texts to each other? Whose is the iPad?'

'It's Kerryl's. She's been texting herself.'

Charlene was incredulous. 'She's been exchanging messages between her own phone and her own iPad? How? Why?'

'The how is easy,' said Adam. 'The networks packed in weeks ago, so these must have been sent and received over the local Wi-Fi here on the farm, which is still working.'

Charlene still couldn't believe it. 'Let me get this straight. She's been sending lovey-dovey texts and then pretending to be someone else and answering them.'

'She's not been pretending. As far as she knew at the time, she *was* someone else.'

Sandy put her index finger to her temple and made a screwy sign.

Adam shook his head. 'Remember what I told you about how the virus affects the brain. One of the phenomena we've seen at Oxford is what we call "acute personality dislocation", APD. A sufferer seems to have two – sometimes more – distinct personalities that they switch between. Often the switches are random but in a few cases they seem logical, planned even. Like here. One of the texters is Kerryl herself; the other is an imaginary correspondent, a boyfriend maybe. She becomes that other person in order to send messages from them.'

'And she doesn't know she's doing it?'

'The "real" Kerryl thinks that she's sending messages to a stranger, and the stranger is replying. She's completely unaware of what her other persona is doing.'

'And when she replies?'

'Then she is somebody else, another person distinct and separate from the real Kerryl.'

'But that's incredible.'

'Not really. People on their own often talk to themselves. There are plenty of examples of APD in cases where prisoners have been placed in solitary confinement. This is just an extension of those. In solitary confinement it usually takes a long time for APD to manifest itself. In this case the stress of her situation, maybe compounded by the virus, has accelerated the process. Fascinating. Fascinating.'

Adam looked at the texts again. Suddenly he leapt up. 'Jesus! Why didn't I see it? I know where Kerryl is.' He rushed from the room.

A COLD WIND pierced them as they crested the hill. They could see nothing ahead but the bare, black rocks and it looked as though the Bride Stones were deserted. Until they got close. Then they saw her.

Kerryl was lying on her back, in the centre of the pool and slightly below the surface. Her hair made a halo in the water and her dress ballooned around her. They ran the last few metres to the bank and Jackson and Mahmood plunged in. Between them and with help from Charlene and Sandy they pulled her out.

Sandy knelt beside her, feeling her neck, wrist, ankles.

'Shouldn't we be giving her the kiss of life, or something?' said Jackson.

'Only if you want to catch the Infection,' said Adam.

'Too late, anyway,' Sandy said. 'There are early signs of rigor mortis in her hands, face and neck. She's been dead at least a couple of hours.'

'She's drowned herself?' said Adam.

'Looks like it,' said Charlene.

'Mm,' said Sandy. 'It's possible but I'm not sure. I can't see any marks or signs of a struggle on her, so it doesn't look like she was forced under the water. There's no indication of an attack by an animal, and it doesn't look as though she fell in as the result of an accident, either. But it's very difficult to kill yourself in a flat, shallow pool like this. As soon as you get water in your throat your reflexes kick in and you cough it out. You can't hold yourself under long enough to make yourself drown.'

'So what happened?'

'She might have fainted after coming up the hill, but there's another option. She looks extremely under nourished. It's possible she went into an anorexic coma. If she was standing in the pool at the time she'd just collapse, and that would be it.'

They looked down at Kerryl. Her eyes were closed as if she was sleeping. She wore a pale, ankle-length dress, strapless, with a design of flowers and birds embroidered across her breast. Her skin was marble white, her hands together on her chest. She looked like an effigy on a tomb in some ancient cathedral. The wet fabric clung to her and showed her ribs and hipbones, sharply angular beneath the silk. Her arms and shoulders were skeletal.

Charlene pointed to her left hand, where a band of gold gleamed. 'That looks like a wedding ring. She wasn't married, was she?'

'I don't think so,' said Adam. 'No, I know she wasn't.'

'So why is she wearing it?'

Adam thought for a moment. 'These rocks are called the Bride Stones. They have romantic and supernatural associations for local people. The texts invited her to meet somebody here. She's dressed herself like a bride and put on a ring. I think she came here expecting to meet her groom.'

'And who was that supposed to be?' said Sandy.

Adam shrugged. 'I think her alter ego, the other texter.'

'Poor girl.'

'I found these,' said Jackson, who had been exploring

the rocks. He gave a plastic bag to Adam, who took out two notebooks: one green, one purple.

It took some time to deal with the body. While they waited for the support to arrive they continued searching the area around the Stones and found the coat and the shoes Kerryl must have worn to walk up from the farm.

When the recovery team arrived they were brisk and business-like. They zipped Kerryl into a body bag, lifted her on to a stretcher and took her to where their helicopter waited. Charlene, Sandy, Jackson and Mahmood left to walk back to the farm.

Adam watched the helicopter's rotor spin up. It rose, banked and headed south. He waited until it was a distant speck, then he sat down on the flat stone where, not long before, Kerryl had undressed for her swim. Even then she'd looked emaciated, scrawny. Shouldn't he have foreseen what was coming? Couldn't he have done something to save her? His orders had been unambiguous: keep your distance, don't interfere, don't let her know she's being observed. But he'd had discretion. He could have done more.

He took up the green notebook. It was almost full, every page densely packed with her neat script. He turned to the last entry.

I am here for you. You promised you would come to me but you have not. Now I think you never will.
What shall I do? I cannot go home.
There is nothing for me there without you.
There is nothing for me anywhere if you are not.
To lose you is to lose my self.

I shall stay here. I shall rest in this pool, where a bride once rested before.
I shall close my eyes and I shall think of you, remembering last night and all the times we have been together.
Goodbye, my love.

Kerryl's misery and pain were beyond bearing and Adam's eyes filled with tears. He flicked the pages of the notebook and caught sight of his own name. He stopped. He was there. She was addressing him, writing for him. Had she known about him all along? He fingered the cream paper. He could see her now, head bent over her task, the breathless, loopy script spilling from page to page, transported on the swell of her coursing thoughts. He put down the green book and opened the purple one.

'You should read this one first,' the flyleaf said. So he began.

My name is Cheryl. Cheryl Alison Shaw. They call me the Paradise Girl.

Acknowledgements

There are a lot of people to thank when you finish a novel. At the top of the list are long-suffering family and friends, who have put up with me either being grumpy or not quite with them (and sometimes both) over lengthy periods. Not only that but they get the manuscript inflicted on them in its raw state. My deepest thanks go to my wife, Sally, who read drafts, talked over options for the plot, discussed characters, helped me work through knots and continuously raised my spirits, as she does in everything. Next I want to thank my children, their partners and their children: John and Kathy Featherstone, Hailey and Ella Featherstone, Sarah Featherstone and Jeff Durber. Family may feel they have some sort of obligation to read my work but friends have no such, and so I'm especially grateful to those who have taken the time to do so, even more if they gave me feedback: Rod and Helen Collett, Judith Shorrocks, Catherine Corry, Lynn Broadbent, Madeleine Hoyle, Sonny Marr, Alan and Carol Durber, Denis Connors, Canyon Stewart. I am flattered by your attention.

There were several reasons why I put *Paradise Girl* in the hands of Troubador. I was told they are the best, and I can see why. I would like to thank Morgan Langford, Alice Graham, Jasmin Elliott, Hannah Stewart, Katherine

Ward and everyone who has helped get my work into print. I also want to thank Moira Hunter for her eagle-eyed editing of my manuscript. I am astonished what a difference a first class editor makes.

I would like to thank Harry Bingham at the Writer's Workshop for his advice. Finally, very special thanks go to Sarah Vincent, who read a draft of *Paradise Girl*, made some invaluable suggestions and gave me a lot of encouragement. If you have not read her novel *The Testament of Vida Tremayne* you should.

Extract from Phill Featherstone's latest novel,

THE GOD JAR

PRAGUE, BOHEMIA, MAY 1584

'WHERE
IS
MY
GOLD?'

RUDOLF II, KING OF GERMANY, King of Hungary, King
of Bohemia, King of Dalmatia, King of Croatia, King
of Slavonia, Archduke of Austria, Duke of Burgundy,
Brabant, Styria, Carinthia, Carniola, Luxemburg,
Württemberg, Upper and Lower Silesia, Prince of
Swabia, Princely Count of Habsburg, Landgrave of
Alsace, Lord of the Wendish March, by the grace of God
elected Holy Roman Emperor, was angry. That was a rare
occurrence. For the most part Rudolf was a mild man,
a reserved home-body who preferred his own company
and shunned that of others. Occasionally, though, when
he felt he was being deceived or advantage was being
taken, he flashed with the fire of his father, Maximillian
II, and burned with the spirit of the Princess Maria, his
Spanish mother.

'YOU UNDERTOOK TO PROVIDE ME WITH
GOLD BUT YOU HAVE DELIVERED NONE.
WHERE IS IT?'

The half dozen courtiers who were with him shrank back, except for his particular favourite, Court Chamberlain Wolfgang, who smirked. It was not he who had recommended to his highness the ancient wretch who was now on his boney knees on the stone floor.

'Your majesty, my most gracious lord, I crave your indulgence,' said the old man. 'I am so close to producing gold, my lord, so close.' He pinched his forefinger and thumb together to show exactly how close he claimed to be. 'My formula nears completion. One ingredient is lacking, but one, to achieve the alchemical harmony which will ensure success.'

Rudolph made a sound reminiscent of the lion he allowed to roam free in the grounds of his Prague castle. 'And what is this ingredient?'

'My lord, as yet I know not. That is the subject of my present research. Once I find it my compound will be complete, you shall have all the gold I can make.'

Rudolf's mouth turned down, his nostrils flared and his breathing quickened. 'I already have all the gold you can make, sir, and that is NONE.'

The old man had been engaged by Rudolph to transmute base materials into gold. God Himself knew how hard he had tried. He had worked for hour after hour, remaining at his bench late into the night, day after day after day until he could no longer stand upright. Experiment after experiment, trial after trial had failed, yet he was convinced he could do it. Why, had he not only the other day seen a tiny, yellow speck twinkling in his crucible? It was no larger than a grain of pollen, but it was gold, it really was gold. It was a start.

He had been at the court for seven months. Before that he had lived and worked in a small shop just off the main street in his home town of Třeboň, a day's ride south of Prague. He had been happy where he was, distilling potions, offering cures, digging through the old books he had acquired over the years. Then one night at the inn he had too much to drink and got involved in a heated discussion about the nature and value of his work.

'What does an apothecary do but peddle slops?' asked Gross Henry, who had been trying for some time to provoke him, so far without success.

'They are slops for which you were grateful enough last year when I cured you of the fever,' said the old man.

'You did not cure me, sirrah. It was my wife's poultice that cured me.'

'Made herself into a poultice, I shouldn't wonder,' someone else said. 'Laid herself on your stomach till you forgot all about your fever.' There was a roar of laughter.

The old man should have left it there, but he was reluctant to let the matter go. 'At any event,' he said, 'I am more than a common apothecary, I am an alchemist.'

'That carries no weight with me, old man. What can an alchemist do that I cannot?'

'I have transmutative powers. I can change the state of materials. I can translate one thing from itself into another.'

'He can transmute pig shit into a turnip,' somebody at the table said. 'He can transmute that wine into piss,' said another. Again there was laughter. 'He can transmute your crowns into his purse,' said a third.

The old alchemist felt he was losing ground. 'I can make gold!' he shouted above the din. 'I can turn base metals into gold! I have the power.'

There was even more shrieking, but somebody must have heard. Somebody who took his claim seriously enough to pass it on. Two weeks later a summons arrived from the Emperor.

He had worked in Rudolf's castle in Prague for seven months, the Emperor becoming increasingly dissatisfied. Now, it seemed, his patience was exhausted.

'Shall he be dismissed?' Chamberlain Wolfgang asked.

'Yes. No. I do not know.' Rudolf sank into a chair and put his head in his hands.

'Sire, I think the man is of no use,' said the Chamberlain. 'He should be whipped and then dismissed.'

'But if he goes I will have no chance of producing gold, no way of financing my great projects. I need gold. I must have gold if I am to achieve my aims for the church, the city.'

'I believe we have an alternative to the old man, my lord,' said the Chamberlain. 'I have here a letter from Count Laski, in Poland.'

'Oh the blessed saints preserve us,' said Rudolf, 'what does he want now? Money again, I'll be bound.'

'No, sire. Well, not directly.' He offered the letter to Rudolf, who flapped it away.

'Read it to me, if you think it worth my time.'

'Yes, sire.' Wolfgang began to read. '"Most excellent and gracious prince, by the grace of God elected Holy

Roman Emperor, King of Germany, King of Hungary, King of Bohemia, Dalmatia, Croatia..."'

'Yes, yes, yes,' said Rudolf impatiently. 'I know my titles. Move on to the matter of it.'

'Indeed, my lord. Count Laski writes, "I commend to your gracious majesty Dr John Dee, from the court of Queen Elizabeth of England, who has been with me in Krakow and at other places this past year. Doctor Dee will be known to your majesty as one of the pre-eminent scholars of our age. Doctor Dee and his assistant, Mr Kelley, are skilled in the arts of transmutation, by which they are able to manufacture gold. They are with me, with their households, and await only your agreement to receive them, and to perform for Your Highness the feats they have already undertaken for me. I am, my lord, your most loyal and obedient subject..." et cetera, et cetera.'

'Doctor Dee?'

'Yes, my lord.'

Rudolf began to smile, for the first time that day. 'Doctor John Dee? Adviser to Queen Elizabeth of England? Correspondent and associate of Gerardus Mercator and Tycho Brahe? I have in my library a copy of his *Monas Hieroglyphica*, and of his *General and Rare Memorials*. They are truly outstanding works, both of them.'

'Yes, my lord. He is a learned man. A well travelled one, too. He was in attendance at your father's coronation.'

'I know, I know. Doctor John Dee, with Laski, in Krakow. Well now.'

'Yes, my lord.'

'Send for him. Send for him at once.'

It did not occur to Rudolph to question why, if these men really were so adept at making gold, the impoverished Count Laski would be willing to part with them.

★

The God Jar will be published late in 2017. For information see: www.phillfeatherstone.net